African Dream

The dawn of a new day

Chief Suleman Chebe

Copyright © 2011 Chief Suleman Chebe

ISBN 978-0-9564100-2-3

Papers used in this book are natural, renewable and recyclable products sourced from well-managed forests and certified in acordance with the rules of the Forest Stewardship Council.

FSC
www.fsc.org
MIX
Wood from
responsible sources
FSC® C021018

Print production management by Gilmour Print www.self-publish-books.co.uk

Contents

Chapter 1: Roadmap to Africa

"I believe in Africa, I believe that Africa can make it," said Professor Mandingo. He was delivering his keynote lecture to the first congress of Africa's Philosophers' Union in Addis Ababa, Ethiopia. His message was entitled *The Road Map to Africa's Economic Freedom.*

"Africa, as we know, is the richest continent in the world, and Africa has everything she needs to fulfil the dreams and aspirations of her people. Yet, there are millions of innocent children starving every day in Nairobi, Kinshasa, Dakar, Banjul, Johannesburg, Lagos, Ouagadougou, Kampala and almost anywhere else you can think of in an already over-blessed continent. As concerned citizens of the world, we have a collective responsibility to ask ourselves today: is poverty in Africa due to a curse, brainwashing or compounded stupidity on the part of the African people?" Professor Mandingo took his time to outline the direction of his road map to a packed conference hall. The congress was attended by more than 500 philosophers, both students and masters, from all of the 54 countries in Africa.

"Delegates," he called and continued, "after almost half a century in my academic career as a philosopher I have come to the sound logical conclusion that poverty is not a living curse on any human society but, rather, a man-made disease. In my expert opinion, extreme poverty is not only wrong and inhumane, but also completely criminal in the eyes of the Lord, who made us all." Professor Mandingo added that people who have little or no food to live on often suffer from self-degrading pain and misery. This pain, he said, takes away the love and happiness of humanity, which we are all supposed to enjoy as God's children on earth.

I tried to write, as the continent's most ardent philosopher asserted his case for a new belief in Africa. But, my pen began to play mental tricks on me. I scribbled and pressed hard on the writing pad, but the pen remained blunt. It was like trying to cut through an elephant skin with a piece of wood. A Zimbabwean student philosopher sitting next to me gave me his spare pen to use as the short, stout professor continued. "Without doubt, poverty is a mental condition which has a perfect mental solution, as the Chinese continue to show the world today." Professor Mandingo argued that success or failure in this life is all down to the way we plan before we do things. "If Mr God did not have a perfect master plan to create the universe, He would not have succeeded in creating a perfect universe in seven days." The distinguished professor maintained that people who fail in this life often do so because they have either *failed to plan* or *planned to fail*. "That is why I am convinced that through sound philosophical thinking, effective planning, better organisation and maximum individual and collective action, we can change Africa's misfortunes today and turn our negative progress into a brighter future through hard work and play. I believe that this new generation of African patriots around the world possesses the power of intellect, willing determination and the necessary ability to reengineer, reorganise, build and transform Africa from a living hell into a prosperous living paradise." The professor continued at length, trying hard to establish his case for a new African Can-Do Mentality. "Before we can succeed in achieving our goals, we need to believe in ourselves." The veteran philosopher argued that Africa has, so far, failed to prosper because of too much doubt and negative belief in the minds of African people. "Let me tell a little story about the power of belief!" he said, breaking into an infectious smile. He paused for a few long seconds to pour a glass of water. "A long time ago, a man called Mosongoro Wongara lived in a remote Tanzanian village. Everyone in the village of Tabora was a cripple and, among them, Mosongoro was the only one who could climb up to the top of the famous village mountain, Kilimanjaro. Because of this extraordinary achievement, the village chief, who himself was a cripple, was so impressed that he allowed Mosongoro to marry his only daughter. When I first heard this story, I couldn't believe it. I asked myself: how did Mosongoro Wongara manage to climb all the way to the top of the tallest mountain in Africa?" Professor Mandingo took a large sip of water from his tall glass.

"Exactly, Prof. That is the question I wanted to ask. How can a Tanzanian cripple climb the tallest mountain in Africa? That is absolutely impossible," said Jonathon, an anxious Nigerian philosopher.

"Nothing is totally impossible; it is all in the mind," Professor Mandingo argued, before explaining that it took Mosongoro many, many years of hard work and numerous unsuccessful attempts before he eventually developed enough stamina to climb all the way to the top of Kilimanjaro. He pointed to the fact that, although the rest of the cripples in the village also tried to climb at some point in their lives, most of them gave up after a few failed attempts. He said that, in this life, those who give up on the way never get to where they wish to go. And that is why an Englishman will tell you that *all quitters are losers.*

"So, how can we set Africa free from economic enslavement? To do this successfully, we first have to devise a way of setting the African people free from the harmful residue of mental slavery. It is important for us to understand that the mind is a complex universe, which can be nourished with good thoughts or poisoned with junk and harmful information. Like a computer, a mind has basic components, or what I describe as the essential tools of the mind. The five most important tools of the mind include a torchlight, an eye, a databank, a central processing unit and a recycle bin." The professor claimed that, without a proper understanding of these essential components of the mind and how they function, any human being will continue to fail, regardless of the opportunities around them.

"The moment you have a thought or a distant dream, it is the torch of the mind that shines the light or points you towards the right direction. Right now, if I mention the word Kilimanjaro, it is the invisible torch of your mind that points your imagination towards the tallest mountain in Africa. Now, while you are thinking of that mountain, it is the powerful eyes of your mind that show you an image of a cripple sitting on the highest point of that tall mountain. It is the powerful eyes of your mind that let you see your own imaginary cripple sitting so high he could just stretch and touch the sky above him. Your mental eye follows the direction of your mental torch everywhere, even whilst you are sleeping. That is why, in your dreams, you can roam to many beautiful places or see yourself doing amazing things somewhere else far away from your sleeping bed."

Philosopher Mandingo also explained that once you have a thought, that thought can be stored in the databank or deleted and put into the recycle bin. "The processing unit is the most crucial component of the mind because, no matter how many good ideas or dreams you have, if you continue to delete them or merely store them in the databank alone, you will never achieve your dreams or accomplish your goals in life," the professor said, taking out a handkerchief to wipe the sweat from his face.

"Now that we know of the powerful tools of the mind and the basic functions they play, I want to take you a little further into the path of progress. As I have already said, what is possible or impossible is directly related to the mind and the belief you have in it. Therefore, the good data you store in your databank will remain useless to you until you attach enough belief to make it work. So, if 80 per cent of the African population today start to believe in Africa, for example, and all support African institutions, African products, culture, family, agriculture, sport, education, markets and economy, then the transformation of Africa is not merely possible but inevitable."

As I sat and listened from a back seat, I continued to jot down my notes as fast as I could. One tall, slim and fair-coloured student stood up to ask a question. "Professor, surely some things are definitely impossible in this life. I mean, I believe that the God I worship everyday is high above the sky. But, I know that it is totally impossible for me or any other man to stretch high enough to see, touch or talk to God directly," said the Angolan student.

"Yes, you are right," said the professor. "What is also true is that, in every rule of nature, there are always some reasonable exceptions. Let us not forget that after his painful death on the cross, Jesus Christ rose from his grave and spoke to God in the heavens above the skies. So, it is not totally impossible to see God or talk to him directly if you are determined to do so. In fact, if you ask anyone who believes in Jesus or Allah, they will tell you that they do not only see God, but they also talk to him in their thoughts and prayers every day. That is why I say that belief is a product of the mind."

"Now, let me tell you something important," he said and paused to organise the direction of his thoughts. "I conclude that the problem of poverty in Africa is not a curse, because I believe in the existence of a good God. I believe that the God who created the universe and placed his people on earth to multiply and enjoy the fruits of creation does not possess the will, the intention or the heart to make any man or any nation remain in poverty forever. However, the man – who God created in his own image to live on his land and take good care of it – is capable of not only keeping himself or his fellow men poor forever, but is also willing to do so at any given opportunity." Professor Mandingo stressed that as no condition is permanent in this life, what is possible or impossible sometimes changes with time. He pointed to the fact that: "half a century ago, no one in their right mind would think that it was possible for an African American man to govern the United States." As I listened and wrote at the same time, the radiant professor continued with his crafty circumambulation, passing through the thick bush as far as he could to create the mental path to Africa's Economic Freedom.

"Student philosophers and fellow African academics; let us now concentrate our thoughts on one powerful logic today. Let us use our best intellect and wisdom, as well as our spiritual know-how, to create a clear visible path that we can use as a foundation of our own economic freedom. Let us create a vivid road map, which the new generation of African youth can follow, and live to enjoy the promise of the African dream." After clearing his throat, a middle-aged bald-headed man raised his hand and stood up to say something.

"My noble professor, "my name is Charles Chingwalu from Malawi. I am sorry, but I find it impossible to see that your African dream will ever come to real life. I believe that the Western world will never allow Africa to develop, because that is against their every interest. They want our cheap gold and diamonds to use and decorate their halls and living rooms. They want our steel to build their fancy cars, and they want our land to grow their fruits, vegetables and flowers. They want everything from Africa for free or next to nothing." Immediately after he sat down, another student stood up to share his views.

"Sir, my name is Samba from Zimbabwe. I agree with Charles that Africa will remain the way it is forever. But, I also disagree that it is the outside world that is keeping Africa from progress. Just look at the situation right now in my own country. Look at what Mugabe is doing to the people of Zimbabwe and you will see why the problem is internal. I don't believe the white man is the enemy any more. I believe that Africa's number one enemy today is the African man himself. I say this because, if you look anywhere around the continent, there is still far too much corruption, greed, tribalism, conflict, war, mismanagement, evil conduct, dictatorship, et cetera. In my view, Africa is failing because of internal madness!" After Samba spoke, many of the delegate students laughed and cheered, especially when he mentioned madness in relation to Mugabe's behaviour. Many nodded in support of Samba's grim and pessimistic assessment of Africa's future.

"Yes, of course. Madness is one way of describing the condition of a man who is filthy rich and desperately poor at the same time. Madness is also the only way you can perfectly describe the situation of an Africa that is so blessed with natural wealth but still continues to struggle as though we were in the dark ages of economic civilisation. That is the reason why I believe that we have a duty as African academics to show our people what is possible. Let me remind you that, everywhere in this world, people have worked together to achieve impossible dreams. Not so long ago, the Chinese were regarded by the Western world as a poor, failing race. Today, the Chinese have worked together to change that image for good." Professor Mandingo challenged the new generation of African students around the world to think outside the box to find solutions to Africa's chronic problems.

"The land of Europe is not of any greater value than the land of Africa, and the African man is no any less intelligent than the European man. Yet, the difference between the two continents in terms of economic wellbeing is like day and night." Professor Mandingo stressed that African countries such as Kenya, Ghana, Burkina Faso, Uganda and Egypt could enjoy the same level of development and a similar standard of living as the people in Singapore, Thailand and South Korea. Equally, the people of Nigeria and the Congo, he said, should be entitled to the same or a similar standard of living as the people in Brazil, Russia, Germany or China. "It is up to you – this new generation of Responsible African Citizens around the world – to make this dream come true. We know that the world places a heavy burden on Africa's neck. We are aware of the destructive power of constant control, duplicity and underhanded influences of the outside world. We also know how much Africa suffers from constant internal bleeding, as Samba perfectly described with regard to the situation in his own country. Yet, there are still more than one billon exemplary reasons why I say nothing is entirely impossible in this life. I believe that the word WISDOM is the key to our collective success. I believe that wisdom is not only the key to unlocking the greatest mysteries of the earth, but also the only way of overcoming all impossibilities of life. Now, I want to proceed to the second half of this lecture by laying the foundation of the African dream."

Chapter 2: The Power of Vision

"My fellow African patriots, students and distinguished academics, I have a dream in which I see the wind of fortune blowing in Africa's direction. In my dream, I can see a peaceful Africa with beautiful landscapes; great buildings, cutting-edge schools, good jobs, better hospitals, an abundant and reliable electricity supply, much improved communication networks and better roads; connecting our villages, towns, cities and countries together in peaceful civilisation. In my dream, I see mass movement of people, like a flock of sheep, returning home to Africa." Professor Mandingo was sweating heavily as he conveyed his dream to the African Philosophers' Congress.

A person without a dream is a person without ambition, hope or the belief that his or her living conditions can improve and change for the better. I have a dream that a time will come in Africa when every man, woman and child will be able to eat at least two good meals a day, have enough clean water to live on and good medicine to wipe out the deadly impact of unnecessary killer diseases.

Dreams, dreams, dreams, what are we without our dreams?

A life without a dream is like a journey without purpose.

A people without a dream are like a forest without roots.

A nation without a dream is like a building without foundation.

A child growing up without his or her own dreams is a child without hope for a brighter future.

A dream without a vision is like a castle in the air; it will always be an empty dream. This is why we need a new vision for Africa to make our dreams come true." Professor Mandingo spoke with enthusiasm, courage and a great expression of belief on his face.

"Now that the talking and preaching is over, it is up to you – the new generation of African students and African patriots around the world – to help make our own African dream come true. Today, we are in the twenty-first century and we can do so much better for ourselves and our future generations. It is up to you, the new Facebook generation of African patriots, to come together and free Africa from disease, hunger and negative tribalism. It is you, the students of today, who will be remembered as the heroes of tomorrow. It is your job to go out and spread the message to the whole world that Africa is no longer a land of stupid fools and third-class citizens of the world. From now onwards, Africa and her people are free from self-imprisonment. I want to encourage and entice you all to leave this great city of Addis Ababa, feeling inspired with enough pride, courage, belief and determination to succeed in the African Dream. Yes, we can, because we have the wisdom, the desire, the willingness and the ability to change our appalling status as a laughing stock in the eyes of the world.

Finally, I want to end by saying that too much talk alone can never build a chicken coop. As we walk on our own path to economic freedom, a thought or belief in the mind alone cannot yield fruitful results. We need to generate good ideas and forward them from the databank to the central processing unit where our actions will lead us to success. I believe that what we need is AAA: Action, Action and more Action. Africa needs you all today. Africa needs her own heroes and her own heroines. It is up to you to go out onto the streets, interpret and help to translate the African Dream to the total benefit of all Africa's children on earth.

Crucially, I want to add that no man in this life can follow or pursue his own dreams without believing in his own worth. I believe that, in the twenty-first century, those who fail in pursuing their dreams do so because of the lack of ambition and not because of the lack of opportunity.

Let us remember that the American people prospered because they were ambitious with their American Dream; the Europeans developed because of a common belief. The Chinese have copied their tricks and are performing unbelievable economic miracles, using the unbreakable power of collective reasoning. Brazil, Mexico and Venezuela are leading the way to prosperity in the former poverty-ridden South American subregion. The Russians, the Indonesians and the Indians have all managed to turn their past difficulties into new challenges and better opportunities. In the twenty-first century world, true progress is developing yourself and your neighbourhood. Developing yourself alone is a thing of the past, which will, in the future, only lead to backwardness, needless isolation, internal tension and self-destruction.

The good news is that everybody can take charge of their own destiny and no one can stop the African people from following our own chosen path. As I have already said, what is possible and impossible is entirely in the mind. If you believe something is possible, you can make it happen.

Let me tell you one last thing before I leave the stage. A long time ago, two brothers accommodated the insane belief that a man can fly from one place to the other, like the bird in the sky. Everyone around them laughed in disbelief, but the two men were convinced by their idea. With the right amount of belief attached to this seemingly insane notion, the brothers gained enough courage to persevere and developed their idea into a vision plan, creating a vivid mental path of action to follow. After many years of trials and tribulations, the two Wright brothers finally succeeded in inventing the first aeroplane in the world.

I believe in Africa. And I believe that, within a decade from this exciting moment, we will find a way to invent and manufacture our own African aeroplane; we need an African Airways to take us off! Those of you who agree with me that all things are possible, I want to assure you that through the little positive step of action that you take, we can together help to bring a happy ending to a sad African story which has been going on for far too many centuries."

Professor Mandingo concluded in perfect tune to a rapturous standing ovation. As he left the stage, many of his fellow philosophers rushed to shake his hands and thank him for his encouraging wisdom. For a good while, we all remained on our feet, clapping and rejoicing to the true spirit of oneness, and singing: "We believe in Africa."

Chapter 3: Sunny Glasgow

After a very warm, inspiring African Philosopher's Conference in Ethiopia, I left Addis Abiba on a Sunday evening and returned to Glasgow. It was a long exhausting flight.

Finally, as we descended high from the clear blue sky, I looked down from my small window. There were many thoughts going through my mind. From my seat, I could see a beautiful landscape covered with hills, houses, villages, towns, rivers and trees, all spread perfectly across large stretches of fields underneath my feet. For a brief spell, the pilot flew through a thick blanket of cloud and the plane juddered like a bus driving over potholes.

"Will all passengers please fasten your seatbelts and prepare for landing," one of the aircrew spoke over the loud speakers. After a long journey, I sighed with relief when we finally landed.

What is the next step? I asked myself stepping out of the British Airways plane at Glasgow Airport. It was one of those rare glorious sunny evenings in Glasgow and magic was everywhere I looked. All the passengers seemed happier as we followed each other out of the terminal building.

Beeeeeeeeeeeeeeeeeeeep, the taxi driver blew the horn.

"Alright, pal. This is a scorching day ae? My name is Tom by the way." The driver spoke in deep Glaswegian ascent. I told Tom I was returning from Addis Ababa.

"Are you Jamaican? Are you here on a holiday?"

"No, I live and work here in Glasgow."

"How long have you stayed here?"

"Fifteen years."

"Don't you fucking miss home? It must be warmer wherever you come from than Glasgow," he said before pulling away from the taxi rank. "So, what were you doing in Ethiopia?" he asked looking at me through his driving mirror. Tom had a bald head and well-trimmed beard. He was wearing a white short-sleeve shirt. I explained to him that I was in Addis Ababa to attend an African philosopher's conference.

"What was the conference about?"

"The African Dream," I replied.

"It is about time," he said and continued, "oh, I feel ashamed anytime I see the poor African we'ans on the TV, with nae food to eat and nae clothes to wear. That's not right. This world is a bloody disgrace. It makes me sick to see what is happening over there in your country. But, the trouble is," Tom said shaking his head, "there is nothing we can do about it. It's all about power, money and politics, pure greed!" Tom spoke very passionately about the unfair nature of the modern world before turning his attention to domestic issues.

"Look at what happened here in Glasgow, when Maggie came into power in the eighties, she fucking wrecked everything here in Scotland. She brought in the poll tax and closed all our mines and shipyards in Govan and the Clyde. Maggie wrecked Scotland. That's why nae-body votes for the Tories in this country. I tell you something, if Maggie was a storm, she would have been worse than Hurricane Katrina."

Tom and I had a good laugh on the way. He shook his head repeatedly in disbelief at what is happening in the world today. "So, big man, what are you gonna do to make your African Dream come true?" he asked as we drove into a long queue of traffic at the Kingston Bridge.

I sat on the back seat looking through the windows admiring the silver blue sky and the bright light it shone on Glasgow city. I could see newly built high-rise buildings on both sides of the river, blending well with the old architecture of the city. The Clyde River runs underneath the Kingston Bridge, splitting Glasgow into two equal halves. I could see the BBC Scotland building standing far to the left, next to the Glasgow Science Museum. There was a blue flashing light on a tall building to the right of the bridge, towards Argyle Street. "Hilton Hotel," I read the sign before Tom took a left exit towards Charring Cross.

"What am I gonna do to make my African Dream come true?" I pondered to myself, trying to think of an answer to give to Tom. In the end, I told him my mission now is to demonstrate to myself and hopefully the rest of the world that what is good for the goose is also good for the gander. So, if Asia, America, Europe and Australia can develop and enjoy the comfort of modern civilisation, a United Africa can also do the same. I told Tom my goal was to write a compelling book to convince the new generation of Africans around the world that we can have what the Europeans and the Americans have. But, if that is what we really want, we have to plan properly, like the Europeans, and prepare ourselves to do what it takes to make our dream come true.

"Good luck with your African Dream, big man. Keep praying as well," he said, laughing and waving. As I waved back to Tom, I knew that every journey in this life, short or long, always comes to an end. At the same time, I also realised that, the end of every journey is also the beginning of another.

I prayed to God to give me the courage and the wisdom and show me the way to make the African Dream come true.

Chapter 4: Back to School

I barely slept on the first night I returned to Glasgow. The next day, I woke up early in the morning to go to school at Mid-Calder. Mid-Calder is a small village outside Livingston, which is the biggest town off the M8 motorway between Glasgow and Edinburgh. I remember driving along the motorway that bright summer morning and thinking to myself: I wish I had a magic wand that I could just wave in the air to touch the soul and spirit of every African man and woman in the whole world. I wish the people of Africa would come together and work hard to improve the image of Africa. I never stopped thinking until I arrived at Mid-Calder.

The school car park was busy but, after a few careful manoeuvres, I managed to park my van next to a disabled parking space. As I locked up, I saw many parents dropping their children off in the school playground. I headed for the office.

"Good morning, are you the African Chief visiting our school today?"

"Yes, I am."

"Come with me, the main entrance is this way. My name is Mrs Morrison; I teach Primary 7."

"Good morning Mrs Morrison, nice to meet you" I said and followed. When we got to the double door entrance, she took a card from her handbag and swiped the automatic doors to get in.

There was a tall woman in her mid-fifties standing by the school office as we entered. She wore a deep pink suit with a nice pair of black court shoes.

"Good morning, Chief Chibi. I am Mrs Anderson, the head teacher. You are very welcome to Brave Heart Primary School," she greeted. "Can I get you to sign in our visitors logbook? I have to get you a badge to wear for the day," she said. We stood by the window to the reception.

I put down my bag searching frantically for a pen, but with no luck.

"Here," the school secretary stretched her hand through the office window.

After filling in the logbook, she took me to the staff room, where I could get tea or coffee at break time.

"This is the gent's toilet," she pointed and said: "Unfortunately, there are only two male staff in this school: Mr Smith, the PE teacher, and Mr McColl, the janitor. The rest of us are female," she said with a warm smile. I liked Mrs Anderson from the onset. She was warm, sweet and very welcoming. "All the children have been looking forward to the assembly this morning. I told them an African Chief is coming to our school today to talk about the impact of fair trade."

Mrs Anderson showed me around the large dining hall where the school assembly was scheduled to take place.

"We have arranged for you to set up your PowerPoint presentation here," she said and pointed me towards a giant screen and projector in front of the stage.

"Do you have any other equipment to bring in?" I told Mrs Anderson I had my djembe drum and a few baskets of fruits and other fair trade products from Africa to show the children as part of my presentation.

"Don't worry," she said, "I will ask a few pupils to come out to the van and help you carry your equipment." After leaving the hall, we returned to the reception area. I stood next to the double door looking outside to the car park as Mrs Anderson went upstairs to fetch a few boys. It was a hectic morning at the school, with many children still arriving through the doors.

"Here they are," she said returning with half a dozen enthusiastic-looking boys, all wearing black trousers and brown school shirts.

"Good morning, young men, you all look happy today, come with me," I said and took the lead to the car park.

"Excuse me, sir, what is your name?" asked the tallest boy.

"His name is Chief Chibi, Mrs Anderson told us your name."

"Wow, Chief Chibi, you van is so cool." I opened the back door and first removed my hand carved djembe drum before taking out the three baskets of fruit.

All the boys immediately scrambled over the djembe drum. Every single one of them wanted to have a go at it. "This is a really cool instrument, is it a bongo drum?" I told the boys that the djembe originally came from the Gambia.

"What is the top of the drum made of?" asked another boy.

"Goat Skin," I replied as we carried everything back into the school. Inside the hall, I had only about ten minutes or so left to get ready. By then, the presentation was already set-up.

"The assembly will start at 9:15, is that enough time for you to get to ready?" asked Mrs Young, the deputy head teacher. "Can I get you something to drink? A cup of tea or water?" she spoke with a polite but firm teacher voice.

"Some water will do me good," I said before going to the toilet to change into my traditional costume. Time passed very quickly and before I realised, the children had already begun to troop into the hall. They all sat in rows according to their ages and classes. The Primary 1s sat in the front rows closer to me and the Primary 7s were at the very back.

"Good morning, boys and girls."

"Good morning, Mrs Anderson."

"As you can all see beside me, today we have a very special visitor in our school dressed in his colourful African clothes. Boys and girls, this gentleman here is called Chief Chibi. He is from Ghana and he is here today to teach us about the importance of fair trade and how fair trade is helping poor farmers in Africa. I want you all to listen carefully and pay attention to what the Chief has to say.

"Now before I hand you over to Chief Chibi, can you all please say a warm good morning to Chief Chibi?"

"Good morning, Chief Chibi," all the children intoned upon instruction from the head teacher.

"By the way, I like your traditional robes, very colourful," she whispered into my ear and walked towards the side benches to join the rest of her teaching staff.

"Good morning, boys and girls. Are you all happy today?" I asked.

"Yes!" After the greetings, I asked the children to stand up and join me for a few warm up exercises. After breaking the ice, I began the short presentation by displaying my first clip on the screen. It was the map of Africa with the cursor on Ghana, my country of origin.

"I have heard that many of you have been learning about Africa for the past few days and weeks. Now, I want to ask you a few questions. First of all, how many countries do you think there are in Africa?" There was little boy in the front row who put his hand up first, smiling as he stood up to give his answer.

"One hundred," he said and laughed. Everyone laughed as well. He was a funny little character; like Horrid Henry! There were many hands up from the back row too, so I pointed to an older girl who stood up and introduced herself as Rebecca. "There are 53 countries in Africa, and Mrs Morrison told us the biggest country in Africa is Sudan." I asked the whole assembly to clap loudly for Rebecca before moving on to the second clip on the display.

"Boys and girls, as you can all see, this is a detailed map of Ghana, my country of origin. How many languages do you think are spoken in Ghana?"

"One," replied a little girl from the middle row. There were several other wrong guesses before I told the assembly that there are at least 54 distinct languages spoken in Ghana alone, with over 200 languages in Nigeria. Most of the children including some of the teachers were shocked at the number of languages spoken in Africa.

"Chief Chebe, how many of the 54 Ghanaian languages do you speak yourself?" asked one tall boy from the back row. He had brown spiky hair with side scrubs like David Beckham. I told the children that although 54 languages are spoken in Ghana, English is still our official language because Ghana was colonised by the British.

As I flipped through the presentation, we eventually got to the photo of a little boy called Kofi. He was working on a cocoa farm. I told the children that Kofi and his Uncle Yaw work very hard every day on their cocoa farm. Yet, they only earn 50p a day as a family because of the unfairness and the unjust nature of world trade. I asked the children what they think 50p can buy in Scotland.

"A packet of crisps," said one little girl. I told the assembly that most farmers in Africa get very little money for the goods they produce. I explained to the assembly that the unfairness of the world trade system makes it extremely hard for many African farmers to get out of poverty and that is the reason fair trade is the key to a positive global future. Before I took some questions, I told the assembly that through the power of ethical consumption and fair trade, many Ghanaian cocoa farmers like Kofi and his Uncle Yaw are now able to earn up to £3 a day for their hard work on the farm. I asked the children to think of what a poor farmer can do for himself and his family if he can get a fairer price for his goods.

Many hands went up, I called a girl to come to the front of the school and explain her understanding of the benefits of fair trade to the world. She stood up and looked nervous for a few seconds before overcoming her fear. When she walked to the front of the assembly, I asked her name first.

"My name is Chloe," she said and looked at me with a little smile.

"Chloe could you please tell the rest of the school why you think fair trade is good for the world?"

"Emmm, fair trade is good for Africa, because the farmers get more money to send their children to school," Chloe spoke, touching my heart. I felt the future is bright when we have children like Chloe speaking out from a small village in Scotland and sending a positive message to the world. I got the whole school to give Chloe a standing ovation before she walked back to her place.

"Fair trade is good because when the farmers get a fair price for their goods, they can build better homes. They can buy medicine and new clothes to wear," said one Primary 7 girl.

"Fair trade is good because the farmers can buy toys for their children," said another.

Whilst I was talking, I noticed that one or two kids were beginning to yawn. I knew I had to improve my dialogue. I decided to introduce a bit of African beat to the show.

"Boys and girls can you all stand up and chant the following words after me," I said and continued.

> Lead: Che-Che Kule
>
> Response Che-Che Kule
>
> Lead: Che-Che Kofinsa
>
> Response: Che-Che Kofinsa
>
> Lead: Kofinsa langa
>
> Response: Kofinsa langa
>
> Lead: Langa tu langa
>
> Response: Langa tu langa
>
> Together: Oops! Ayinde! Oops! Ayinde!
> Oops! Ayinde! Oops! Ayinde! and back to
> the beginning again!

When they got the song right, I added the drumbeat. The whole school chanted and sang along in their beautiful voices. It was the best moment of the assembly as all the children stood on their feet, wiggled their bums and shook their bodies in response to the sizzle of the irresistible African drum beat. What a wonderful time we had together!

After the assembly, it was Mrs Morrison who approached to take me upstairs.

"Chief Cheebi, I have brought some kids to help you take your stuff up to our classroom," said the teacher.

"Chief, can I carry your drum?" asked Rebecca. The rest of the kids took my baskets. I followed them and Mrs Morrison upstairs to set up a fair trade market.

"Wow, this classroom is amazing. The children have been working so hard," I remarked on entry. Although I have visited hundreds of schools throughout Scotland, the UK and other parts of Europe, I'm still surprised when I see how much effort many Scottish school children put into global education, especially their studies of Africa.

"Yes, all these masks were made last week," said Mrs Morrison. The whole classroom was decorated in a jungle theme with bright colours and drawings of giraffes, elephants, lions, snakes and other wildlife that brought a real feeling of Africa to the Scottish classroom. One of the walls was decorated with different masks from Kenya, Tanzania, Nigeria, Uganda, Ghana, amongst others. I felt very excited as the children spoke about what they have been learning about Africa as part of their global citizenship week: a week run every year in Scottish schools to celebrate the spirit of one world.

After admiring and commenting on the decoration, I got the children to help move the tables and chairs to the sides of the classroom so that we could start the fair trade market exhibition. I began by spreading my African mat in the middle of the classroom, then asked all the children to sit on the floor in a circle around the mat. I squatted on my knees and began the show. As the children and their teacher looked and wondered, I removed and spread out all the food and vegetables on the mat, one by one.

"Boys and girls, as you can all see for yourselves, this is my fair trade display to show you some of the food items produced by African farmers. Now, I want to invite three people to pick an item each which you have never ever seen in your life until today." Almost all the children had their hands up, even before I stopped speaking. I chose the first boy and asked his name.

"Craig," he said and smiled in an agitated way.

"Craig, please select any item from this mat; something you have never seen in your life until today." Craig stood up and edged forward into the circle. He scanned the foods before bending down to pick up a large tuber from the mat. I asked Craig if he had any idea what he had in his hand.

"It's a chunk of wood," he said and the rest of the class laughed out loud.

"I think it's a giant turnip," said one girl in the circle.

"I think it's a cucumber," said another.

"But a cucumber is green and this is brown," said Craig. He still had the tuber in his hand. None of the other children could tell what Craig had. Finally, it was the class teacher who came to their rescue!

"I think it is like a sweat potato, or is it a yam?" she asked and took the tuber from Craig to feel and examine properly. I got the whole class to clap for Mrs Morrison as Craig returned to the circle. I told the class that yam, cassava and maize are the most common sources of carbohydrate in West Africa.

"Boys and girls, I now want one or two of you to stand up and come into this circle to pick an item which you are familiar with. Something you think your Mum can buy from Tesco or ASDA today." One little blonde rascal put up her hand first. "What is your name?" I asked.

"Emily Russell," she said.

"Emily, I want you to pick up something from the mat; something you think your Mum can buy from Tesco or ASDA." Even before I finished giving Emily her instructions, she moved forward to select her choice.

"Emily what is that you have in your hand?"

"A banana," she replied.

I turned round and asked the rest of the class: "Boys and girls do you all agree that what Emily has in her hand is a banana?"

"Yes, it's a banana," they replied.

"Emily, where do you think banana's come from?"

"Tesco" she said and tickled herself into an infectious giggle.

"I mean, which part of the world do you think bananas come from?"

"Africa and the Caribbean," she said. I asked Emily if she knew why bananas only grow in Africa and the Caribbean, but not in Europe.

"It is hotter in Africa, that's why. We can't grow bananas in Scotland because it is too cold," she smirked.

I asked the children to show by hands how many of them eat bananas and almost 90% of the class put their hands up. I then took a little bit of time to explain the nature of our interdependent world today. I explained that fruits like bananas, pineapples, mangoes and cocoa beans can only be produced in tropical countries, but the farmers who produced them are usually paid very little money for their hard work, and that is what brings about poverty in Africa.

The bell rang interrupting our flow. It was time for break and I was relieved because I was gasping for a cup of tea. I followed Mrs Morrison downstairs.

The staffroom stood at the end of a very long corridor. Inside, there were many teachers, 18 of them I counted and not one male. It is always a scary experience sitting in front of so many women! It was a newly kitted staffroom with new carpet, new chairs, a new fridge, dishwasher, microwave and two automatic water boilers mounted beside the sink. I couldn't help thinking to myself how nice it would be if a Ghanaian school staffroom was kitted with the same or similar facilities.

"Chief Chibi, can I make you a cuppa?" Mrs Morrison asked placing her black leather handbag on the seat next to me.

"Tea would be great."

"How do you like it?"

"Hot, sweet and strong," I replied.

"I am sorry but we don't have any sugar. Will you take some sweeteners?"

"There is sugar in the cupboard, Maureen brought some yesterday," one young teacher pointed, she was texting with the other hand.

During the short 15-minute break, all the teachers gathered round me to find out a few things about Africa.

"So, Chief Chebe, is it true that one African Chief can marry as many wives as they like?"

"Err... yes, that is true, although this tradition is fading out now," I said feeling the heat.

"So, basically, one man is allowed to marry ten wives if he wants? How does it work in practice, are the women allowed to sleep with other men as well?" asked another teacher.

"My God, how can you keep them all motivated? How can you go to bed with ten wives?" asked Mrs Young the deputy head. Everyone laughed thinking about the potential practical problems of managing ten wives.

"Are any of these women ever happy at all?" asked another. There were more questions being thrown at me than I could answer! I tried to explain that sometimes polygamy works well in Africa but other times there are marital problems, which can lead to divorce, just like anywhere else in the world. I told the teachers that the situation is changing rapidly. In Ghana for example, about 20 years ago the average number of wives per man was four but today most Ghanaian men see even two wives as a huge burden on their shoulders.

"So how many wives do you have yourself?"

"Two," I said.

"Two wives, my goodness, you must be a greedy man. How do you keep them both happy?" I told Mrs Young that in my tradition, I have no choice but to have two wives. "My first wife is my grandmother. She is my spiritual wife and my lifetime mentor. My second wife is the chosen one, my true love."

"Oh, I see, but that is very strange. I suppose every culture is different," said Mrs Young.

Krrrrrrrrrrrrrrrrrrrrrrrr. The loud school bell rang to my rescue. I was beginning to feel the heat in my cheeks. Thank God I don't blush! I like talking openly about everything in this life, but in a fast-paced world, sometimes the risk of being misunderstood or misinterpreted is high. Anyway, I sighed with relief as I stood up and carried my half empty cup to the sink. "Let me put it in the dishwasher," a teacher said collecting the blue mug from my hand.

I returned to Primary 7 and showed them a game of Oware. Oware is a board game from Ghana, which is played in pairs. It proved very popular with all the pupils in the class. I spent the rest of the morning with them and we finished with a final dancing session where each boy was allowed to invite a girl of their choice into the middle of the circle. Initially, it was a struggle as the children all felt shy, especially about dancing with their opposite sex.

One little boy broke the ice by inviting Rebecca into the circle for the first dance. After moving and jumping around in the circle, they finished by hitting their bums together. The rest of the class laughed and cheered.

After the first dance, they all joined in and took turns. It was going great until the final bell rang for lunch. And, that was the end of my lesson.

"Chief Chibi, thank you so much for coming to Brave Heart Primary School today. This was the best day ever in school," said Rebecca.

"Me too, Chief Chibi, you are the best teacher in the whole world," said one of Rebecca's friends. I felt shy as they all sang their praises, thanking me left and right. I felt like a real hero or a celebrity (without the money!).

"Well, boys and girls, I want to thank you all for being the best Primary 7 class in the whole world. You have all been very good listeners and excellent contributors. I hope and pray that you will continue to learn everyday about the world around you, as you will soon progress into high school. I want you to promise me and yourselves that, when you grow into adulthood, you will continue to do everything you can to help make this world a better place for the future generations of children like you today."

"Well, boys and girls, haven't we had a wonderful day today?" asked Mrs Morrison.

"Yeahhhhhhhhhhhhhhhhhhhhhhh" they replied.

"I want you to give Chief Cheebi a big thank you. Hip, hip,"

"Hurray!" the children screamed and clapped loudly before rushing out of the classroom to go for some lunch.

Chapter 5: Tipping Point in Africa

It wasn't until three weeks after I returned from Ethiopia that I finally stumbled across a vital clue to solving the African Conundrum. What is the African Conundrum? The African Conundrum, in my mind, is a mathematical problem, which is the root cause of poverty in Africa. The fact is that, in simple mathematics, one plus one always equals two but, in Africa, one plus one equals zero.

On the first day that I began to see the answers, I was up in Aberdeen to teach global citizenship at a high school. For those of you who are not familiar with Scotland, Aberdeen is famously known as the oil capital of Europe. With an estimated population of a quarter of a million people, it is the third largest Scottish city next to only Glasgow and Edinburgh. The city has many nicknames including the Granite City, Grey City, Silver City or the City with Golden Sands. Aberdeen is also considered to be the Flower Capital of the UK because; it is estimated to have a staggering 2.5 million roses, 11 million daffodils and 3 million crocuses.

Anyway, I had a brilliant day at the high school and after work I drove along Queen's Street looking for the Aberdeen Youth Hostel to spend the night. When I arrived at the hostel, it was teaming with life. There were half a dozen people standing by the steps outside the main entrance, smoking cigarettes and chatting. I greeted them before heading to the reception to check-in.

"Good afternoon, can I get your name, date of birth and nationality, please," asked the lady at the reception. As I gave her the information she needed, she typed in and stared at her monitor to see if my details came up. "I am sorry; could you please spell your name?"

"C for charlie, H for hotel, E for echo, B for bravo and E for echo," I spoke, a little agitated.

The lady eventually got my details right. "This card allows you into the building at anytime, but the reception is closed after midnight," she spoke with an Australian ascent. Her name was Anna and she had a big Alsatian dog standing by her side. "Sit down, Jake," she ordered as the dog wagged its tail and panted with its long tongue stretched out as if it could not fit properly in its mouth. This is just like a domestic wolf, I thought to myself feeling a bit uneasy. "The kitchen is available to all guests and we have a laundry room in the basement where you can pay to wash and dry your clothes," Anna said and gave me a blue bed sheet and a white pillow to take upstairs. "You are in room 48 on the second floor. You can choose any bed which does not have a bed sheet and a pillow on it already."

"How many people am I sharing the room with?" I asked.

"There are only eight beds in your room, four guests have already checked in, you are the fifth," she spoke looking at the sheet in her hand. Anna told me that my room was one of the smallest in the hostel. "Some of the rooms can host up to 18 people," she said as I picked up my stuff to go.

After dropping my bag off, I went back downstairs into the kitchen to make myself a cup of tea. I was desperate for one. It was there that I met a group of people who were having a deep debate about the nature of unfairness in the modern world.

"The West has enjoyed too many privileges over the rest of the world, for far too long," said Raj, an Indian Master's student. There were about four Indians in the kitchen and they were all students in oil engineering. Two Nigerian oil student workers were also there cooking and they joined the debate as the food sizzled and steamed in the background. One of the Nigerian students was called Josh. A good international flavour of food and politics permeated the whole kitchen.

The talking and cooking continued until the conversation got too loud for the quiet room next door, so, some of us decided to go out to the garden. Josh and the other Nigerian man joined us after they had eaten and as we continued the debate, one charismatic Chinese man came to join us. He was also a Master's student in journalism at the Robert Gordon University. We spoke about the rise of China and India and how that could have significant impact on the lives of everyone in the world, especially the fat, bloated West. There was unanimous consensus that sooner or later, the greedy West would be forced to change its already overexaggerated and gluttonous lifestyles and unsustainable consumption patterns, which we now know causes so much damage to the environment and spreads material misery to far too many people in the developing world.

"The only way forward in this world is for everyone to work together to save ourselves and the planet. We can no longer continue to compete and outdo each other," said the Chinese man. "Now is the time we have to cooperate and coexist, and we need to build powerful human institutions like the UN, and improve its capacity as the unmanipulated government of the world." I was overjoyed with Mr Chang's rhythm and enthusiasm. "If we all continue to compete at a fast pace for a long time, we will fall and die together," he warned before he was duly interrupted.

"Look at the financial crises in the world right now, it is all because of greed," said Raj. "Look at all the earthquakes and hurricanes, look at all the natural disasters around the world and you will know that, global warming is no longer an issue we can ignore. Even God is getting angry with us every day!" Raj exclaimed. And we all laugh at the prospect of our Mighty Creator getting angry with his little creatures. What a dangerous predicament to find ourselves in, I thought.

"I tell you something," said Chang. "The world is not only a bad place to live, it is also a very good place, and many things are getting better every day. Look at where we are right now. We are sitting here in Aberdeen, eight different nationalities, all talking about the future of the world. These are all signs of positive global change.

This is why I chose to be a journalist. I want to travel around the world and do anything I can, to portray a good image of China and paint a better picture of the world." He spoke from the bottom of his heart.

Inevitably, the conversation gradually turned towards Africa. "Look at the situation in my country, Nigeria, right now. We have so much corruption in the country. If our leaders were not corrupt, why would any young intelligent Nigerian leave Nigeria to go anywhere else in this world to look for jobs? We have all the resources; oil, gold, diamonds, timber and, above all, the best agricultural land in the whole world."

"I don't think Africa will ever grow unless you do what we did in China after 1948. Look, we brought all the different Chinese tribes together to form the People's Republic of China. After that, we went around the world to learn from everybody and now we make everything that we need. What we don't need, we sell to the world. That is what you need to do in Africa. You have to learn from the West and go back to Africa with the knowledge to build your own economy. I have a book for you, if you want to change Africa."

"Where is it?" Josh asked.

Mr Chang took the book from his bag and showed it to us: "This book can change everything in Africa," he said pointing. Curiously, I stretched my hand to collect the book, but Josh was quicker. Josh took a long stare at the front cover before turning it over to see the back page. It was a white book with a bold title: *The Tipping Point*. There was an unlit matchstick in the middle of the front cover with some small writing in red. I took the book from Josh and read the text: "How little things can make a big difference."

"My brother, what this Chinese man is telling us is very true. I have read this book already and I believe that we are at the tipping point in Africa," said Josh. I asked why he believed so. "Look at the situation in America right now. The idea of an African-American president in the United States should be the greatest source of spiritual inspiration for every African man and woman in this world today. We have to consider what happened to our people in the past and feel proud about Obama." I felt mesmerised sitting on the garden bench with the book in my hand. I asked Josh why he thought Barack Obama provided the most important opportunity for Africa to unite for her own good.

"Obama is like a bridge and a connector. He is a man who can bring two worlds together. He is the man who can help Africa recover from our past wounds. By the way, I believe that this book can change Africa for good. If you have not read it, I strongly advise you to go to W.H. Smith tomorrow and get yourself a copy. There is one on Union Street," said Josh.

"My advice to the African people is simple. You must copy what we do in India," said Nadir, the shortest of the Indians.

"What can we learn from the Indians?" I asked quickly.

"Learn to grow your own food and improve education and you will win in Africa, that is the only way to succeed in the twenty-first century." Nadir stated that in India, they had to go through several Agricultural Revolutions before the country became stable enough in recent years. During the conversation, I wondered whether some things in this life are truly meant to happen or are just coincidence. I asked myself: why I am talking to these people? I didn't plan to meet any of them, but we found ourselves sitting and talking about exactly what was going through my mind at the time. The rest of the conversation simmered and boiled like a cooking pot on the fire. There was a very good atmosphere in the garden and, in the end, I felt both mentally and emotionally constipated and went to my bed thinking: what is the next step?

That night, I struggled long and hard to sleep. The room was so hot. Even after opening the windows, it was still impossible to relax. It didn't help that there were so many men sleeping in a single room, with some snoring like pigs and cows.

Later on, around midnight, one Portuguese man exacerbated the situation by arriving late, clearly plastered. He argued that one of the Indian guys was sleeping on his bed.

"You must get off and give me my fucking bed," he demanded. After a heated debate, it was the hostel manager who came into the room to quench the fire.

The next day, as advised, I went to Union Street and got myself a copy of *The Tipping Point* before leaving Aberdeen. A few days later, I managed to squeeze some spare time to visit the library. I was determined to read *The Tipping Point* so that I could understand why Mr Chang believed that this book can change the injustice of the world. I especially wanted to find out why Josh believed that this is the book that offers a definite solution to a successful African Revolution.

That day, I went to the Mitchell Library in Glasgow: one of the biggest and best-equipped in Europe. The library was busy and it took me a while to find an ideal space. When I eventually got myself a quiet spot on the third floor, it didn't take too long to get my teeth into the book, turning page after page in a breathless effort to unravel the truth for myself.

In this fascinating book, the author Malcolm Gladwell argues brilliantly that: 'there are magic moments when people's aspirations, ideas, dreams and other social behaviour cross a threshold, tip and spread like wildfire.' After the opening pages, Mr Gladwell stepped forward and offered step-by-step explanation as to how social revolutions often come about by the unlikeliest means.

Using real life stories to paint a vivid picture, Mr Gladwell wrote flawlessly about the epic story of a ten-year-old American schoolboy, Thomas Jefferson Junior. Through ingenious craftsmanship, Mr Gladwell explained how innocent Thomas sparked a word-of-mouth epidemic, which led to the brutal battle with the British for America's Independence.

According to Mr Gladwell, the story of American independence began on 18 April 1775. Little Thomas was returning from the stables in Boston when he overhead something about: "Hell to pay for tomorrow." When Thomas returned home and told his Uncle Paul Revere, who became convinced that the British colonial army was planning to attack the area and seize control of the strategic town of Lexington the next day. Mr Gladwell explained that earlier that afternoon, Mr Revere received a warning from a friend that the British were planning a major military assault on the area. What happened next, Gladwell argued, has become part of historical legend, a tale told to every American school child of today.

Mr Gladwell wrote that at ten o'clock that night:

> Mr Revere met his friend Warren: They decided they had to warn the communities surrounding Boston that the British were on their way, so that local militia could be roused to meet them. Revere was spirited across Boston Harbour to the ferry landing at Charlestown. He jumped on a horse and began his midnight ride to Lexington. In two hours, he covered 13 miles. In every town he passed through along the way he knocked on doors and spread the word, telling local leaders of the coming British, and telling them to spread the word to others. Church bells started ringing. Drums started beating. The news spread like a virus as those informed by Paul Revere sent out riders of their own, until alarms were going off throughout the entire region of Boston.

> When the British finally began their march towards Lexington on the morning of the 19th April 1775, their foray into the countryside was met, to their utter astonishment, with organised and fierce resistance. In Concord that day, the British were confronted and soundly beaten by local militia, and from that exchange came the war known as the American Revolution.

There were many questions in my mind as I sped through page after page until I finally got the message.

The Law of the Few

According to Mr Gladwell, what is very important to the success of any human revolution is the explicit realisation that, in this life, it is not every human being who has the power or wisdom to cause a chain reaction over the boiling issues of society. On the contrary, he argued that there are only a critical few in every society who matter most. He explained that this critical minority of people among us have that rare but essential ability to kick-off a word-of-mouth epidemic or social revolution. He cited Mr Revere as an excellent example of those critical few in society who matter most. To explain the impact of this category of people in our lives, Gladwell coined the term: "The Law of the Few".

According to the logic of Mr Gladwell, there are some people who are more socially connected than others. These types of people, he argued, have a much greater effect on the spread of an epidemic in any given context. In relation to a social phenomenon, they know the right people to talk to and they can cross any social boundaries. These types of people are always capable of living comfortably under any conditions.

In every society, the powerful contribution of a few dedicated people can be more important than the lackadaisical action of the masses. As I read on, I couldn't help agreeing with every single claim of the author. I felt inspired by the story of Thomas Jefferson, the ten-year-old American schoolboy. I continued to wonder if there are any special little boys like Thomas in Africa today who could perform similar magic for Africa. Who is going to light that critical torch for all the people of Africa to see and escape from our long days of darkness? To escape from the very long dark tunnel we have been going through for so many dark centuries? I asked myself again and again, time after time.

In a nutshell, Mr Gladwell's argument about the law of the few can be better explained as follows:

If, for example, 100 per cent of the people in Africa believe that Africa deserves to achieve better economic status but takes only 1 per cent of the action required to make a difference all the time, then Africa will remain in her hellish position forever. In other words, it might not be true that little drops of water alone can always fill a mighty ocean.

But, on the other hand, if only 20 per cent of the enlightened population of Africa today believe that hunger or malaria, for example, are preventable and they take 80 per cent individual and collective action towards this belief, Africa will be freed from the devastating impact of hunger and malaria in a matter of a few hardworking generations. In the fields of economics and social anthropology, this powerful and influential minority is described as the "critical mass". This is why an economist will tell you that in most businesses, 80 per cent of the work is done by the critical 20 per cent of the workforce. Many criminologists also believe that in almost every country of the world only 20 per cent of the population carry out 80 per cent of the crime. Similarly, only 20 per cent of dedicated and committed daily drinkers in Europe consume a staggering 80 per cent of all the alcohol drunk in Europe every year.

Mr Gladwell explained that even in this critical mass, there are a crucial few who can make the biggest impact. These crucial few he described as connectors, mavens and salesmen. Painstakingly, he argued that, without the vital and necessary contribution of these three categories of people, there can never be a successful social epidemic in any given scenario.

The Role of the Connector

According to Gladwell, connectors are people with a special gift for bringing the world together. These are the kind of people who are usually popular and well-liked. They are also the kind of people we can all look up to and believe to be sincere in what they say. A good example of a connector is Mr Revere who rode his horse spreading the news all night about the planned British assault on Boston. Gladwell argued that without the vital contribution of Revere, it is possible that the British could have won that vital battle to take Lexington.

After reading about the role of connectors in bringing positive change to society, I couldn't help but ask myself: who can we trust and believe to play the role of the African connector. Nelson Mandela immediately sprang to mind but, then I thought to myself, our humble Mandela may have all the wisdom, the heart and the likeable personality to connect Africa but, he no longer has the horsepower like Mr Revere to go round and tell the new generation of Africans to unite for our own collective good. So, who else has a powerful image like Nelson Mandela with the power and a believable and convincing personality to connect the people of Africa? This was a question I found easier to ask than to answer!

The Talent of the Maven

The second most critical category of people who can force and bring about positive change in society is the data banker. Gladwell argues that, just as we rely on connectors like Revere to bring people together in times of social anxiety, we also rely on others to provide us with new, credible information. "There are people specialists and there are information specialists. But sometimes, of course, these two specialists are one in the same," he wrote, citing Paul Revere as an example of a man with both credentials. Gladwell explained that Mr Revere wasn't only an effective connector or just the man with the biggest Rolex in town. "He was also actively engaged in gathering information about the British. He set up a secret group that met regularly at the Green Dragon Tavern with the express purpose of monitoring British troop movements. Paul

Revere was a connector. But he was also a maven, and this is the second of the three kinds of people who control word-of-mouth epidemics."

The Power of the Convincing Salesman

Finally, Mr Gladwell explained that, for social epidemics to break and spread to the masses, there is an essential group of people who have the power to persuade us to take certain action. "In a social epidemic, mavens are data banks. They provide the message. Connectors are social glue; they spread the message. But there are also a select group of people, Salesmen, with the skills to persuade us when we are unconvinced of what we are hearing, and they are as critical to the tipping point of word-of-mouth epidemics as the other two groups."

I read the tipping point over two days and, at the end, I was left more confused than before. I was confused because, I could not immediately identify a single man or woman in Africa who I could point to and say, this is the person who can connect the people of Africa together. We have big personalities, such as Nelson Mandela, Kofi Annan and Desmond Tutu, but at the end of the day, I wondered if any of these guys had the horsepower and the stamina to unite Africa?

I have my own doubts and sometimes wonder if Africa will ever unite and prosper. Sometimes I get frustrated, thinking too much about Africa. Every day, I say to myself: "I wish I could be that amazingly, irresistible salesman who can sell sand to the Arabs." Unfortunately, although I consider myself a good salesman, I know that trying to sell some sense to the African man might prove to be a harder challenge than trying to persuade the Arab man to buy some extra sand from me to put in his desert.

So, what next? If I am not enough of a salesman to persuade the people of Africa to unite, what else can I do? I asked and asked myself these questions repeatedly until I finally came to a perfect realisation. I read the story of Bill Gates and discovered that although he was not necessarily the most convincing salesman in the world, he managed to become the richest man in the world.

Bill Gates sold his software to 80% of computer users in the world for two important reasons:

First of all, Bill knew from the onset that he had a great product to sell to the world. If you ask any good salesman or woman you meet, they will tell you that in every sales environment, having a good product is a bonus to the salesman. But, the second and perhaps the most important reason Bill Gates became exceptionally successful with his Microsoft empire was because he hired the best salesmen in the world to do the job for him.

In the end, I convinced myself that, although a blind man cannot see for himself, he can use his sense, get a walking stick or a guide dog to get from A to B. In other words, if I cannot directly sell my sense to the African people, I can at least employ or hire the services of a good salesman, maven and connector like Barak Obama to help to interpret and spread the full gospel of the African Dream to the African people: this is why I believe that at this moment in time, we are going through a tipping point in Africa!

Chapter 6:   Barack Obama: Yes, Africa, We Can

One day in Glasgow I was sitting in the church next to my friend DJ Yaw. As the pastor continued his preaching, I became a bit bored. I decided to close my eyes briefly to say my own little prayer: "God the Almighty," I called and said: "please show us some magic in Africa today to convince me that you are there and alive. God, please do something to prove that you really care about the people of Africa." In my prayers, I said to God: "If seeing is believing, please open your curtains from the sky and show us your face in Africa so that we can believe and follow your will. God, do something to convince us that you are interested in helping to bring an end to our pain and suffering in Africa." As I prayed, I was almost in a trance when my friend Yaw hit me on the shoulder.

"My brother, it's time to go home, the christening is over. Were you sleeping there at the end?" I told Yaw about the little prayer I was making to God.

He laughed and shook his head and said to me: "But why do we need to see the face of God in Africa before we can convince ourselves to do the right things? Don't you think that God has already performed enough miracles for us in Africa?" Yaw asked and pointed his finger: "Look at Obama, since the Lord Jesus Christ came to the world, can you think of any other ordinary human miracle on this earth as big as the story of Barak Obama?"

"No," I replied as we followed each other out of the church. Yaw told me that, in his view, Obama is the new face of God in Africa. "It is now up to me and you and every African in the world to believe Obama as our God's messenger or not." Yaw pointed to the fact that through Obama, God has already shown to the people of the world that, a man of an African origin is not a man of an inferior ability. He said, "If we fail to unite ourselves as Africans whilst Obama is in power, we may never ever again get a second chance till judgement day.'"" As I listened to Yaw, I kept asking myself: can Barack Obama really play the role of African Messiah from the awkward position of the presidency of the United States of America? And if he can, what must Obama do to break the chains of mental slavery from the hands of the African people? Finally, what do we know about the man we all call Barak Obama today?

The Son of a Shepherd

Luckily enough, I had a good person in mind who I knew could give me inside information about Obama. This man is a true African maven, a retired Kenyan professor in Edinburgh, who I believed could help me unveil the story of Obama from an African viewpoint. Professor Kenyatta, as we call him, because of his striking similarity to the first Kenyan president, Jomo Kenyatta. When I thought of Professor Kenyatta's, I called to arrange a meeting with him in Edinburgh.

I remember that Friday when I got to Edinburgh to meet the professor. I was so anxious to hear what he had to say about the Obama dynasty. "The ultimate truth," Professor Kenyatta said and paused as the barman arrived to take our order. "Barack Obama is a young, dynamic, but previously unknown, African-American politician, who suddenly emerged from almost nowhere to gain prominence." Kenyatta talked with charisma, good pace and great sense of wisdom like a true African elder. "It is important to remind ourselves that, in spite of the global media hype and all the glamour surrounding Obama today, just a few years ago before this 2008 presidential election campaign, hardly anyone in America knew about Obama, never mind the rest of the world."

Professor Kenyatta intimated that, unlike any other normal aspiring US presidential candidate who often originates from the privileged and upper ruling classes, Obama's own story is rooted in an ordinary humble beginning. "The son of a hard-working shepherd turned distinguished Harvard-trained Kenyan academic." The professor told me Obama's father was among the first 81 brightest Kenyan academics taken to the United States to train and return home to build their country after independence. "Their mission was to gain new knowledge and go back home to take over from the British Colonial Government." Professor Kenyatta spoke about Obama's father with a great sense of pride and dignity. I could see every glimmer of hope expressed vividly on his face during my interview. In the professor's view, Obama's outstanding record and ability to rise from common ground to the top of society can only be properly interpreted as: "A like-father-like-son episode unfolding before the eyes of the world." I sat and listened with ears open and tuned to my Kenyan brother's reassuring, authoritative voice and his authentic account of a man who many believe can offer the necessary spiritual hope that we so badly need in Africa today.

"Obama Senior," he said referring to the father again. "He was a rebellious young man with a positive vision for Africa. When he left Kenya to study at Hawaii University in 1959, he told his friends at his leaving party that after his studies, he would return home with his knowledge to change the African economy. He refused to attend the first school he was enrolled in, because his teacher was a woman. He told his father that as a young male, he preferred to be educated by a man.

In his youth, he was a ladies' man, like many other super-talented African youths of his days."

Professor Kenyatta told me that Obama Senior was a very brave young man: "Especially in relation to women. He was always confident. Let me tell you a story about Obama's father," he said and paused a little. "One day, he went into a local village dancing competition. During the dance, he spotted a beautiful lady called Kezia and approached her. There were many other beautiful young ladies at the dance, so Kezia was surprised that she was the chosen one." According to Professor Kenyatta, Obama Senior danced happily with Kezia that night and three days later, he married her by giving 16 cows to her father. He only needed to give eight cows, but he doubled the dowry because he loved her as much. "Take it this way, Obama Senior was a very romantic man," the professor said with a wise smile.

It was at Hawaii University that, Obama's mother and father met. "Stanley Ann Dunham was 17 at the time. Ann's father, Stanley Dunham, desperately wanted a son. He was a little disappointed when Ann was born. So, he gave her the name Stanley Ann. Obama Junior, otherwise President Barack Hussein Obama, was born in Hawaii on the 4 August 1961 at 7:24 p.m.

Unfortunately, after a short spell of happiness between his parents, the relentless pressure of family life soon led to an amicable and blameless divorce arrangement when the little star was just a toddler aged only two. Kenyatta explained that shortly after the separation, Obama Senior moved on to study for a PhD at Harvard University. After completing his academic work in America, he returned to Kenya, where he lived and worked happily for the rest of his life, until his death in a car crash in 1982.

"Although Obama Junior had very little time with his father during his childhood years, as a young man, he grew very fond of him. He was deeply inspired by his father's story of struggle and remarkable success, stretching back to the very remote Luo village of Nyangoma Kogela, which is more or less a roadless settlement in Western Kenya. His father's inspiration led Obama Junior to write one of the bestsellers in the US book market – *Dreams from My Father*."

After deliberating on the Kenyan side for some time, Brother Kenyatta turned the page to the maternal side of the Obama's unfolding story.

"Obama's mum, Anne Dunham also moved on quickly and married an Indonesian gentleman. After the marriage, she migrated to

Indonesia with the six-year-old Obama Junior, where a brand new chapter began for him." I asked Brother Kenyatta how little Obama coped with such an extreme move from America to Indonesia.

"From a very early stage, it was obvious that Obama was a bright rising star." Mr Kenyatta said Obama spoke the Indonesian language fluently within six months and subsequently achieved much of his early education in Indonesia, which is the largest Muslim country in the world. As I jotted my notes, my maven brother continued, adding that after Indonesia, "Obama returned to Honolulu and spent his teenage years with his maternal grandparents where he carried on with his education. He clearly understood from an early age that a good education would later play an essential part of his father-inspired dream, to aim for the top through hard work and determination."

Finally, he explained that "As a bright, colourful, easy-going, fun-loving and extremely intelligent young student, Obama Junior, like his father, achieved high academic standards and won many scholarships throughout his education, which eventually led him to the Law School at Harvard University. The very place his father had completed a doctorate degree a few decades earlier."

Before we finished, I told Kenyatta what my friend Yaw told me in the church. In his response he said: "Of course, if you believe that Moses was a messiah to the Israelites, then Obama is an even bigger messiah to the Africans today, it is up to us to believe and follow what he says or not," he said. I had a fantastic interview with my Kenyan brother in Edinburgh. We left the Sheraton Hotel together. Brother Kenyatta walked me along Lothian Road, passing through Princess Street to Waverly Station to catch my train back to Glasgow. In the station, Professor Kenyatta said something, which completely changed my life. "My brother," he called and said as we bought coffees. "Have you ever heard the Nigerian saying that: what the people of Sokoto are looking for outside Sokoto can only be found inside Sokoto?" I stood in silence for a moment and took a sip of my cappuccino. "The reason I ask you the question is that if you believe Obama has an important message for us in Africa, then, you have to go home and find out what the people of Africa are saying about Obama. I believe the answer to your African Dream is waiting for you in Ghana, not here in the Scotland. Remember what the Sokoto man is looking for outside Sokoto can only be found inside Sokoto!" Kenyatta advised before I ran to catch my train.

"I wish you a safe journey home," he added.

Glasgow to Accra

And that was it; I knew I had to pack my bags and leave Glasgow as soon as possible. I said to myself: this is the moment of action. I have to go home and find the sticky glue I need to start spread my own word of mouth epidemic to bring positive change to Africa.

I must admit though that, my decision to go home was so much easier said than done. Things were tough and tight and there was no way to turn or twist. I thought a lot on my own and with people. At the end, I said to myself, it was either to go home or sit back in Glasgow and regret the rest of my life for not doing what I feel I can do to make Africa a better place. I was ill-prepared, but at the end I convinced myself that where there is a will and determination to do something, there is always a way to do it. I left Glasgow towards the end of July, by then the 2008 American presidential election campaign was already brewing to a bubbling sensation across the Atlantic. Radio and television coverage spread waves, hitting every corner of the world. I remember when I flew to London; every global media network had Obama mania. Amazingly, it appeared as though Barack Obama had changed, almost overnight, the dull and uncool image of American politics into a desirable, sexy, global, Hollywood movie show. It was like witnessing the birth of a new son from Big Brother's House.

It was my friend Anthony who picked me up from Gatwick. I asked him why he thought Obama has managed to perform such amazing miracles overnight.

"My Brother let's forget about Obama right now and discuss why you are going home in such a haste."

"I want to do something to unite Africa that is why I am going home. I want to find a convincing message to touch the hearts and minds of our new generation."

"Challae, make we enter this Somalian shop, make I buy goat meat. I have invited a few friends to join us for dinner," Anthony diverted as if he was not interested in the answer I gave.

That evening I had a sudden twist of faith. Some of my London Ghanaian friends were unconvinced about my trip home, especially my friend Winfred. "My brother let me ask you a straight question," said Winfred. "First of all, I have to be very honest with you. I am still totally unconvinced as to why you are going home. What about your own business in Glasgow? Who is going to look after your interests while you are away trying to solve Africa's problems? Can't you see that you are being totally crazy?" Winfred told me that he could not understand why any normal Ghanaian man could just get up and leave the comfort of his home in the UK to go to Ghana and write a book about: *African Dream.* "Let's enjoy ourselves here in the UK and forget about Africa; Africa will never develop because we are greedy. You are wasting your time following an empty dream," Winfred said and forced a large chunk of goat meat into his mouth. "If I can be totally honest with you, I think you are wasting your time. Africa is poor because there are big powers behind the scene that control what is going on and there nothing poor men like you and I can do to change the system," Winfred continued. In response, I told him that a journey of a thousand miles consists of billions of small steps. I argued that if Africa is the richest continent with the poorest people, it is because those among us who know better and should do better for Africa are not taking enough little steps to improve the situation. I told my London friends that those of us who feel frustrated enough about the poverty in Africa have a duty and a right to change our attitudes and behaviour in a way that reflects the changes we wish to see in Africa.

The next day, I woke up early and got ready to go to the airport. Anthony was working that day, but Winfred had the day off, so he gave me a lift. When we got to Heathrow, everything happened in precise, military style. The security was tight that day and there were long slow-moving queues on every direction. I checked in my luggage. Winfred and I went up stairs to share a last pint.

"My brother, I wish you a safe journey home and please don't worry about the doubts I created in your mind last night. I know you have a good heart and good mind, please make good use of both while you are home. Please look after your body. You know all the dangers at home. Home is not always sweet. Sometimes home is more bitter than we wish to taste. Be careful with yourself and don't drink carelessly in public places because there are many wicked people who can poison unnecessarily. I leave you in the capable hands of the Lord Jesus Christ to take you home safely and bring you back safely to the UK. In Jesus' name, Amen," he said. "Amen'" I replied, before trotting frantically towards the departure gate. When we finally took off, the plane skidded along the runway before rising from the ground, pointing its nose first and lifting up high towards the sky. As we rose into the sky, I sat and thought for a while, and then began to doze.

"Excuse me, sir, can I offer you tea or coffee?" asked one of the flight attendants. She was pushing a trolley of drinks and beverages along the narrow cabin.

"Strong black coffee with two sugars, please," I replied, still half asleep. I couldn't keep my mouth shut with yawning. After a few sips of coffee, I gave up and decided to go back to sleep, but was distracted by a lively debate which began to gather pace. Many passengers got involved.

"Obama will be remembered differently from every other president of the world because of his universal identity." A lady passenger argued. She said that through the image of Obama, the Blackman can see the good side of a white man and through his image; the whites can also see the good side of the black people." The lady passenger caused laughter in the plane when she said Obama is the only one in the world who resembles the people of every nation on earth. "It is true," she said and continued. "If Obama goes to China today, he will blend in perfectly well with all the good people of China. If he goes to India, he looks like and Indian man, in Cuba, he looks like a Cuban. In Arabia, he will look like an Arab. In Brazil, Ireland, Jamaica, Ghana, or anywhere in Africa, he will have no problem connecting with the people. Who else can do the same in the world today?" She asked before she was duly interrupted.

One man fuelled the debate to a higher level by questioning if Barack Obama was any different from any other glamorous, self-seeking politician in the world?

"Personally, I believe it is crazy and wishful thinking for Africans to sit and think that Obama will bring any change for Africa. You see, let us not fool ourselves as Africans. Barack Obama cannot do anything for Africa because he is an American man. His loyalty is to the American people. Those who are going to elect him on the 3rd November," he argued. He was an elderly Ghanaian with bushy hair and a touch of grey.

"Excuse me sir, why do you think Obama cannot help Africa?" I asked.

"Don't call me sir, my name is Papa Yanky. I say Obama can't do anything to help Africa because it is up to us in Africa to change the way we behave. Look, I have lived and worked as a doctor in America for 25 years. And, I can tell you that Chicago is beautiful because the people of Chicago are proud of themselves. They do whatever is expected of them properly everyday and at the right time. That's the only reason Chicago is beautiful. We Africans, on the other hand, are not proud of ourselves and we don't serve our public institutions with pride and dignity." Papa Yanky argued that although many Africans are disloyal in serving our own countries, we are often the most honest, dedicated and hardworking employees when we travel to Europe, America or anywhere else in the world.

"Challae, I totally disagree with you that Obama is an American man who cannot do anything to help us in Africa. That is completely wrong," said one Nigerian passenger. He was a charismatic and bubbly man; wearing a cowboy hat. He argued that everyone in this life has a father and a mother. "A woman can never fertilise her own eggs. Obama's father is Kenyan. So, I believe that even if he cannot help Africa as a continent, he must at least show some American love to the people of Kenya when he gets into the White House."

I sat back with my seatbelt fastened; the debate continued like beans in a boiling pot. Many passengers chipped in and out as the aeroplane flew on passing over oceans and cutting across continents.

"Obama just seems to me, to be a man I can look straight in the eye to see whether he is telling me a lie or the truth," said one beautiful young Ghanaian woman. She was also returning home for good. "I have worked as a nurse in the UK for ten years but now I am going home because my country needs people like me," she said with a proud Ghanaian smile. Then explained how she had teamed up with two of her colleagues in London to set up a business. "Three years ago, we all decided to pull resources together and build our own clinic in Accra. That is why I am going home. "I like Obama, but I just wish he was not already married to Michelle!"

"Forget about Obama, my name is Oga, I am the best man for you" the Nigerian man said adjusting his hat. "I bet you Barack Obama is not as romantic as I am! You are a very fine Ghanaian lady. I can see from your hips that you can bear more than ten children for me. Just come with me to Lagos and I will make you the happiest woman in the whole world." Like the rest of the men, Oga was enjoying the spirit of the moment to the limit.

The seatbelt light flashed and everyone returned to their seats to prepare for landing. The captain took a deep dive in the air and descended abruptly through the thick clouds, manoeuvring skilfully. When I looked through the window, I could see lights spread across miles and miles of land. Wow, Accra looks so beautiful from the air, I thought to myself. I knew I was nearly home, but the feeling of anxiety in the air made my nerves ache in the few seconds before landing. Finally, after six amazing hours of floating through the air like a giant bird, the large British Airways passenger bus screeched onto the runway, touching Ghanaian soil. Everyone inside cheered and clapped to show their appreciation for the pilot for bringing us home safely! The atmosphere inside the plane was like the moment of the final whistle in a game of football, when you know your team has taken the cup. When I got out of the aeroplane and my feet touched the ground, it felt like touching on the surface of Heaven. The air was dusty, but warm and fresh to breathe. In actual fact, there is no adjective in the English dictionary that could describe how I felt touching Ghanaian soil again. Home sweet home!

Chapter 7: Voices on the Streets

My hotel room was hot and sticky and the mosquitoes were on a rampage, making an excruciating noise and piecing through my innocent flesh without mercy. In a raging anger, I slapped and killed one nasty bloodsucker, which had sneakily bitten me on my neck. The blood splattered on my palm, like red paint. I tried to cover myself with the blanket but it was too warm and sticky, perhaps a mosquito net would have been useful!

As I lay and struggled to sleep, the ceiling fan above my head produced just enough cold air to give me a little comfort, but the rackety noise it made also added a different degree of pain to my agony. Around midnight, I grew restless and decided to call for help.

"My brother, please come and rescue. What is your name?" I asked.

"Sir, my name is Luke-man, what can I do to help you?" the hotel guard said and approached me with his shirt on his shoulder and a small radio in his hand.

After hearing my predicament, Luke-man thought of an immediate solution. "Sir, give me five Ghana cedi. I will go and get you some mosquito spray from the filling station." Luke-man told me that normally, the mosquitoes are not too bad, but the previous week the first rains of the season had begun and fell heavily. "That is why the mosquitoes are wild these days." I gave Luke-man some money and sat on the bench in the compound with a few other guests while he rushed off to get the mosquito spray. About ten minutes later, he returned with some news. "Sir, I am sorry but there were no mosquito sprays at the station. But, I bought some coil. Let me go and light it for you," he said before collecting my room key. Fortunately, the burning coil chased away the little devils, but the smoke it produced filled the room; making it uncomfortable to breathe in the warm choking air. I sneezed and sneezed, asking myself many "whys?" I began to wonder whether I was biting off more than I could chew. I asked myself, could I really do anything as a small individual to help the Africa that I love and believe in so much? And if I could, what exemplary role could I play to inspire and make others proud enough of Africa or believe in Africa like I do?

I felt very lucky that I was able to purchase a coil to get rid of the mosquitoes in my room. The question that remained in my head all night was, what about those who do not have the money to buy mosquito coils? Why do millions of poor innocent people in Africa die each year from treatable disease like malaria?

I began the next day by treating myself to a hot Ghanaian breakfast; kenkey and tilapia fish with a large glass of freshly squeezed home-grown pineapple juice. That bright morning, I broke my fast at the "Country Kitchen" breakfast club.

After my early morning gastronomic feast, I decided to visit Makola market, the busiest open-air market in West Africa. Makola is situated in the hub of the Accra commercial district. I had to catch a bus at the Neo-plan station, so I headed there by foot. The sun blistered onto my face as I walked towards the Kwame Nkrumah Circle.

On my way to the station, I saw many billboards showing slogans of the new African Prophet.

"Yes we can," a man shouted walking by. He was wearing an Obama T-shirt, the latest in town. I watched many taxi drivers passing, displaying American flags in their cars to show their support for Barack Obama. The magic floated and lingered in the air catching everyone along the way like influenza. It was as though there was a new African pope in town.

On the way, I met hundreds and thousands of people all going in different directions. Cars beeped their horns and traders rang their bells, others roared at the top of their voices to catch passing trade. Before Nkrumah Circle, I saw a group of children sitting on a patch of green grass and begging. One of them saw me and immediately ran in my direction. He wore only a pair of pants and his bare belly showed signs of malnourishment.

"Sir, give me dollar. I didn't eat any food last night," he said. He was a foreign-looking boy with browner skin, probably of Somalian origin.

"How old are you?" I asked.

"I'm seven years old, I need dollar to go and eat," he said slightly aggressively. "I want dollar," he said again and again.

"Where are your parents and why are you not at school today?"

"I have no mother or father. They died when I was two years."

"How did they die?" I asked, unconvinced. I saw a few adults sitting under a tree looking at the little boy and me. I looked and wondered if the boy was working for them.

"Where do you come from?" I asked unable to judge by his accent, which had a slight American twist to it.

"Sir, I come from Liberia. I lost my mother and father in the war. My aunt brought me to Ghana." Out of guilt, I dropped a few coins for the boy and continued.

Inside the Neo-plan station, there were queues of passengers and rows of stalls selling everything from second-hand clothes to household and electrical goods. I saw some smoke rising in front of me. I tried to walk past, but a man called me to come and buy.

"Nice kebab," he said and used a sharp knife to cut a small piece for me. "Sample before you buy," said the tall Chin-Changa man. The tribal marks on his face suggested that he was probably from Burkina Faso. After navigating through hundreds of packed pedestrians, I boarded a tro-tro, the local transport, heading to Makola market.

The seats were tight and, to make matters worse, a very fat lady entered the bus and no one moved to let her sit next to them. Out of some naive kindness, I squeezed to the middle seat and allowed her to sit next to me. Perhaps, that was my first mistake of the day.

Before the bus left the station, a man with a battered briefcase jumped in. He was about six feet tall and in his mid-thirties. He was smartly dressed in a brown suit. His infectious smile made it impossible to keep my eyes away from him.

"Good morning my brothers and sisters," the man greeted, "it is nice that our kind Lord Jesus Christ has given us all good health today. Let us rejoice together and say Hallelujah. Good health is the most important thing in this life, which so many of us take for granted every day," the stranger in the brown suit continued. "As I speak to you right now, there will be some people going through pain, not because they do not have a good bank balance, but simply because they cannot get out of their sick beds. That is real poverty." The pastor spoke rather convincingly before opening his briefcase to retrieve his bible.

"Let us pray," he said again and opened his bible. "Prayer is the strongest weapon in this life. Prayers combine belief and hope and turn them into thoughts, visions, dreams, ideas and plans which can then be translated into deliberate actions; actions which can produce successful outcomes." As he spoke, the driver manoeuvred his tro-tro to get out of the busy morning traffic at Nkrumah Circle.

"Praise the Lord," said the Pastor.

"Hallelujah," the crowd responded. This is unbelievable, I thought. Only in Africa where church services are conducted in buses, taxis and trains!

"Now let us pray together for hope. Let us pray for freedom and final glory. Let us pray for our dear brother. Let us pray that God will deliver Obama into the White House with dignity and honour. Let us pray to God to cleanse his heart and give him greater wisdom to bring lasting peace to his country America, and to his great kingdom of Africa. Let us pray as we sit in this bus today, that come 3rd November 2008, our chosen brother Barack Hussein Obama becomes the 44th President of the United States of America. Let us pray for unity and prosperity, not only in America but also right here in Ghana and throughout our motherland Africa. The bible tells us in Mathew 12: 25 that: 'Every kingdom divided against itself is brought to desolation; and every city or house divided against itself, shall not stand.' So, let us pray for unity and lasting peace in the world. In Jesus' name, please say Amen."

"Amen," every single passenger replied including the bus driver.

"Yes we can," the driver shouted out raising his right hand. Everybody repeated his phrase. As he drove along the busy Accra road, the pastor continued with his preaching. I sat watching the social commotion unravel with no idea what was to come next. At a point, I felt like a million dollar lottery winner sitting among the most diehard Obama supporters and enthusiasts. That was exactly the situation I most wanted to be in: the very reason I was home. It was one of those moments when everything is exact, including the time. The feeling was simply priceless.

The bus stopped frequently, dropping and picking up new passengers along the way whilst the pastor continued with the morning prayers.

"The Holy Bible I hold here tells us that a messiah will come after 2,000 years," the pastor said as we approached the next stopping point. The bus drew to a halt to drop off the Makola passengers. I felt a breath of relief after such a tight squeeze in the middle seat. I took my bag and got out feeling energised and inspired by what the pastor said. I thank God for giving me good health and promise to do the same everyday that I am well.

Arriving at Makola market, everywhere I turned to look teamed with life. The feeling I had standing by the pavement reminded me of the Glastonbury music festival which I'd attended several years ago in England; lots of buzzing music, bells ringing, roaring noise, colourful umbrellas, concrete walls, congested pavements, hundreds and thousands of market stalls and packed shops on the roadsides, colourful and noisy traders and shoppers moving in all directions like a large colony of bees.

That morning, I walked round and spoke to dozens of traders and other market visitors until noon, when I stopped for some lunch. I was thirsty and hungry, so I ordered some fufu and goat meat. In a desperate hurry, I sat in the busy bar and ate my food before sinking down a bottle of water to clear my aching throat. The heat of the day was unrelenting and I bled with sweat.

Before I left the market, I had one last important interview to conduct with Mami Dakunu, the President of the Makola Market Women's Association. I wanted to ask her what she thought about life in general and the Ghanaian economy in particular. Adisa, a tall beautiful dark-skinned Kayayo woman from the north led me to see Mami Dakunu. As we approached the shop, I saw a bright yellow sign: "Mami Dakunu Imported Food Supplies".

"I am sorry, sir, but Madam has gone to her other shop. Please come with me, I will take you to the other shop," said Adisa. Kayayo are like market slaves, the lowest ranked paid workers in Makola market. As I followed Adisa through the busy crowd towards the other side of the market, I asked for her own views about the economic situation in Ghana.

"The economy is hard these days," she said. Adisa told me she had come to Accra two years before, after running away from her husband in the north. I asked her why she left her husband in the village and ran to city. "My husband was greedy," she said and smiled broadly, showing her perfectly kept white teeth. "He fell in love with another girl from my village. I advised him not to marry her, but he refused to listen to me."

"Do you have any children with your husband or ex-husband?"

"No, that was the problem in the marriage. He told me that he wanted to have ten children with me and I agreed to give him ten if

God permitted. But after four years, there was no child. God did not give us a child. My husband used to blame me, as if it was my fault. I am a woman and every woman wants a child, but God refused me children: what can I do about this?" she asked waving her hands. We were approaching her boss's second shop. We both spoke in a northern language, Hausa.

"So, what are your plans for the future, do you think you will ever go back to your ex-husband or would you prefer to marry a new and better man in the city?"

"These days, men are the same everywhere in the world. There are so many spoiled apples among them. They are all like goats." Adisa told me that all the good men are dead and gone, leaving only the bad ones. "Those in the city are much worse than the village ones," she argued. I asked her why she thought so. "The men in the city are not interested in marriage. All they want is a bit of sex. In Accra here, if you see a man with a BMW today, tomorrow you will see him with a brand new Mercedes." Adisa spoke referring to the different shapes of girls Ghanaian men prefer these days. "After they see the colour of your pants, they disappear to go and look for a new model. That is the nature of Ghanaian men these days." Adisa explained as we arrived at her boss's second shop. I was amazed by her knowledge and wondered why such an articulate young woman should be reduced to the bottom of the economic pile as a Kayayo woman.

"Mami Dakunu Electrical Shop," I read when we arrived at the bright blue painted shop.

"Good afternoon, Madam. My name is Chebe. It is nice to meet you. Thank you for agreeing to give me a few minutes of your valuable time for an interview," I said and bowed slightly to show respect. Mami Dakunu was a slim, vivacious lady in her forties. The store was busy that day with heaps and piles of goods hanging on the walls from kettles to extension cords. There was hardly any space to walk but Mami Dakunu managed to pave a way. I followed her and squeezed myself through into her back office.

"My brother, you are welcome from the UK, how are the people in London?"

"Fine," I said and took out my notepad. I began by asking Mami Dakunu her thoughts about life in general.

"Bibia ye ska sem - it is all about money in this life," she said in Akan before turning to the English language. "Without money you are nothing these days in Ghana. If you are poor, you cannot make yourself or anyone happy in this country," Mami Dakunu said, adding that no matter what amount of rubbish you talk in Ghana today, people will listen, agree and even believe you, provided you have the money in your pocket to support your views. "But, if you don't have money, your own brothers will cast you out of the family decision-making process." I asked Mami Dakunu what she thought about the Ghanaian economy.

"The country is growing but people are getting poorer. They say the economy is getting better, but many people I know are suffering because they don't have any money to spend," Mami Dakunu explained, hinting that there was a two-tier economy operating within the country: one tier for the unfortunate poor and the other for the privileged rich. I asked her how she felt personally, as a businesswoman, in this two-tier economic system.

"To be honest, it's not bad if you are a trader like me. I started my first shop eight years ago and now I have three shops. I go to China, Europe or America once every two months to import my goods," she said using a very sophisticated slang of her own. The shop we sat in sold household goods and electrical products from China and Dubai. "In my other two shops, I sell imported rice, sugar, milks and other food products from Europe and America." As I sat and spoke to Mami Dakunu in her backroom office, I had the feeling that, life for her was probably as jolly good and comfortable as she could make it. We had a long chat about many things: it was exciting to hear a successful story in the Ghanaian market. Now, I wanted to talk to a trader from the bottom of the ladder to hear what they thought about life and the Ghanaian economy.

Pure Water Business

"Yes, pure water," a faded voice called from behind. I turned around and saw a slim girl. She was carrying a large basin on her head; walking across from the other side of the street. By this point, I was exhausted. My throat croaked with drought and dehydration.

"Ice-water girl, please come and sell me some, how much is one sachet?" I asked.

"Please sir, one bag is five pesewa," she said. At the time, one Ghanaian pesewa was equivalent to one American cent.

"Pure-water girl, what is your name and how old are you?"

"My name is Abiba; but my friends call me Abi. I am 14 years old."

"Abiba, why are you not at school today?"

"Sir, I don't go to school. My father is blind and my mother is dead, that is why I sell water on the street. If I don't sell this water everyday, we cannot get food to eat," she said turning her head away in despair. I could see a few tears dropping from Abiba's innocent face. She told me that her father used to be a butcher at the Keneshie market in the north of the city but, through an unexplainable illness, he became blind. A few years later, her mother also died of breast cancer. "That is why I was forced to leave primary school. My dream was to be a nurse one day," she said in a sorrowful voice. She wiped her face with one hand with the other hand supporting the basin on her head. She still had about 20 bags of water to sell.

It was heartbreaking talking to Abi and seeing all the sweat pouring down from her face and the tears, which she tried hard to hold back. Why should any Ghanaian child today be growing up without a dream they can believe and follow? Ghana is a land of many riches; gold, diamonds, bauxite, manganese, copper, iron, cocoa, timber, oil, you name it, Ghana has it all, in abundance. Yet, far too many of Ghana's children are growing up without hope. These were the thoughts that were floating through my brain as I continued to talk to Abi.

"If you sell one sachet of water at five pesewa, how many sachets of water do you have to sell a day to make a living in Ghana?" I asked helping her to put the basin down on the ground. She gave me a sachet, which was cold in my hand.

"My target is to sell 500 bags of water a day."

"Where do you get the water from and how many of these cool water bags can you carry in your basin at a time?"

"Where I get the water is ten minutes walking this way," she said pointing her hand. Abi told me she could only carry 50 plastic sachets of water at time. Finally, I asked Abi how much it cost her to buy the water from the foreign company which bags free Ghanaian spring water to sell. "I buy each bag for four pesewa; I make one pesewa a bag. Sometimes people leave their change as a tip, but that is only down to luck," she said looking anxious to go and carry on with her business. I felt an agonising pain in my conscience as I spoke with little Abiba. I felt guilty that I was wasting her time because she needed to catch other customers to meet her ambitious daily target. I told her to go and carry on with her business. I prayed that her conditions would change one day. I encouraged her to keep working hard and never lose hope. I told Abiba that no condition is permanent, so she should never give up her dream, even if it seems impossible to accomplish.

Before she went away, I gave Abiba five Ghana cedis, the equivalent of her sales target for the day, approximately £2.50. She looked overcome with joy. "Today I am going to cook a nice meal at home," she said. After that, I left Makola and returned to the Accra station to catch my next bus. I felt angry that a 14-year-old girl with a dream to be a Ghanaian nurse is out of school selling water on the street. I couldn't help going through the same pain anytime I saw a little girl in Accra with a basin on her head. When I returned to my hotel later that evening, I tried to work out: how many hours does Abiba have to spend in a day to sell 500 bags of water, so that she can feed herself, her two little brothers and her blind father?

Chapter 8: Be a Chameleon!

The current of the mighty Atlantic Ocean roared in the background, whistling from time to time like a blue whale. My eye caught sight of a fishing boat with about half a dozen fishermen sailing further out to sea.

"Let me remind you of something very important," said Professor Ababa, an elderly friend from the Institute of African Studies, "don't forget that there are many different types of knowledge systems: We have knowledge in quantity and knowledge in quality. We also have traditional knowledge, modern knowledge, good knowledge and bad knowledge. Finally, we have emotional, technical and spiritual knowledge. What I want you to know is that, Africa is poor because we rely too much on spiritual and emotional relationships. But we don't invest enough time and energy on our social and technical knowledge."

Ababa told me that only technical knowledge is good for wealth creation.

"Culturally, Europeans are not better than Africans, but, technically, they are more advanced. That is why they have advanced economies." I told Ababa about my theory of the African Conundrum and he said: "If one plus one amount to zero, it means that we are suffering from technical impotency in Africa." We finished our drinks whilst looking out over the mighty ocean. Before we parted my friend gave me one last piece of advice.

"You have to use this trip to find a better path to your own financial freedom. That is my best advice for you," he said and continued, "the people of Africa are copy cats: if you can make your own dream come true, others will be prepared to believe and follow your vision for Africa. If not, you can forget about everything and go back to Glasgow right now to look after yourself and your family."

Over the next few days, I struggled with indecision, confused about my future path. Eventually I went to see the local juju man, Malam Yusuf, for some spiritual advice.

"If you want to find the truth at home, you have to be careful with the way you are. Don't let people know who you are and always remember that your true friends are the poor ones." Malam Yusuf told me that a poor friend is more considerate than the rich friend, especially when one is in need. We were sitting on a cow-skin prayer mat with a lantern placed between us. He threw a handful of white cowrie shells onto the mat and spread them carefully with his right hand. "My brother, close your eyes and choose one shell," he said and moved the dim lantern to the side. The rest of the large juju room was in pitch blackness. I closed my eyes and stretched my hand to pick. I had never before paused to realise how difficult it is for one to close his eyes for as long as the juju man instructed me to do. I collected one shell from the mat and still kept my eyes closed as Yusuf began the prayer. I held the cowrie shell in my clenched fist as the prayer continued. After more than ten minutes in solitary darkness, Malam Yusuf allowed me to open my eyes again. Oh, what a relief!

I stared at him, unable to imagine what he was going to make me do next. He continued to whisper some sacred words with his head lowered, looking directly into the water inside his juju pot. "My brother, drop the cowrie shell into the pot," he instructed and pointed the juju pot towards my hands. I hesitated for a little moment, my muscles tense as I stretched forward and released the shell into the dark water. It was boiling in that dark room and the sweat of fear and the worry of the unknown poured from my face.

"You need to change your clothes and disguise yourself like a chameleon. That is the only way you can find what you are looking for," he said as he returned the juju pot to the darkest corner of the room. "If you want to be a friend of the poor, you must live with the poor. The best way to find the truth is to live with the truth," he said. Malam Yusuf warned me to be careful about choosing friends wherever I went. In the end, he told me that I must say a special prayer that Friday. "If you do what I tell you, you will be a very happy man soon. Your dream will come true. But, don't forget to come back and see me," he said.

I must admit, I felt a little disappointed that Yusuf thought I would become a happy man one day. I am already a very happy man. That is good enough!

The problem with living in Europe is that, after a long time away from home, most African people like me begin to doubt our traditions and cultures. For many Africans abroad, the mention of juju is something we don't want to believe anymore; especially those among us who think we are advanced or civilised. As I struggled to clear away the creeping shadows of doubt in my mind, I wondered, why? Why is it that the African man is so poorly educated about his own traditions and ways of life? Why is it that almost every educated African man and woman you see on earth would rather associate themselves with foreign traditions and cultures as opposed to our own traditional beliefs?

That night, I twisted and turned for some time before reaching a crossroads in my mind. I saw the light pointing only in one direction. I knew it was the right direction. I had to adjust myself to fit into a new reality. Like the Juju man said, it was true that if people knew I was a returning European resident, they would think I was a charity worker with lots of money to donate to people on the street. Usually, people's behaviour changes and the dialogue they have with you changes accordingly. So, in the end, I came to the conclusion that I must follow the strict advice of my Juju man and change my clothes. I had to change my identity like a chameleon in a tree if I was going to find the answer to the African Conundrum. I had to avoid all those who were rich enough to have their own car, including my friend Godson who picked me up at the airport. I knew this was a radical path but if this was what it would take to survive at home, that was exactly what I was prepared to do without fear of compromise or shame. I have always felt that in this life, there is no gain without pain or endurance. Equally, I was convinced that there was no problem without a solution and this was the time for me to prove myself wrong or right.

Finally, on my eighth day in Accra, I made a critical move. It was my own moment of evolutionary transition. So, I checkout of my hotel early in the morning and carried my bag onto the street with no idea where to go next. Now that I was warned against the rich, I had to look for a poor man to live with. By then, I had already spent half of the money in my pocket, leaving only a £125 and a few Ghanaian cedis of loose change.

I was aware of the fact that although the money I had left was peanuts, especially if I hung around the rich boys, this amount of money in Ghana could make a poor man very rich immediately. So, I promised myself that I would give all the money to any poor friend I could find on the street of Accra who would host me. I walked heedlessly without any sense of direction. For the first time since I arrived home, a completely strange feeling of loneliness and despair spread through my veins.

As I walked passed a busy filling station a taxi pulled in. The driver waved his hand but I continued to walk towards the busy Accra ring road asking myself, why? Why am I choosing to go through this radical path to demonstrate my sincerest belief in Africa? As my friend Winfred had asked: why must anyone in their right mind leave their comfortable way of life in Great Britain to come to Ghana and roam the streets thinking they can change Africa for good? For a brief moment, I felt like a lost soul and nothing made sense to me, walking along the busy pavement. I even began to worry in case I bumped into people I knew. I knew that if anyone heard my story, they would have their own legitimate reasons to say I have lost a few knots or bearings.

As I reeled through the pain of feeling powerless, it suddenly dawned on me that I had reached the point of no return. In my own stubborn mind, I convinced myself there was no going back to my comfortable position until I found enough answers to satisfy my own curiosities about life once and for all. Even if I reached the bitter conclusion that there is absolutely nothing a sensible man like me can do to change myself and my own society, then I could at least live the rest of my life without further complaint or regrets that Africa could be a better place to live, if ordinary people like me made a difference.

It was like day-dreaming, walking in the spirit of loneliness, a certain realisation came to my mind, but I got a shock when a taxi driver repeatedly beeped his horn at me, asking if I wanted a lift. I am sure it was the driver I saw at the filling station a moment earlier. I jumped into the taxi without another thought. "Good morning, sir, where will I drop you?" asked the driver.

"I don't know yet, please just drop me anywhere far away from here," I said. The driver laughed and asked again if I was serious. As he spoke, I remembered a poor friend of mine, Mark. Mark lived in the Art Centre village, which is adjacent to Nkrumah Museum. My friend Mark is the type of guy I knew would accept me in my new conditions. "How much will it cost for you to drop me at the Art Centre Village," I asked the taxi man.

"Fifteen cedis!" he replied. And that was it. I removed my last change and counted it; it all amounted to exactly nine Cedis and fifty pesewas. Fortunately after a little persuasion, Kwame, the taxi driver, agreed and drove me to the Art Centre Village where a brand new chapter began. I remember walking towards Mark's shop on this dusty sunny day. There were rows of shops and wooden huts with goats, sheep, chickens, cats, dogs and people all moving in different directions. There were many hardworking carvers and craftsmen and women working in front of their shops. A few people called me to come and buy stuff. I remember arriving at

Mark's shop with my bag on my shoulder that day. He was sitting on his bench with his head resting on his knees; it was as if he was in a deep trance. He got a big surprise when he heard my voice. I asked Mark how he was feeling.

"I was just praying to the Lord Jesus to perform a miracle in my life today and here you are." Mark spoke and shook my hand by the door before inviting me inside his broken shop.

"How are you? You look a bit stressed," I said.

"To be honest, I am not fine at all today. But I believe now that I have seen you, I will soon be fine." I asked Mark why he said things were not good to him. "I have been suffering from some serious coccidiosis for the past few days," he said crudely referring to the painful condition of an empty stomach. "That is why I am so glad to see you. When did you arrive home?" he asked offering a weak smile. I told Mark that I'd arrived a week ago and that I had brought little money home with me. I asked if he could be my host for some time.

"I am afraid it is too dangerous to live here. You will die of malaria in one week. Don't you realise that you are a boga?" he asked. Boga is the local name for a returnee Ghanaian. "Let me put your bag under this bench in the corner. That is where I sleep." Mark collected my bag and tucked it neatly under the bench before reaching for my hand again. I asked him what happened to his shop.

"Just three days ago, I went to the church in the night. When I came back, a thief had broken into my shop. I think the thief was looking for money but I he couldn't find any. So, he removed all the plywood from the side panels of my shop to go and sell. That is how wicked Ghanaian thieves are these days. I am so glad I was not sleeping in my shop that night. I think the thief would have stolen my body and sold it to a juju man at Konkon-ba Line." Konkon-ba Line is a notorious crime-ridden settlement in Accra where anything can be bought and sold, including human body parts. "Some people are so dangerous." Mark spoke with anger, pointing his hand to God in the sky. "I have left the thief in the hands of Jesus. My pastor told me not to worry: God is going to punish the thief very soon." Mark is a pious Christian who never says more than a few words without mentioning his Lord Jesus.

"What about your business, have you not been carving any drums or xylophones to sell lately?" I asked Mark in our native language.

"I have not had the money to buy any wood for the past three months. One Nigerian man came and bought all my goods and took them to Germany on credit. Since then, I have not received a single payment from him. That is why my business is completely dead. If it were not for my Lord Jesus, who loves me so much, I would be a carcass by now."

After all the greetings and catching up, Mark told me that he was worried about me staying with him because his shop was no longer secure. He suggested taking me to another friend who had a better shop. I refused the offer and insisted that I was going to lodge in Mark's broken shop for as long as he would allow me to do so. "I told you already that the mosquitoes alone will eat you to death in one week. You will never survive this place: I swear to you." I asked Mark why he was still alive. "I am immune to mosquito bites; they find my blood too bitter to swallow."

After a short argument, I removed the £125 in my pocket and gave it all to Mark. I told him to buy some wood and carve new musical instruments to kick off his business.

"This is the very reason why I believe in Jesus. The whole of last night, I never slept. I prayed so much to him. Now, look at the miracle the Lord has performed in my life today," he said unable to believe that there was the equivalent of almost three million old Ghanaian cedis in his hand. "With this money, I could go to the north and marry a brand new wife today if I wanted." This time Mark's smile was as bright as daylight. He looked completely confused but excited by the timing of my arrival. He really believed

Jesus had sent me to deliver the good message to him. "I know a carpenter at Akuma village," he said referring to the other side of the Art Centre. "Let me go and bring him right now to get an estimate. I have to fix this shop immediately. If you insist in staying here, we will have to secure ourselves a little bit," Mark said and took off. I sat in the stark shell wondering where I would be laying my head come night. It didn't take too long before Mark returned with a carpenter. He had a hammer, some nails and a measuring tape in his hand.

"My brother, this is Thunder," Mark introduced his companion. Thunder was about five and half feet tall, a tough-looking guy with short dreadlocks. I got a fright when he shook my hand; his palm was as hard as solid brick and rougher than crocodile skin. I couldn't imagine how it would feel if he used his elephant hands to slap me on the face.

Thunder made his estimate and charged Mark 45 Ghana cedis, the equivalent of £20.

"Benin man, that is too expensive. I will give you 30 Ghana cedis," Mark bargained. As they continued with their discussion, I left the Art Centre to go for a little wander.

Chapter 9: Africa's Forgotten War Heroes

I had an intimidating first night in the shell of the shop. The next day, I decided to forget my nightmare experience and visit Nkrumah Memorial Park: Dr Kwame Nkrumah was the first president of Ghana and a Pan-African spiritual hero who attracts thousands of visitors to Ghana every year from Europe, America, the Caribbean and other parts of the world. Luckily, that day, I met one of the museum's guards. He was also a local Ghanaian historian. He told me the story of the African Independence Movement.

"Five Ghanaian soldiers lit the flame that sparked the Independence Movement for the whole continent," said Mr Opoku, the museum guard. "I feel very sad that most Ghanaian youths today do not know about the sweat and toil of our own World War II veterans." Mr Opoku told me the extraordinary story of five Ghanaian soldiers known as the Big Five. Their struggle to free Africa from colonialism began on one boiling hot evening in 1948, at Burma Camp, the headquarters of the Ghana Arm Forces. The five men had just returned from their tour of duty in Germany as part of the King's African Rifles. The five soldiers were: Corporal Atta, Sergeant Kofi, Sergeant Luri, Captain Wayo and Brigadier Mahama. Mr Opoku told me that, on their return from duty in Germany, Sergeant Kofi and his colleagues met on one crucial evening to discuss the shock of what they experienced whilst they were fighting to save Europe from blowing itself apart in flames.

"We have to act now. We need to let everyone know that the white man no longer holds the legitimate right to be our master," said Brigadier Mahama.

"So, how can we spread this news to the Ghanaian masses? I don't believe that our experiences in Germany can make any difference to the nation. The British system is too strong to break away from and besides, I don't think anyone in Ghana will believe our stories," Sergeant Luri erred on the side of caution.

"I completely disagree with your pessimism," said Kofi. "On the contrary, I believe that if we can let enough people know about our experiences in Europe, people here will soon come to realise that we can govern ourselves. It is up to us to convince our fellow countrymen that we are capable of doing what the European man can do plus more. If we spread the message, people will start to ask why they force us to serve them." According to Mr Opoku, there was one immediate problem confronting the Big Five in their attempt to inspire ordinary Ghanaians to fight for independence. Although they had a strong product to sell, they needed a powerful vehicle to carry their message to the people. They needed a good salesman who could convince the masses on the street to act for freedom and justice.

As it happened, Brigadier Mahama had some contacts with the Workers Union, a movement that campaigned actively against colonial rule. Brigadier Mahama got in touch with the Workers Union hierarchy to see if they would be allowed to attend their next rally at OSU, the then colonial district headquarters. Unsurprisingly, the Workers Union agreed and the Big Five set out to lead the people on the street in the long walk to freedom.

At their first ever rally, each of the five soldiers gave personal statements about their experiences. On stage, they each spoke at length in their effort to incite, fuel and provoke local anger against British colonial rule.

"Before I went to fight in Europe, I used to think that the white man was immortal. I mean, I was shocked to see them lying dead in the battlefield. Now I believe it is my duty to tell you today that the white man is no longer a God to be worshiped, followed or feared anymore," said Brigadier Mahama. There were warm claps and cheers as each soldier took turns on the stage to give their own moving accounts.

"The European man is no longer immortal. We saw many thousands of them dead in Germany," said Sergeant Kofi. "From now onwards, we should fight tooth and nail to take control of our own destiny from Great Britain. The African man in his fullest sense must no longer accept the poor and inferior position of perpetual slave and the permanent servant of the European man," Sergeant Kofi spoke deep from his heart.

During that important rally, the five soldiers came across a man who shared their pain and sympathized completely with their anger and frustration.

"That man I am talking about is Osagyefo Dr Kwame Nkrumah, the redeemer, and the greatest hero of the African independence movement," said Mr Opoku. As he spoke, the water fountains leading to Dr Kwame Nkrumah's memorial statue sprayed high into the roasting air.

Mr Opoku explained that, like the Big Five, Dr Kwame Nkrumah had a similar experience in both Europe and America. As an international student, he had witnessed something in Europe that was completely hidden from the African people throughout the colonial era.

"Dr Nkrumah was committed and totally determined to bring to an end to the insane claim that a European man was a semi God; and therefore had the legitimate status to remain the master of the human race. He was convinced that the European man must be stripped of his self-proclaimed god-like status with immediate effect.

After listening to their emotional tributes, Osagyefo, the redeemer, seized the opportunity to work with the veterans and help them spin their yarns and emotional accounts to fuel maximum anger against the colonial masters." Mr Opoku said that in the weeks and months that followed from the first meeting with the Big Five, Nkrumah organised tours, rallies and peaceful demonstrations to spread the message. He travelled with the Big Five throughout southern Ghana, connecting and attracting more ex-servicemen onto the streets. "Dr Nkrumah also encouraged other grassroots activists to stand up against everything that had the colonial label on it. The movement continued unabated until Ghana gained independence: the first African nation to set herself free on the 6th March 1957." As Mr Opoku spoke, I began to see Nkrumah as a Paul Revere, the man who ignited the flame for American Revolution as I'd learnt from *The Tipping Point*. I wanted to know more about the message and philosophy Nkrumah brought to the people of Africa. I asked Mr Opoku to give me a flashback into the early life of the man whom, he believed, every enlightened African student of today must know about.

"Dr Kwame Nkrumah was not only the best African messenger but also our best thinking mind. I will tell you the short version of his philosophy." Mr Opoku said. "First of all, Dr Kwame Nkrumah was born in a little village called Nzima in the south-west corner of Ghana. After a bright but humble start, he left Ghana and studied in both America and Britain. From the onset, he was a radical, a dedicated and sincere pan-African. After completing his studies abroad, Nkrumah, returned home in 1947 to become General Secretary of the newly established United Gold Coast Convention (UGCC). Following some internal disagreement with members of the UGCC, he left the party and formed his own Convention People's Party (CPP)." Dr Opoku said that Nkrumah had a lot of grassroots support, especially from veterans' groups and the then disenchanted and highly mobilised Ghanaian youth, who were angry and fed up with the malicious nature of colonial rule. He spoke at length and gave me some old newspaper articles containing one of Nkrumah's early speeches.

My fellow countrymen and women, we must bring all our experiences together and fight for total liberation of our country and establish our right to self-determination. We have dignity and pride in our own ability to govern our people and manage our own resources, for our own good. We can build our own roads and our own schools and hospitals. We can build and develop our own economy and create our own industries. We can because we are capable by virtue of our own creation: And not because someone else so far away from Ghana wants us to believe in him and his deplorable perception about us and our ways of life. This is a long and difficult journey to freedom which will cost many lives and needless hardships along the way. But, I believe that if we continue to peruse and give our maximum effort to this important call, Ghana will not only be the first nation to regain independence in the continent, but the people of Ghana will also be paving the way for the eventual and total liberation of Africa – our motherland.

This speech was made at Nkrumah's first rally as the leader of the Convention People Party in Cape Coast, the then capital city of the Gold Coast.

According to Mr Opoku, many, many things happened in the years that followed which eventually led to Ghana's independence on the 6 March 1957. In his maiden speech on Independence Day, Dr Kwame Nkrumah declared that: "The Independence of Ghana is meaningless unless it is linked or leads to the total socio-economic and political liberation of the wider African nation."

From day one, Nkrumah argued that Ghana's independence alone was not good enough for Africa. He committed huge resources and fought tooth and nail to free, reunite and rebuild the African family as one great people and, ultimately, a strong force for good in the wider world.

"Unfortunately, he was unduly prosecuted and driven to an early grave by the CIA and other sophisticated secret Western intelligence agencies: people who saw Nkrumah as too close to the East, the socialist, the communist or the 'evil world' as they would like us to believe. Frankly speaking, the colonial masters hate it whenever a good African leader tries to unite the continent and prove that we can run better systems of governance for ourselves" Mr Opoku continued.

I had a very enlightening visit to the Nkrumah Memorial Park that day. In the end, I came to the conclusion that Nkrumah was not only a great African philosopher but also a strategic master planner. He knew that the African style of social living was similar to the Chinese way of life and the Soviet Union communal style of governance. He tried to encourage African leaders to copy good examples from both West and East. I felt sad and disappointed that such a great African hero was seen by the Europeans and Americans as being too friendly with their enemies. It is difficult to accept that a man of Nkrumah's wisdom should have been unduly victimised for having a positive vision for Africa. I wished that we had men like Nkrumah today to continue the necessary battle for African unity.

After listening to the stories of Nkrumah and the five World War II soldiers that day, I began to realise how much responsibility lies on the shoulders of the new generation of Africans today, especially, those of us who are privileged enough to live in Europe and America. It is these privileged and enlightened generations and all Africans abroad who could play a similar role to the Ghanaian World War II veterans who came to the conclusion after their time in Europe that enough is enough.

I also realised how we can learn some crucial lessons from the good examples of great men like Osagyefo Dr Kwame Nkrumah whose contribution to Ghana and Africa are still hard to match by any of us, even in the twenty-first century world. Today, if you look around anywhere in Ghana even with your eyes closed, you can see clearly why some people still believe that Dr Nkrumah was the best ever African leader to live on the surface of this planet.

"If you ask people on the street, many will tell you that Nkrumah alone probably did more than the rest of the other Ghanaian leaders put together since independence in 1957. His greatest achievements still rank highly with the best. Some of Nkrumah's greatest work includes the construction of the famous Akosombo Dam. A dam that was built to serve the industrial and domestic energy needs of Ghana as a country, and also to supply electricity to neighbouring Côte d'Ivoire, Burkina Faso and Togo. Today, the Akosombo dam is still the largest man-made lake in the whole world.

Furthermore, his scheme for the Accra Tema motorway created the longest stretch of first-class motorway in West Africa. Additionally, the Tema community estate housing scheme he implemented still remains the greatest example of the dream that an African man and his family can live in a nice modern environment and enjoy the comforts of modern life, while simultaneously maintaining his culture and African ways of life," Nkrumah's continental achievements include the establishment of the OAU or the Organisation of African Unity. He argued with his fellow African leaders that the OAU, which was a political union of independent African States, must form the solid foundation of a strong African economic union based on the principle of a single currency.

"Union government is a prerequisite for control of Africa's wealth for the benefit of the African people," he said in one of his numerous addresses to the OAU leader's summit.

Nkrumah was not only a great African leader but also an honourable, sincere and caring world leader, who was totally committed and motivated by peace, freedom and justice, not just for the smartest few or his own people but for all of humanity. Fundamentally, this is the same message Obama brings to the twenty-first century world: equal opportunities, peace and prosperity for all, without the need to discriminate or divide and rule in favour of the privileged minority.

"Unfortunately, Dr Nkrumah was overthrown while he was abroad trying to mediate a peaceful solution to end the totally unnecessary war in Vietnam. While he was on an aeroplane en route to China, he was informed by the Chinese authorities that there was a coup d'état which had overthrown him at home. What a great shame to end the noble life of a very great African peaceful warrior in this way. Nkrumah lived in exile in neighbouring Guinea until his death in 1972 in a Romanian hospital. One of the best ever quotes from Africa's greatest Messiah:

By far the greatest wrong which the departing colonialists inflicted on us, and which we now continue to inflict on ourselves in our present state of disunity, was to leave us divided into economically unviable States which bear no possibility of real development. We must unite for economic viability, first of all, and then to recover our mineral wealth in Africa, so that our vast resources and capacity for development will bring prosperity for us and additional benefits for the rest of the world.

Chapter 10: African Genesis

In the beginning, there was nothing, and then, a voice spoke out loudly and said: Let there be light. And, there was light. Out of light, man appeared, walking across the Valley of Creation in Ethiopia.

"Hello, my name is Adam, God created me in his own image. What is your name and who created you to be so different from me?" Adam asked a stranger who he met standing naked by the River Nile.

"My name is Eve," she replied shyly and covered her face.

God spoke through an angel and told Eve; "Don't be shy. There is nothing you can hide from Adam. He is all yours and you are all his. I made you man and woman and put you in this garden to live and multiply. Between you and Adam, I will give you two children: one boy and one girl. Your children will grow and multiply to fill the earth. Your children's children will be divided into many nations. But, I want to place these holy apples under your control. This is the only forbidden fruit in my holy garden. Never let your husband Adam or any of my angels touch it. If you obey my command, you will live and enjoy an everlasting life, a life without pain or endurance. But if you break my covenant and allow anyone to touch these apples I have placed on your chest, I shall punish you severely."

After God spoke, Eve and her husband Adam held each other's hands and walked away. They lived happily in the Garden of Eden until trouble broke out in Heaven. One of God's most trusted angels started to feel envious that Adam was the only one allowed to live with Eve in the Garden of Eden. He told God that it was not fair for man alone to have total dominium over the earth and all of its vast resources.

"Satan, don't be jealous. I made you and all the other angels in my Heaven. I made man in my own image to rule over the earth. I put Adam and Eve in the Garden of Eden because I trust them over all other creatures including you, Satan."

"But that is not fair. I am better than man, because I am your most powerful angel. I should be the one controlling the earth, not man." Satan was very angry and disappointed with God for making Adam in charge of the earth.

Satan waited until God was sleeping. He sneaked and stole a powerful wand from God and flew away from heaven. Satan came down onto earth with a mission to deceive, capture, confuse, manipulate and control the actions of man against the will of God. For Satan to succeed with his plan on earth, he turned himself into a desirable man. One day, he approached Eve in the Garden of Eden.

"Eve, come here and let me teach you something you will never regret knowing."

"What is it? Who are you?" she asked looking confused.

"I am Satan. I am God's most trusted friend in Heaven. I am here to teach you the first lesson of creation."

"Satan, what do you want from me?" asked Eve.

"I want to have sex with you. Trust me, you will enjoy it so much, you will never regret it. Sex, is the sweetest thing on earth. It is sweeter than honey and sugar put together."

"No, my God told me not to let anyone enter through the forbidden gate. Stay away from me." At first, Eve turned her face and covered herself with her hands. But Satan used many tricks to persuade her.

That day, Adam was away on a hunting trip. When he came back later in the evening, he noticed a dramatic change in his wife's behaviour.

"Adam, please sleep with me tonight and let us enjoy some sex together."

"What? Let us do what together? Why are you talking about sex today?"

"Please, Adam, I want to have your baby. Don't you remember that God promised to give us a son? How are we going to have one without intercourse?"

"It is up to God how we multiply. It is not up to us. Let us not sin against God's will."

"Come on, Adam. Don't be a coward. Please touch my breasts and sleep with me. Don't be afraid of God. He will never find out because he is too far away in Heaven."

"Absolutely not! That is the road to our self-destruction. My God told me not to commit any sin in his Holy Garden."

"Adam, please don't be a coward," Eve said and stretched her hand to hold his manhood.

"No, Eve, this is wrong. I don't want to touch your breasts, but I love you so much. I am confused," Adam said and felt his penis swell hard. He tried his best but Eve rolled her body over him and they fell into each other's arms.

After breaking the rules of God, Eve became shy and immediately climbed a tree and brought down some leaves to cover herself. She gave some leaves to Adam to cover himself as well. And that was the beginning of sin on earth.

God was very angry with Adam and Eve and told them they would be punished severely. He told Eve she would endure many months of labour for committing sins in the Holy Garden. God also promised to punish the rest of humanity for all our sins from then onwards.

Nine months after breaking the covenant with God, Eve gave birth to twins. One was a good twin but the other was a bad boy.

"Eve, I don't understand why the twins are so different. Are you sure they are both my sons?" Adam asked feeling confused about the striking differences between the two boys. One of the twins was identical to his father, but the other was completely different.

"Of course, they are both your sons. Who else lives with us here?"

"But surely, God only promised us one son and one daughter, why do we have two sons? How will they multiply and fill the earth?"

"That is a question you have to ask God, not me." Eve tried as hard as she could to protest her innocence. And that was how it all began. Two years later, God performed his second miracle by giving Adam and Eve another set of twins. This time they were identical twin girls. When the two girls and two boys grew up, they fell in love with each other and married. From then on, the two sons and the two daughters multiplied and spread from the valley of Creation across east to the land of Kush. That is the story of the African Genesis and the truth about creation. Thank you for listening to this reading. Now you can call me with any questions and comments, I will be happy to take your calls for the next half hour.

The pastor announced before the first caller rang.

After listening to the pastor on the radio, I wanted to call and air my own views, but the line was busy as callers queued to comment.

"Hello, good morning, Pastor. Thank you for a very interesting reading. You make me feel proud that I can now trace my ancestry back to Adam and Eve. My question is, do you think that a European or American will ever accept that they came from Africa?" the caller asked.

"Forget about what others have written to mislead and control us about creation. What you have heard this morning is the truth. Without a doubt, Africa is our motherland, the origin of life and all human civilisations," the pastor said and continued. He told the listeners that: "Everything good you see on earth here today, including civilisation, trade, democracy, money, et cetera, all originated from the ancient world of Africa." I sat back, listened and jotted down some notes.

"The first known tribe or family on earth were called the Nubians. We are all children of Nubia. There should be no doubt in your mind that Adam and Eve were the first Nubians in the world," the pastor said before another caller interrupted.

"Pastor, do you have any evidence to prove your claim that Adam and Eve lived in Africa?"

"Of course, there is mounting evidence around the world about the origin of the human species. According to European scientists, for example," he cited "the earliest prehistoric human remains ever found on earth were the scattered bones of a girl they called Lucy. Her bones were found in Ethiopia." The pastor argued that the solid remains of 16-year-old Lucy offered the greatest scientific evidence that human life began in Africa. "We also know from documents and other prehistoric evidence-based accounts that Ethiopia is the oldest country in the world."

"Good morning, Pastor, my name is Mary, my question for you is: if the journey of humanity began in Ethiopia, what happen from then?"

"From Ethiopia, the Nubians spread to the west into modern day Sudan. From Sudan, they multiplied and expanded, stretching to the east, west, south and north. So, you can say that, if Ethiopia is the fatherland of our common humanity, it is reasonably safe to conclude that Sudan is the mother of all human civilisations. It was from Sudan that a very powerful son of Africa was born. This son was named Egypt. And out of Egypt came the rest of the world."

Chapter 11: Meaning of Civilisation

After three long weeks of sleeping on the rough edge of a single bench, I hit my head on a solid rock. Don't get me wrong, I was very well prepared in my mind to face the dangers at home, but I never imagined things were going to be so bad. The vicious, evil mosquitoes had managed to pierce enough of their killer venom into my body's cells to inflict maximum pain and suffering on me.

"My brother, you don't look well at all today. Let's pray for the Nigerian man to come and pay me the money, you have to go to hospital tomorrow," Mark said and gave me a long sympathetic look. His Nigerian friend had arrived from Germany the previous night and had promised to come and pay his debt.

Later that afternoon, I began to shiver. My stomach grumbled constantly, like a beating drum. I twisted and turned on the bench. Soon, the situation developed into a desperate fever. I struggled to believe that my condition was deteriorating so fast.

With the pain increasing every passing minute, I started to worry: how can I suffer like this by choice? Some people suffer because they have no choice, but, here, I had chosen to come home and endure this pain of my own free will.

The mosquitoes in Mark's shop were so bad, no words I have in my limited English vocabulary can explain the trauma that I put myself through. I remember lying on the bench thinking to myself: truly, the mosquito has got to be Africa's number one indigenous enemy, worse than our deadly and corrupt African dictators.

On the second day of pain, my condition grew worse. I needed to go to the toilet but felt embarrassed to go out. The toilet facilities in Akuma village were much worse than the most basic conditions anyone can ever imagine. I remember the first morning my diarrhoea began, Mark took me to the nearby toilet station. I followed him through rows of concrete jungle style huts and shops. As we walked along the narrow path, there were many women bathing their children in buckets of water. Others were preparing breakfast in their coal pots and clay ovens. A few people greeted and watched me with expressions of concern on their faces.

"Is that the Boga who came here three weeks ago? Ayeee, he has lost too much weight, ooo," said one of the women.

"I think he is not well," said another. The women gossiped among themselves as we passed by. I could hear them, so, I turned and looked. Mark and I continued through the narrow lane all the way to the coastline. As we approached the final point, there was a man sitting beside a yellow broken kiosk with a crossing rope. It was like a private road barrier. I was desperate for freedom. "Where is the toilet," I asked Mark as my stomach roared with internal thunder. It was about to explode. I walked with clenched buttocks and struggled to hold onto my brakes and clutches, fearful of an uncontrollable disaster.

Mark edged forward and whispered a few words in Dagara language to the toilet attendant. I watched the waves in front of me, trying to take my mind away from my desperation. I saw Mark collect a portion of old newspaper from the toilet guard. After conducting his secret negotiations, Mark brought me an old piece of Italian newspaper.

"Nan don, la mobal kamua choal mini," Mark spoke in the native language, saying, "Please take the mobile and use the light to see in the dark tunnel. Be careful not to slip into the gutter," he warned and waited for me beside the kiosk. It was a steep slope down to the tunnel; the end of a long underground sewage tunnel which carries organic waste material from Accra city into the innocent ocean.

How can this be the toilet facility for the residents of Akuma? I asked myself in staggered silence. There were other people in the tunnel; all squatting and floating away their early morning garbage into the sea. At some points, I had to switch off the light from the mobile phone, because I felt guilty at shining the light on other people's private gadgets. As I edged forward, the creeping noise from the gutter gave me a dark, cold feeling of sadness and overwhelming pain. Why do we not have proper toilet facilities in Ghana? I asked myself in despair. There were small mounds of excrement everywhere on the pavement, making it difficult to walk without slipping and falling into the piles of residue. I could smell raw sewage everywhere; the smell was poisonous like an exhumed grave. I numbed my feelings, tried to ignore my sense of smell and continued.

Finally, I found a clear section, five metres away from another man. He was squeezing hard and making loud noises. I ignored the noise and slipped down my trousers before squatting to carry on with my own business. Then, I heard a rustling noise; I shone the touch in the direction of the noise, but saw nothing.

"Don't worry, my brother, it is the rats that are making the noise. Nothing to worry about," a female voice spoke in the dark. I started. She was just a few metres on the other side of the gutter; I followed her advice and continued with my mission.

It was one of those strange moments where the mind proves to be stronger than the body. It was as if my sickness almost disappeared because my mind was too busy to think about the pain I was going through. Why did I put myself through this? I asked myself many difficult questions in that dark tunnel. Why do we not have basic functioning public toilet facilities that are fit for purpose in the twenty-first century? What is the point in economic growth without human progress?

My pain subsided as I began to think about all the possible solutions in the world. How can I translate my difficult toilet experience into a powerful insult that would force my fellow Ghanaians to think for themselves? For a brief moment, I felt that the best way to be controversial was to partially agree with the notion that the African man's poverty is evidence of his uncivilised status.

Let me tell you why I am forced to think of this crazy impossibility. Once, I watched a BBC documentary about the life of a supposedly moderate Nazi general. I can't remember his name. He was asked why the Nazis were so cruel to the gypsies and the Jews. In his reply, the general argued that the Nazis hated the gypsies, in particular, because they believed the gypsies to be the most uncivilised people in the world. When the general was asked to explain what he understood to be the definition of civilisation, he said: "Those who flush their toilets are the civilised people of the world, and the uncivilised ones are those who shit behind their houses." Anytime, I remember the unholy remarks of this Nazi general, I think about Dr Nkrumah and his idea of "an African personality" in which he argued so vehemently, that the African man deserves a better civilised status in his own backyard.

On the third day of pain, my worst nightmare finally materialised.

"My brother, I think your condition needs some medical attention," Mark said, his face riddled with the wrinkles of fear. It was early in the morning. I grew more worried myself as I began to vomit. "I believe it is the mosquitoes in this shop and I blame everything on that stupid Benin man for not fixing it," Mark spoke angrily. He was referring to Thunder, the carpenter he gave 30 cedis to repair the shop. He left and went to the timber market to buy some wood on the day Mark gave him the money but had since then not been seen in the Art Centre Village again.

My condition continued to deteriorate. I knew I needed to go to hospital, but there was no means to do so.

"I have a friend, he is a pastor, I want to go and beg him for some money to take you to the hospital before you die," Mark said before going away to solicit some help. Whilst he was away, I moved inside the little locked cabin, or the bedroom, as Mark referred to it. My knees were in agony and my shoulders ached with relentless pain. I closed the door and stretched myself on the solid bench. It was uncomfortable as usual but my eyes were heavy. I tried hard to steal a little sleep because I had barely slept for the past three days.

After a little while, my body collapsed into relax mode and I managed to doze away for a brief moment until there was an unexpected arrival.

"Bang, bang, bang," at the door. "Hello, is there anybody in here?" a voice spoke. At first, I heard the knock but pretended there was no one inside the room. The visitor continued to call for attention. "Bang, bang, bang," he knocked again and again.

"Who is it?" I asked faintly.

"It is me, brother, Shaibu." By this time I had begun to recognise the voice.

"It's your brother Shaibu, I just returned from Takoradi today and heard that you had come home and you are not well. I did not know you were home," Shaibu said and pushed opened the door. I sat up on the bench and witnessed the disappointment in his face as he tried to understand why I suddenly found myself in such great misery.

Shaibu and I are not direct brothers, but we both come from the north and that is enough of a foundation for our solid brotherhood. We have known each other for more than ten years and we are like brothers to each other. In the past, I have bought hundreds of djembe drums and other musical instruments from him to ship to the UK. Those were the days when I used to go around the summer festivals to sell handmade drums and other African arts and crafts.

Anyway, from the moment Shaibu came and saw me on the bench in Mark's shop, everything changed.

"Brother, please I am begging you with all my heart to come with me. I want to take you home. I have a good room in OSU. You don't have to sleep under these conditions to bring change to Africa," Shaibu pleaded. I tried to argue back but he began to weep. He twisted one long dread to calm himself as he spoke. He was on his knees. "Brother, I want you to come and stay with me. I will look after you and you will recover from this terrible malaria. I want to show you my love," he said and continued, "I want to prove to you that whatever goes around always comes around, true!" I asked Shaibu why he was being so emotional. "Brother, let me tell you something you did to me," he said and looked at me directly in the face. "Do you remember about eight months ago I called you and asked for some money?" he asked and waited wordless to see if my memory was as good as his. "The money you gave me that time, I used it to hire my room in OSU where I want to take you today. You can come and stay with me for as long as you want. I will do anything I can to help you because; you took me out of shame, the shame of roaming in the street as a homeless man." This was one of the most difficult moments of my whole trip home. Shaibu wept and wept. After about ten minutes, he stood up and said, "Brother, wait for me, I will go up to the road and bring a taxi to take you home!"

Chapter 12: From Bench to Mattress

"Driver, my house is on the left after you pass the filling station," Shaibu spoke before we passed the Shell garage.

"How much is the fare?" he asked and got down from the front seat. Brother, you can come out," he said and opened the door.

I was still in desperate pain and after I managed to get out, the driver took off and driving past the OSU Police station on the right before taking a sharp turn.

"Brother, this is my room, we can stay here together. I beg you brother, please wait for me. I want to go outside to buy some meat at OSU Market. I have to make you some light soup, right now."

After Shaibu left, I laid myself flat on the mattress feeling like the happiest king in the whole world. The table fan blew cool air onto my aching body and some reggae music played joyfully in the background. There was a small television and a video recorder in the room as well as two buckets of clean water beside the door. Even under the worst pain, it felt like heaven moving from a hard bench to a soft bouncing mattress.

I lay on my back and tried to keep a positive mind.

Shaibu took a little longer than I expected. I went outside to relieve myself, the toilet was just a bucket underneath a concrete wall but the comfort of my own privacy in the little cubicle gave me a tiny taste of hope and the belief that life can get better.

"Brother, I have put a bucket of water in the bathroom for you." Shaibu spoke and proceeded to light the charcoal in the coal pot. I wrapped myself in a brown towel and went out into the compound. There was an old lady, Nana, sitting in the left hand corner next to the toilet block. Her sister was staying in the room to the right of her, with a young male relative in the room in the opposite corner from Nana's room.

Initially, I was frightened and deeply troubled by my attack of malaria, but, in the end, I managed to overcome my worst fears, thanks to Shaibu's timely intervention. He fed me well and gave me medicine to survive.

Time passed and once I was fully recovered, I got out on the road to look for answers to solve my African Problem.

I realised that, in order to survive the conditions at home and achieve my goal, I must devise an *action plan*.

There are six ways in which we can transform Africa into a land of happy dreams and wealthy ideas. The six steps I had to take to solve the African Conundrum were: History, Religion, Culture, Politics, and Economics and, most importantly of all, COMMONSENSE!

Chapter 13:   History of Africa

Are you proud to be an African and are you proud about your history? This was the question I set out to ask as many people on the street of Accra on one dull cloudy day. That day, my brother Shaibu and I left OSU and walked by foot to the Ghana National Art Centre, a journey of about four miles. On the way, we met a short man from the North pushing a wheelbarrow full of coconuts.

"How much is one coconut?" Shaibu asked.

"The small ones are 50 pesewas and the big ones are 80."

"Ayeee, that is too expensive. How can you sell one small coconut for 50 pesewas? That is too much! What is your name?" Shaibu asked.

"My name is Abu from Navrongo." I asked Abu what he thought about the history of Ghana.

"Me? As for history, let's forget it. It is easier that way. My life is too hard to worry about history. I want to concentrate on what is happening today, not yesterday," he said before using his machete to cut open two coconuts for us. We left the coconut seller behind and walked passed Independence Square. As we entered the Art Centre, Shaibu told me about a man he was convinced I had to meet.

"Alhaji Sokoto is the wisest man in the whole Art Centre. His shop is over here," he pointed as we approached. "Morning brothers, where is Alhaji today?" Shaibu asked the shop assistants. As we greeted the hardworking men, a football flew by and only missed my head by a narrow margin. The ball was fired by a group of teenage boys on the dusty football pitch directly in front of Alhaji Sokoto's Shop.

"Hey small! I will beat you well, well if you hit the ball into this shop again," said one carver. Alhaji Sokoto's shop was situated near the entrance to the Art Centre, facing kente line, adjacent to the Akwaba drinking spot.

"Master was here a few minutes ago," said Atinga Frafra the shop assistant. There were at least half a dozen craftsmen; carving, sanding and polishing giant nude sculptures for export to Europe and America. "I saw Alhaji going this way with two white men, I think they were going towards the kente line," Atinga Frafra spoke and pointed his hand towards a large building with red roof tiles.

"This cripple, he likes roaming far too much. I have never seen a cripple who doesn't like sitting in one place," said Eric, the shop supervisor. "Please take a seat, master will be here soon," he advised. I entered the shop and sat on the middle of the bench. There was a lot of sawdust and chips of wood all over the floor. Brother Shaibu sat on my left and Mr Ofori, one of Alhaji's friends, sat next to me on the other side of the bench.

"Me too, I am here to see Alhaji. That man is so hard to catch." Whilst we sat and waited for Alhaji to arrive, I asked one of the carvers if he was proud to be an African.

"I am more than the word proud. Africa is the greatest," he said catching the attention of the rest of the carvers. I then asked what he thought about African history and if he is proud about it?

"I don't worry about history or the future. I only worry about today and what I can get to chop."

"We have to let bygones be bygones. Too much history to me confuses the point," Senior Ofori interrupted. I opened my ears and listened with curiosity. A few more people gathered around to take part in the conversation. One of them was drinking a bottle of beer he had brought from Akwaba Bar. This is the way of life in the Art Centre. Like almost anywhere else in Ghana, two people cannot just sit and have a private conversation without others inviting themselves in. Gradually, the chatting matured into a full-blown political debate.

One retired teacher came around and provoked the debate to another level by suggesting that there is little to be proud of African history.

"Of course I am proud to be African but I am not at all proud of a history of failure, tribalism, political corruption and all the crazy things that have happened here in the past. As a matter of fact, when I was a teacher, I used to encourage many of my students to learn about European and American history and forget about African history. We need to study European history so that we can learn to know how to do things the right way and become successful." The retired teacher argued that the reason why most Africans are not enthusiastic about our history is because it is full of tragedies and failures. "Who wants to know about how his grandfather failed? And what positive lesson can we learn from a history of failure?"

As we sat and debated, two young German student girls arrived at the shop. They were accompanied by a dozen or so young hustlers who were all desperately seeking to sell them some artefacts: bright colourful leather handbags, beads, jewellery, woven hats, djembe drums and other musical instruments. One of the German girls wanted to buy a nude sculpture to take back to Germany. Their arrival disrupted the flow of our lively conversation. So, I left the growing pandemonium and went to the Akwaba Bar to catch a little gossip.

"Good afternoon, Obama Brother," Sister Ama, the owner of the bar greeted. Because I talked about Obama everywhere, people, especially in the Art Centre, had begun to call me his brother.

"Did you hear about the Obama Match on Saturday?"

"Which match?" I asked.

"The Rastafarians against the Evangelical Christians; it is at Labadi beach this Saturday."

"Rasta's against Christians, what has that got to do with the American presidential election?" I asked.

"They want to boost local support for Obama's campaign. I am surprised you didn't hear about it," Sister Ama said offering me a nice cold Star beer. After a little chat, she went away into the kitchen to bring me some soup and goat meat. I asked Sister Ama what she thought about the history of Africa and if she is proud about it.

"Sometimes I feel ashamed about being African today, but I am very proud about our history. Have you ever heard any country in Africa that went and stole or robbed from any country in Europe before? Our great grandfathers were good people. They looked after everyone in the society. But, today we are not good to ourselves. We can't blame the ancestors." Sister Ama argued that it is our wicked mentality that breeds corruption today. It is not our grandfather's fault that we don't have hospitals and good roads in Ghana or Nigeria. I was encouraged by Sister Ama's attitude towards our history but I was also a little disappointed about how disinterested many people seemed to be. I wondered if this was because history is usually such a heavy and boring subject to many people. Or is it simply due to the fact that for some unexplainable reason, we Africans don't feel proud enough of our past records because history brings guilt and shame to us today? I tried to talk to a few more people about the same topic, but the interest was low. In the end, I felt that, although history may sometimes taste like bitter quinine, which is difficult to swallow, knowing, understanding and learning from our past mistakes is the only way forward to a prosperous future in Africa.

Not making any progress on the street, I wanted to see if I could make any progress in the classroom. I went to meet a history professor at the University of Ghana, Legon. When I met Professor Yoho, I began by asking him to define history and explain why he thinks the past is so important to us today, especially to the new generation of African youth.

"History is the observation, study and the understanding of past *important* events which are relevant to us today. For example, how did Africa become 55 countries? This is relevant to me and you today. Why did Abuja become the capital city of Nigeria on the 12th of August 1991? When, how, where and why did such systematic slavery occur in Africa but not anywhere else in the world? Who started the transatlantic slave trade and who benefited from it? When did the Europeans start thinking of colonising Africa and why? Why did the Europeans see themselves to be superior to the African people? We need proper answers for all these questions because what happened in the past has resulted in how we are today. This is very important because it is the foundation of our society. This is why Marcus Garvey once said: A people without the knowledge of its past is like a tree without roots." Professor Yoho told me it is only when we observe study and understand why we are in the mess that we are in at this present moment that we can begin to cleanse our souls and do better for ourselves.

"Knowing our past is not only good for today, it is essential for tomorrow," he said. I sat and wrote my notes, ensuring that I did not miss out any important detail.

"The early years of African history are full of great stories but those stories have been misrepresented and misreported by outside forces for their own strategic interest. Right now, if I mention the word pyramid, you think of Egypt in the Middle East. Yet, very few of us are aware that, the land of the ancient Kingdom of Nubia, which is current day Sudan, has twice the number of pyramids of Egypt. So, Africa was once a great kingdom and this is a fact we have to know and be proud of first before we can properly reflect and learn from our past mistakes." Professor Yoho insisted that – prior to anything modern – our greatest African ancestors already had advanced and highly sophisticated systems and structures, which worked perfectly well in meeting the needs of our past societies.

"Let me tell you another fact," he said after pausing to reorder his thoughts. "Do you know that half of the stories you read in the Bible especially in the Old Testament are African stories? And yet have you ever seen the word Africa appear anywhere in the Bible? This is because, those who wrote the Bible do not like to admit that the stories they told and the people they spoke about originated from Africa. Let me tell you something else that should make us proud about our history." The Professor paused to clear his throat. "Before modern money, there was already a well-established system of barter trade in operation amongst large sections of African society. This was, by far, the fairest and most appropriate means of exchanging goods and services in our continent. Furthermore, it is important to highlight that, even following the barter trade system, the vast majority of African societies moved on to using cowrie shells and other precious beads as a means of exchange. This lasted for centuries, well before the Europeans and the rest of the world came to know anything about paper money, which they use as a weapon to control us today. As a matter of fact, do you know that the word 'cedi' is an Akan word which means cowrie?" the Professor said, referring to the Ghanaian national currency.

I knew that Professor Yoho was making a lot of sense because, even today in many rural African communities, people use cowries as a legal tender and a means of exchange for goods and services. In my own Sissala tribe, we still use cowries as dowry settlement and as an important gift to elderly relatives, especially during weddings, funerals and celebrations.

The Point of No Return

A few days after talking to Professor Yoho in Legon Campus, I travelled on a bus to Cape Coast to visit Dr Mahama; he is the director of the African History Museum at Cape Coast Castle. Originally built by the Swedish as a slave dungeon in 1453, the Cape Coast historic castle was seized by the British in 1462, only to be captured by the Dutch a year later before it was finally retaken by the British again in 1464.

"Dr Mahama, what do you think went wrong in the past and what important lesson can the African youth of today learn from our past mistakes?"

"Look, the answer is simple and straight forward. Before we Africans can unite and make progress, there are two things we have to know: we have to know who we are and we have to know who they are."

"But, who are they?" I asked.

"The Arabians and the Europeans: they were the secondary cause of the downfall of Africa. When they came, we gave them unconditional love, when they left; they took our people away as slaves. Let me tell you a story that will make your blood boil like a pot of beans. A long time ago there was a small desert village in Mali. The name of the village was Medina, 20 miles outside Timbuktu. One day, the villagers returned from their farms as the evening sun sank in the sky. The cows were also returning to the kraal from their grazing fields. The little calves joyously followed their mothers, lowing, playing and fighting each other along the way. Together, more than 200 cows generated a visible cloud of brown dust in the atmosphere as herdsmen followed with their guiding sticks.

Suddenly, a racing wind scattered leaves and dust high into the sky. The herdsmen watched with dismay as nature continued to show its mighty power by turning the roof of the earth into thick dark clouds. The wind generated more dust, swirling it around in circles rising from the ground to about a hundred metres high into the sky. The village dogs picked up the strange smell and followed the tornado, barking and wagging their tails in distress.

The barking continued as the village dogs chased the unusual tornado towards the riverside. Everyone knew there was something wrong; maybe something terrible was about to happen. The entire village gathered to watch on the riverbank. To their complete dismay, the tall wind disappeared into thin air, confusing everyone.

'Look, I can see something across the river. It's a river monster!' said one nervous villager. The creature was resting heavily on its stomach by the riverside. It had drunk so much water it could not stand up and walk. The dogs hesitated to get too close because of its gargantuan size. No one in Medina village had ever seen an animal like this before.

'It does not resemble a cow,' said one bewildered villager.

'It is not a giraffe, either,' said another."

Dr Mahama told me that the animal the villagers saw by the river that day was a camel, which belonged to a man called Abu-Bakr. He was one of the first Arabian men to set foot on African soil.

"This story I am telling you right now has been told as far back as the first century or even earlier." Dr Mahama told me how the villagers in Medina received Abu-Bakr and fed him with all their love and wealth. He said that after receiving the best hospitality from the villagers for three weeks, Abu-Bakr left Medina and returned to Yemen on the back of his camel. On his way, the villagers gave him food, clothes, tools and other precious metals.

"Several months later, Abu-Bakr returned with four camels and two friends. Again, they were well received, fed and sheltered for a few weeks. When they were about to leave this time, Abu-Bakr and his friends gave a bag of salt to the villagers and asked for anything they could get in return. The Medina villagers were generous in their giving. They gave Abu-Bakr and his friends everything they wanted, including clothes made from cotton. The men on the camels were also given bundles of jewellery and spices to take away to Yemen.

Two or three months later, Abu-Bakr returned with ten camels and seven of his brothers from Yemen. This time, Abu-Bakr and his brothers prayed together in the village chief's compound. As they did so, they invited the villagers to join them. They said before the villagers could join them for prayers, they must abandon their own beliefs. And this was how the story of deviation began in Africa. We used to have our own religions and ways of worship, but, it was through our unfortunate willingness to believe and to do anything the outsider says that brought us to the beginning of our doomed days. The first Arabs in Africa knew we love strangers better than ourselves, and that is how they capitalised on our weakness. Because we were always willing to give, they began to reach the conclusion that we were fools. Even today, most Arabs think that a black African man is a slave or a stooge." The cool breeze from the ocean was nice but the heat of the conversation made it uncomfortable to enjoy the environment. Dr Mahama explained that the Arabians first entered Africa from the North (modern-day Morocco, Algeria and so forth) and extracted salt from these desert regions which they then traded throughout the rest of Africa in exchange for gold and other locally produced African commodities, such as leather goods, clothes and other cotton products.

"It is important to highlight here that, in order to maintain this vital gold–salt trading link, the Arab traders also exchanged some salt for African slaves. These slaves were then used like donkeys to extract more salt to be sold to the very same African people."

Dr Mahama explained how the Arabs were successful in bringing Islam to the African continent using the already important and well-established gold–salt trade route. According to Mahama, Abu-Bakr was the first Arabian man to bring Islam into Mali and, from Mali; he preached and spread his culture and religion far and wide. From this small village in Mali, the Arabs devised an action plan to spread Islam to every village in the land of Africa.

Consequently, by the end of the tenth century, many parts of Africa were completely Islamised and huge parts of our land occupied. He cited East Africa as an example, the local Bantu language was dramatically changed by the influence of the Arabic language into a completely new language called Swahili, which is spoken today by not less than 16 countries around the African continent. Dr Mahama mentioned that Hausa, which is the most commonly spoken West African language, also has a third of its origin (syllabus) from the Arabic language.

"The impact of Arabianisation on Africa can never be over-emphasised. Even in today's world, Africa hosts the largest population of Arabs – more than any other continent or region of the world, including the Middle East. The fact of the matter is that the people of Africa have always been kind to the Arab people but the Arabian man has not shown enough appreciation or respect for us. Even today, many Arabs think we are their foolish servants."

After talking about the Arabs for some time, Dr Mahama turned his attention to the Europeans.

"My brother, come with me, I want to take you down and show you the point of no return," he said referring to the last doorway in the castle where captured slaves were loaded into the ships to take away to the Americas. "Slavery, as you know, is a very sensitive issue which has created huge ugly scars and wounds in many people's lives today. Sometimes, some people prefer to ignore the topic and suffer the pain of indignity in silence. Many people just want to get on with their modern day realities and forget about the oppressive past. As a historian, however, I believe what has happened in the past must always be forgiven in the present, so that we can move without pain or hatred into the future. But, we must never ever forget what happened to the African people in the past." Dr Mahama argued that without the burden of slavery on our neck, it is possible that Africa could have been just as developed and advanced as Europe and America today, if not better. He referred to the fact that the slave trade was used to fuel the engine of the Industrial Revolution of both Europe and America.

"Let me tell you the story of how the trans-Atlantic slave trade began right here in this building many hundred years ago," he spoke as we walked through the door of no return. "On a warm October day in 1444, a group of girls were carrying buckets and basins of water on their heads and walking from the riverside. They lived in a little village called Moree, just about ten miles away from this castle," Dr Mahama spoke with great diligence and understanding about the hidden past. "As the girls navigated through a stretch of long grass overshadowing the narrow path, the dew soaked their clothes. Mariama, the oldest girl among them was 14. She took the lead. They could see the thatched roofs of the village in the distance. Ama, the youngest girl, was only six. She had a sore neck and wanted to put her bucket down to get a little rest.

Mariama stopped and put her own bucket down first before helping Ama, her stepsister. While resting they heard a sound.

'Awwwwwww, please help me,' a voice called from the other side of the bush. It was a faint voice in an unfamiliar tongue.

'Please help me. I cannot move. I am going to die.' the voice said repeatedly. Mariama told the rest of her siblings to stay back and she nervously pierced through the thick grass to see who it was.

'Please help me. Don't go and leave me here or else I will die,' said the alien voice. Mariama did not understand a word but was concerned enough to see who it was. After clearing through the grass, Mariama jumped back frantically screaming to her sisters, 'Let's run home. I saw a dangerous-looking man. He is not like us,' she said. In a panicked hysteria, Mariama and her sisters ran back to the village spilling all the water they had fetched from the river. When they got home and explained what had happened, the chief of the village immediately dispatched some strong men to go down to the riverside and investigate the claim.

'Please help me. I need food and water. I need medicine or else I will die.' The villagers stood back nervously unable to decide.

'Why is he a different colour from us?' asked one villager. Before this day, no one in Moree village had ever seen a European man before. At the beginning of the encounter, a few of the villagers were unhappy about taking the white man back to their village.

'Come on, brothers, let us take this man home and give him some food. Look at him, he has no meat left on his bones,' said another sympathetic villager.

'My name is Christopher,' he spoke. From the onset, it was clear that Christopher the Dutchman urgently needed food and medical treatment.

Although the villagers barely understood a word he said, they could see that he was weak and feeble, and they were sure he had severe malaria, as well as all the other hostile tropical diseases that one could think of. Without further delay, the villagers in Moree rushed Christopher in a donkey cart to their chief's palace. The chief ordered one of the village men to leave his house and give it to the new guest as part of their usual village hospitality to strangers."

Dr Mahama explained that, fortunately, Christopher did not die because of the high level of care and attention he received from the people of Moree. The villagers in Moree killed chickens and cooked delicious meals for him. They gave him the best local medicine, which was powerful for getting rid of the malaria that ravaged his body. They healed his wounds, which he had received from wild animals and they gave him the best care any man could reasonably expect from his fellow man.

"Six weeks later, Christopher recovered and decided to leave the village. All the villagers in Moree gathered at the chief's palace and thumped their drums, singing and chanting happy songs and praises as a farewell for Christopher.

Like the story of Abu-Bakr the Arabian man in Mali, Christopher was given plenty of food, medicine and other precious materials to carry away. Our generous ancestors showed love, kindness and compassion. They gave many things away with blind faith. Among the things Christopher took away from Moree village, was gun powder.

One year later, Christopher returned with two friends. They brought with them, a pistol, a Bible and some schnapps. The pistol was loaded with bullets from the powder Christopher took away on his first voyage. As you can perfectly imagine for yourself, Nana Osofo the chief of the village was very impressed with his new gifts. After sharing some gin with his host that fatal morning, Christopher performed his first magic in front of the village by shooting and killing a cow that stood and grazed in the surrounding bush. Afterwards, Christopher handed over the weapon for the village chief to try."

As Dr Mahama spoke, tears came close to dropping point. I had more than a billion questions going through my mind. Why, why and why? There were many whys? Why did the Europeans and the Arabs succeed so easily in bringing shame and despair upon us? Why and how. What did we do wrong? I asked Dr Mahama if he will agree with me that it was not only the outside world that let us down but also ourselves.

"Yes of course, we have to carry half the blame ourselves. This is why I said the outside world was only the secondary factor to the downfall of Africa. We the people of Africa are the primary cause of Africa's failure. This is true both in the past and today."

"Dr Mahama, what was the role and conduct of our own Chiefs during the trans-Atlantic slave trade? Is it true that some of our own leaders have benefited from this ungodly affair?"

"To a very little extent, yes, we know that some disgruntled African leaders colluded with the slave merchants and might have made small gains. But, we are verging on the risk of comparing an ant to that of a mighty elephant in terms of disproportionate benefits and gains. Today, if you meet an unrepentant European man, he will do anything he can to convince you that we Africans sold ourselves. The question I have for the whole world is: how much did the slave masters pay for the slaves they took and shipped away from Africa?" Dr Mahama said that in his expert opinion, there is no way our African ancestor sold themselves.

"But surely before the Arabs and the Europeans came into Africa, there were already tribal conflict and internal rivalry among many sections of African society? How can we continue to point all our fingers on the outsiders alone?" I asked.

"Of course, there is no doubt that Africa had problems just like any other continent of the world. But what I am saying here is that the Arabs and the Europeans came in and exacerbated all our internal problems. Let me give you one specific example," he said and paused to arrange his thoughts. "To a great extent, it is arguable that both the Bible and the Qur'an destroyed our culture. Christianity, for example, is based on a nuclear family arrangement which is in many ways contradictory to the values and traditions of our extended family systems. Equally, Islam, which is my own religion, has come to prohibit many of our positive cultural practices. Do you know for example that even today if you go to most northern Ghanaian Muslim villages, the people are not allowed to play any traditional music because of the wrong interpretation of the Qur'an?"

After taking his time to explain the cumulative impact of Arabianisation and the slave trade in Africa, Dr Mahama touched briefly on another sensitive issue.

"As if 400 years of active enslavement and the total dehumanisation of the African people were not enough, once the nineteenth-century Europeans became too guilty and, to some extent, ashamed about the slave trade, they quickly made laws against legal slavery, but immediately embarked on a system of 'divide and rule' of Africa.

Don't forget that colonial rule was just a pretentious 'change of uniform' from the previous era." Dr Mahama told me that colonial rule, which was masterminded at the 'Berlin Conference' in 1884 and 1885, was, in his view, the worst form of systematic abuse and concrete evidence of racism against the African people.

"The Berlin Conference was where prominent European imperial powers met and successfully devised a new diplomatic agreement about how to break the entire African continent into smaller fragments, which they could then effectively control and exploit for their own benefit, hence the term 'divide and rule'." Dr Mahama told me that the partition of Africa was built on the principle of what the colonial masters describe, in their own words, as "effective occupation of Africa."

"By 'effective occupation', I mean that, in order to justify ownership of a particular demarcated territory in Africa, the various colonial countries had to first demonstrate to its fellow colonialist that it had exercised military control over its territories and failing this could simply result in a rival imperial power taking it away. So, in a way, the Berlin Conference effectively served as a stock market, where the various European nations successfully butchered Africa into smaller pieces and shared the titbits amongst themselves for their own benefit."

I felt sad and happy at the same time listening to Dr Mahama. I was sad because of the shameful realisation of what happened to our greatest African ancestors. But, I was also glad and equally relieved to know that my great grandparents helped significantly to build this modern world we all live in today. I hope and pray that this fresh understanding of Africa's proud and sometimes lamentable history should provoke a new realisation of how our modern-day has come into shape, and why Africa is, consequently, in the difficult position she is in now.

"Brother Chebe, I want to end your visit to this historic World Heritage site by giving you a final message to the people of Africa and the rest of the world. I want to seize this opportunity to point out loudly, that the purpose of history is not to blame and finger point at each other or blame somebody else. The purpose of history is to learn, understand and repent from our bad behaviours. I believe that this is the time for forgiveness and reflection so that we can foster and build new positive relationships between the great grandsons and daughters of former victims and former perpetrators of a very hideous human crime. Finally, I believe that facing up to our history presents us with a genuine opportunity to remind ourselves, as Africans and African descendents around the world, that even though we are all bound by the common tragedy of the past, we have only been weaken but not completely broken. Today, we can recover from our wounds by uniting together as a new repentant generation of the twenty-first century. It is only by working together and not against each other, that we can build a better future for ourselves, our children, grandchildren and great, great, great, great grandchildren."

Chapter 14: God, Religion and Conflict

"Who is God?" my friend Ababa asked as we walked along a stretch of dusty road. "What role should God play in your life? Is God sincerely honest, truthful and fair to every human being in this world or is God sometimes a big hypocrite? Are there any chosen races and forgotten races or are we all equal in the eyes of the Lord. Has God blessed us in Africa or placed a secret curse on our conscience as some enemies of Africa have always claimed? How can we use the power of God to unite the people of Africa today for the goodness of humanity? These are the questions I ask myself everyday and I am so glad to tell you that these are the questions roaming about in every single human mind. Everybody is searching for the same or similar answers about God," Ababa spoke before waving his hand to stop a taxi. It was a bright yellow taxi with long white stripes along the sides.

"Where do you guys want me to drop you?" the driver asked, rolling down his window.

"Legon," we both replied and I opened the back door. I let Ababa in first, then entered and slammed the door. Inside the taxi, the talk about God continued.

"My brother, as I was saying, whether you believe it or not, the most burning issue in the mind of every human being you see in this world today is God. From the day we are born till the day we die, God remains the biggest mystery in our lives. Those who don't believe in God know the name of God. The question I asked already is: who is God? Is God truly one powerful living creature or a thing of the mind?" Ababa asked.

It was meant to be a half hour journey, but we spent over an hour on the road because of the heavy Friday afternoon traffic. The car was boiling and I couldn't help the sweat pouring and soaking my shirt. I rolled down the back windows, but it offered little comfort. I was so relieved when we drove through the campus gate.

"How much is the fare?"

"Oh, give me 20 Ghana," the driver said before turning off his engine. "That is too much, let me give you 15 Ghana."

"No problem," he said and collected his money before we got out. That day we were in Legon Campus to visit the ATR Institute. For those who are not familiar with the acronym, ATR stands for African Traditional Religions. We were there because I wanted to conduct an interview with Baba Wisi, the head of the Theology Department.

"Good afternoon, my brothers, thank you for coming to see me today," Baba Wisi greeted and shook my hand before offering the same gesture to Ababa. "Take a seat and make yourselves comfortable."

The sweat continued to pour and soak my body. There were so many questions I had to ask the expert about God and religion, especially in relation to Africa.

"So, where shall we begin?" Baba Wisi asked sitting in front of his heavily cluttered desk and facing Ababa and me. Papers piled high nearly covered the computer screen.

"I want to know why every continent of the world has a dedicated religion, apart from Africa. What is the indigenous religion of the African people?" Ababa began. I sat quietly with my pen and paper ready to jot down the answers.

"The first known African religion is called Fawfaw or Fafalism, which is the belief in the spirit of our ancestors. Those who believe in Fawfaw also believe that God is everything and everything is God!" Baba Wisi exclaimed and paused for a few seconds to gather his thoughts. "The absolute truth is that almost every religion of the world, including the main three Abrahamic religions, Judaism, Christianity and Islam, originated from the African continent. This is why Africa is not only the birthplace of humanity but also the birthplace of God. Africa is the origin of all traditions, beliefs, religions and cultures."

I asked my lecturer why he relates religion so closely to culture and tradition.

"Culture and religion are both the same," Ababa interrupted, anxious to add his voice to the conversation.

"That is true," said Baba Wisi. "Culture and religion are both ways of life. The way of life of an Arab man is Islam, which is part of his culture. How many times will you see a long-bearded Arabian man going to church on Sunday? Or dressed up in his shirt and tie to go for a Sunday roast? The Arab man will not do so because he is proud of his own cultural tradition and his own religious believes." After stressing the similarities between culture and religion, Baba Wisi then told me his understanding of God, itself.

"If you think of your life as a journey from A to Z, then God is the final destination where every individual journey ends. Every single being you see in this world is on a personal journey to God. Religion, on the other hand, is just one of the means or the vehicle by which you get to your final destination. The individual in this case is like the driver or the passenger in the vehicle of life." Mr Wisi spoke, setting out the parameters and the delicate relationship between religion, God and the conduct of the individual.

"What is God and who is God?" he asked again and continued, "God is a simple thought of the mind. What you think is God, what I think is God, what they say is God and what we believe is God is nothing else but God." Baba Wisi told me that in reality every human being has an idea of their own God and what one knows about God is of no greater value or importance than another. Only God knows it all: no one else knows God better than you do," he said. "We Fafalers believe that God is more than one common identity. As a matter of fact, God is a trinity. In other words, there are three ways to see God from an ancient African perspective."

"So, what are these three dimensions of God?" Ababa asked.

"The first dimension of God is based on a belief in one God. This dimension of God is approximately 2,500–5,000 years old." Mr Wisi stated that Judaism, Christianity and Islam are all based on this doctrine of God as one universal creator who is omnipotent and omnipresent.

"The second dimension of God is based on the understanding that the gods are many. This is the oldest belief system in the whole world and dates back to the very beginning of Adam and Eve. The truth is that even before the idea of the one single God came into our minds, the people of Africa were already following the paths of many gods. In African theology, there are always many gods, or many dimensions of God. In Ghana, for example, there are some who believe in a river god, others believe in a stone god. There are good gods and there are bad gods."

"So, the gods can be two, like twin brothers as there are always two sides to a coin!" Ababa interrupted.

"Exactly," said Baba Wisi. "And if there are twin brother gods controlling the world, one of these gods is a good god but the other twin brother god is most definitely a bad god!"

"Hold on a minute, here, my brothers, surely you must be joking. How can there be more than one God, this doesn't make any sense to me at all," I said.

"OK, if two gods don't make sense, how does one god make sense to you? If you only believe in one god, is this one mighty god a good or a bad god?" Baba Wisi asked staring at me.

"Of course, God is always a good god. I mean, any god who created this vast universe and placed us on earth to live, multiply and be fruitful can only be described as a good god," I argued.

"So, who controls all the bad things in the world and why?" Baba Wisi asked.

"Satan is the man in charge of the evil we do," said Ababa.

"Who is Satan?" Baba Wisi asked. "If there is only one good god in charge of the universe, then who created Satan and why? Are you honestly trying to convince me that God made Satan and gave him the power to destroy you and me and everyone else in this world?"

"That is completely impossible. If this is the case, then, surely God is a hypocrite," Baba Wisi argued that there is an unbelievable amount of hypocrisy and inconsistency that underpins the doctrine of a single all-loving and blameless God.

"Even in Christianity, the image of God has not been fully portrayed as one entity. If you read about the beginning of the earth in Genesis in the Bible, after the gods created everything in the universe, then, one of the gods says: 'Let us create man in our own image.' According to my understanding of the Bible, all the bad gods disagreed with the good god and there was fire right from the beginning. If it was one single god who created the earth, why did he not quench the fire at the beginning? The other problem is, if there is only one god, who created man in his perfect image? Why has man become such an imperfect being? Why do so many people on earth suffer so much undue hardship, social disorder, disease, tragedy, accident, robbery, murder, bullying, malnutrition, starvation and all the rest of the wicked and ungodly human crimes we experience in our world today?" Baba Wisi told me that he does not believe that he shares the same gods with the wicked unrepentant sinner. I began to see a reasonable amount of logic in Baba Wisi's theory of multiple gods.

"The idea of many gods allows us to see God outside of the box. It places greater emphasis on the conduct of the individual as opposed to the path or the vehicle you choose to follow your God." Baba Wisi said that under the second dimension of God, one is able to understand and appreciate that, there are many manifestations of God and it doesn't matter if you are a Muslim, Christian, Jew, Fafalist, Buddhist or idol worshiper, so long as you do enough good to yourself and practice kindness to others in your world, then you are following the principles of a good god which is the surest path to spiritual freedom and the only way to eternal life!

"Now, the third and final dimension of God is the newest and perhaps the most controversial. The third dimension of God is based on the assumption that God is only a child of the mind. This belief originates from the slim possibility that, although every religious person would like you to believe that God created all human beings, it is equally possible that our own thoughts about the origin of humanity has forced our greatest ancestors to think about an almighty creator who they named as God."

"So, does this mean there may not be a God at all?" Ababa asked looking unconvinced.

"Yes, of course. It is possible that there is no God because, nobody knows for sure whether there actually is a God." I was very confused, like Ababa. If there is no God, how can we explain the position of the sky, the stars, the moon and the earth? How can we also explain the origin of life, the air we breathe, the water we drink and the food we eat? How can all these be an accident or a coincidence?"

I asked Baba Wisi for his final advice to the African youth of today. How can we follow the right path of God and unite in Africa for our own good. "We have to go back to our roots in Africa for spiritual salvation," he said hastily. "All Europeans and Americans believe in Jesus, every Arab man believes in Allah, the Chinese believe in Buddha, 800 million people in India believe in Hinduism, which is, after all, a belief in a water god. We the people of Africa today must ignore all our differences and wake up to worship and follow our own traditional religion of Fafalism, which is the belief in our ancestral connection. There are approximately two billion African people in the world today, can you imagine the power we have if we come together under one ancestral spirit? As I told you already, in Fafalism, we believe that God is one big thing made up of billions and trillions of smaller units, including you and I.

Fafalism is the only non-discriminative religion on earth. If you are a Christian and you believe that Jesus is God, then Jesus is God. If you are a Muslim and you believe that Allah is God, then Allah is God. If you a village man in Angola and you worship a river as an example of God, then the river is God. If you believe that Moses was a prophet of God, then Moses was a prophet of God. This is the only path which can bring total unity not only to the people of Africa but to the whole world." Baba Wisi warned that the idea of trying to convince everyone to believe in one doctrine or one religion or one path to God is the most dangerous route to universal spiritual suffocation. "The belief in one super master God or one righteous religion is an extremely dangerous dogma to carry into the future. The best way forward, especially in Africa, is to worship your God, believe in your own chosen path and respect other beliefs. We have to live and let others live and Fafalism offers us all enough room and space to coexist and co-worship. Can you even imagine if we were all Muslims? Don't you think that this world would have been a very dangerous place to live?"

I asked Mr Wisi why he believed that a man who worships a stone or river god is just as important as a man of Jesus or Allah.

"In the eyes of the Lord, every being has equal value. No single man's understanding about God is better than the other because we are all merely blindly in love with God. The danger is, if we put all our eggs in one basket or force everyone in the world to believe in one correct God like Jesus or Allah as opposed to all the rest, what happens if we are all wrong on judgement day?"

God's Role in the Rwandan Genocide

With my head beating like a talking drum, I returned to Art Centre a few days later to find out more about God. I remember when I reached Alhaji Sokoto's shop that day, there were many people gathered, as usual after Friday prayers, heatedly debating.

Unsurprisingly, the topic was international politics. I sat and listened for some time before seizing the opportunity to pose my loaded question. "Who is God?" I asked Alhaji Sokoto.

"God is good and bad," he said and stepped forward. "God is good because he gives everyone a chance to live. On the other hand, God is bad because he blesses some people and curses others like me, I don't know, why?" he said.

"Alhaji, how can you accuse God of placing a curse on you?" asked one of the talkers.

"I am a cripple, that is why I can accuse God," he said with a weak smile.

"I don't believe God is wicked to you at all," said Razak, a good friend of Alhaji and a regular visitor to the shop. "You are a cripple who enjoys more than many normal men in Ghana, here. You have your own shop, don't you?" Razak asked and continued, "Let me ask you a question, how many cripples do you know in this world with two wives and other side issues to play with?" Many people laughed at Razak's comments, knowing that he was stating a gospel fact. There is no doubt that there are many people in this world with two perfect legs who are not as fortunate as Alhaji Sokoto.

"Listen to me, my brothers. There is no point in blaming or pointing all our fingers at God. The problem is not God but rather the numerous foreign religions in Africa. Religion keeps us divided and disunited. That is why our African leaders must seriously consider banning all religion for ten years. This may bring positive change to this continent."

"We have too many religious divisions," said Alhaji Sokoto. I asked him why he blames religion as opposed to God. If most religions are telling us to believe in one God, why do people fight each other over the same one God? Why are we afraid to blame God for lack of progress in Africa?" I asked.

"No, I don't think anyone can seriously blame God in Africa. God has already blessed Africa. He gave us the best land in the whole world. I blame religion because religion, by nature, breeds ignorance and intolerance. If you think I am telling lies, ask any honest Muslim you come across. He or she will tell you that if you don't believe in Allah, you are going to hell. This is exactly the same with Christianity. An honest Christian will tell you that without the love of Jesus, you can never get to anywhere near the gates of heaven," Justice said and continued, "Religion breeds intolerance, bigotry and narrow-mindedness and it is this kind of ignorance which led to the needless carnage and massacre of one million innocent people in Rwanda!" There were tens of people gathered in front of the shop watching a game of football on the dusty field as Justice continued with the story of the genocide in Rwanda.

"In fact, I feel ashamed anytime I remember what happen in Rwanda. People sat in their offices in New York and did nothing to help. World leaders at the UN were busy discussing whether it was genocide or not before they could intervene. By then, it was clear that hundreds and thousands of innocent heads were being chopped off and bodies were being mutilated indiscriminately. It was just like Armageddon." said Justice. Everybody listened to his words. As I listened to the story of genocide, a memory of 1994 brought vivid pictures of cold rotten carcasses lying on the blood-stained streets of Kinshasa. A shame, indeed, I thought to myself feeling the spread of goose bumps on my guilty shoulders as Justice spoke on.

"Within a matter of just a hundred days, over one million Tutsis and Hutus were exterminated from the record books. By the time the rest of the world started to feel a little guilty about what was happening in Rwanda, it was far too late."

I took a brief moment and tried to reflect back. I tried to imagine what the genocide in Rwanda had in common with God or religion.

Whilst I was thinking, Justice searched his briefcase frantically for some time before removing an old newspaper article to give me.

"Take this article and read it out loud for everyone to hear. I want everyone in Africa to see how dangerous it is to follow the path of blind faith," he insisted and passed the article into my hand. It read as follows:

> Missionaries were "the first ethnologists" of colonial Rwanda … for Father François Menard, writing in 1917, a Tutsi was "a European under a black skin". If the church heralded the Tutsi as "supreme humans" in 1917, the same church would turn into a prime site for the slaughter of Tutsi in 1994.

> The biblical story of Ham, one of the sons of Noah, was enlisted for this purpose. Initially this myth postulated that Ham, having seen his father naked and drunk, was disowned by Noah and was driven away. Because of his dark skin, and his propensity for disloyalty, idleness and stupidity, he supposedly became the founder of the black "race", who were therefore cursed and doomed to inferiority to the white man. This piece of biblical nonsense was a justification for the crudest forms of racism, designed to justify the treatment of humanity with a black skin in general like animals. It was one of the key "intellectual" and religious justifications for slavery in the earlier period of mercantilism that preceded the full development of the European empires.

I read out the text feeling wordlessly frustrated and sad. How could religion play such a negative role in the Rwandan civil war?

"And what is it about being black? What is so badly wrong with having a skin colour that doesn't burn under the sun?" Alhaji asked laughing and showing his hand. "Justice, do you not think some of these racist comments are based on jealousy? I mean, personally, I don't think any African man or woman should ever feel insulted or ashamed for being a descendent of Ham, even if that was the gospel truth. In fact, we should be very proud that God made us different from the rest of the world."

"There are two reasons why I gave you this article to read out," Justice interrupted and collected the newspaper from my hand. Neatly, he folded it back into his briefcase and said: "My first reason is to explain how a simple explicit belief or religious statement can become such a deadly catalyst. After Father François made his ignorant and totally racist statement by writing the above article, the Tutsis grow big-headed, believing they were of superior value over the Hutus."

"Obviously, what Father François said in 1917 alone could not have led the Tutsis to believe that they were a superior race with a higher reasoning capacity, like the Europeans."

Justice explained that, once Father François made his ungodly religious diagnosis, this unfortunate divine assessment or belief system was systematically adopted, programmed and developed by subsequent colonial masters, each of whom had the objective of dividing and ruling the Rwandan people for their own selfish goals. "The colonial masters handpicked and selected Tutsis and educated them to the highest standard. They then ensured that although the Tutsis were the minority tribe, they controlled the entire civil service and every aspect of governance in Rwanda for many decades, until disaster struck in 1994." Brother Justice explained that since the mind is a powerful universe of its own, it is important to feed it with the right information. He argued that when you feed people's minds with negative beliefs and hate, then it is not only religion or God we have to blame but, equally, the people who brought their religions to influence our behaviour in Africa.

"What we need now in Africa is a New Belief. We need our own African Bible to guide as and protect us from misleading propaganda," Alhaji Sokoto interrupted.

"Yeah, that is true," the rest responded by clapping and cheering at the same time!

"We Africans need to know that in this life, every action a man takes has a corresponding reaction. This means that whatever goes around must always come around." Justice warned that even today in many parts of Africa, religion is used in broad daylight to mislead and cheat the poor and torture the innocent. "Look around anywhere in Ghana today, pastors and church owners are richer than corrupt government ministers. If you think Ghana is bad, go to Cameroon, Côte d'Ivoire, Nigeria, Uganda, South Africa or Kenya and you will see breathtaking daylight dishonesty among our pastors, priests, and imams. Let me tell you a short story about one famous Nigerian pastor. I can't exactly remember his name but if you talk to any Nigerian, they will know who I am talking about. This pastor has a mega-church called the Winners Church. He charges everyone a fee to come to his church services. He has millions of followers in Nigeria, Ghana, London, New York and everywhere, with numerous branches of Winners Churches all over the world. This Nigerian pastor is so rich, he flies everywhere in a private jet. One day, he was interviewed by a Nigerian journalist who asked him why he lives such a lavish, extravagant life at the expense of the poor. The pastor replied by saying: "Nobody believes a poor pastor anymore in this world. The pastor told the journalist that if Jesus, was alive today, he himself would be using a private rocket to go from one corner of the earth to the other before people will listen to his message." Justice concluded by pointing out that right now in West Africa, the church is the most profitable business.

"Running your own church in Ghana is like operating a GP clinic, except that the pastor receives more patients. Everyday, those who are ill will go to see the doctor. And every blessed day, those who are worried and confused about certain aspects of their lives will go and pay their pastor to pray for them." Brother Justice concluded that, "Although Jesus died on the cross to wipe away the sins of mankind, many of his pastors today are carrying the wrong image of Jesus in Africa and using his name to lie and cheat the poor."

Wobo-Dam!

One rainy day in late October with less than two weeks to the 2008 American presidential election, I came across a man on the road to Makola market who claimed he knew exactly who God is. Everyone on the street called the man Wobo-Dam, meaning "crazy man" in the Akan language.

"Africans are not stupid, we are intelligent fools," he spoke and shook his head. Indeed, Wobo-Dam looked crazy, standing on the street in his wretched clothes, but what he said to me that day was as accurate as the position of the moon in the sky and the billions of stars around it.

"God is me and you," he said, standing tall and dirty. He was carrying things all over his body and his hair was in a complete bushy mess. "God is honesty and honesty is God. If you are not honest, you are following a wrong God," he said and scratched his hair. I asked Wobo-Dam why he believes honesty is the only way to Heaven's gate.

"First of all, I am not a mad man. I am a lawyer," he said and scratched his hair again. "I practiced in New York for seven years before coming home. My sister died exactly three weeks after 9/11. After coming home to bury her, I never made it back to New York again. My family destroyed me at home," he said and shed some tears. "I have not spoken like this for a long time," he said and wiped his face. "We are fools and dishonest in Africa, that is why we are suffering the pain of frustration. And dishonesty is the devil's strongest weapon." Wobo-Dam argued that those who are dishonest often cheat, lie and destroy positive relationships. As he spoke, I noticed that his teeth were yellowish brown.

"Look at the problem in this country, right now," he said and paused for a few seconds looking up into the sky as if he could see God hanging from the roof of the clouds.

"We have fertile land to cultivate all the food we need to live happily as one strong nation. Our land produces gold, diamonds, silver, copper and oil, and intelligent people who are unfortunately dishonest in their service to our own nation." Wobo-Dam told me that nowadays in Ghana people place allegiance to their mosques and churches first, before the nation.

"What is the point in deceiving ourselves everyday?" he said and stood still. I looked at him as his behaviour suddenly changed. He kept scratching his head, showing signs of distress.

"We don't love God in Africa: We are betraying his trust. What is the point in worshiping Allah or following Jesus if you are dishonest enough to tell lies, cheat and steal from the poor everyday?" he said and walked away crying.

Chapter 15: Cultural Change in Africa

"Our culture is more valuable than all our gold and diamonds," said Mrs Adjei, a spokeswoman from the Ghana Ministry of Culture. She argued vehemently that culture is the most important determinant of progress in any human society. "Look at Europe, what do you think they have, apart from the culture of efficiency?" I was listening to Mrs Adjei on Choice FM inside a taxi on my way to Makola market. She was giving an interview about the impact of culture on Economic Development.

"Those who have travelled outside the continent will tell you that Africa has the best culture in the whole world. The problem we have in Africa is that we don't evolve, change, and modify our culture to improve our living reality. That is why an African farmer still uses the same hoe his great, great grandfather used to farm without any modification."

"My brother, that lady on the radio is speaking a lot of sense," said Papa Nii the taxi driver. "We have to change our culture; it is too barbaric," he said. I asked why Papa Niii thought we have a barbaric culture in Africa.

"Look around the whole continent and you will see why I say we are suffering from a culture of barbarism." The taxi driver told me that in his opinion, there are many aspects of African culture which are based on negative behaviour like witch-hunting, tribal wars, jealousy, hypocrisy, backbiting and backstabbing.

"If you think I am wrong, I will take you to my village in the Volta region today; you will see evidence of primitive behaviour. The moment someone is dead, everybody suspects a witch or a wicked aunt or a bad uncle. We don't care if the death is because of malaria, tuberculosis or bilharzia, we always have to accuse and blame someone for anything that happens." Driver Nii argued that any culture which is based on superstition without enough attention to science is a barbaric and primitive culture. He told me that barbarism breeds backwardness because when there is a little argument in society; people fight and kill each other when they can behave like civilised men and woman and talk around the table to resolve their differences.

"Apart from barbarism, there is far too much backstabbing in Africa as well!" I asked him to explain what he meant by backstabbing. "When I scratch your back and you throw sand into my face to make me blind, that is what I mean by backstabbing. Let me give you a perfect example," he spoke as he negotiated his taxi through a shortcut to avoid some traffic he spotted ahead. "Three months ago, a friend of mine sent his girlfriend to the hospital. She was pregnant and he had to abort the baby because she was only in her first year of university. This friend didn't have money to pay the doctor's bill, so he came and borrowed two million old Ghana cedis from me. It was almost the end of the month. He told me that when he collects his salary, he will pay me back. The problem is, the money I gave to him was not my own. It was my sister's money and she gave it to me for safekeeping. When she needed the money to send her son to boarding school, I went to see my friend. That day, he promised me he would go to the bank to withdraw the money from his account and bring it to me at home. I waited till evening arrived but my friend didn't come to give me the money as promised. I tried to ring his phone but it went straight to the answer machine. Since then, I have been trying to get to him but he is nowhere to be found. I feel so angry and disappointed. I feel I have been stabbed in the back because I tried to help my own friend. I believe this is part of the reason why we don't develop in Africa."

The Role of Culture in Society

"Ladies and gentlemen, no matter how much one tries, it is nearly impossible to overemphasise the importance of a good culture," said Master Adam Folie, a senior lecturer at Winneba Teacher Training College. He was giving an open lecture that I had travelled from Accra to attend.

"From an academic viewpoint, I can tell you that the only means by which we can improve our standard of living in Africa is to change those aspects of our culture which have remained static and detrimental to our society for far too long. What we need more than anything else is a new culture of honesty, and it is you the teachers of today, who can make this change happened." Mr Folie said that if we are honest, we can get back to our senses and work together to build a new spirit of African patriotism. Honesty and sincerity he pointed out leads to dedication and commitment and the ultimate determination to succeed.

"Let us start the process of change by assessing the role of culture in Africa. Culture has three important functions in every society," he said, sneezing gently and covering his nose with a blue handkerchief. "The first function of culture is social and economic utilisation. The second function of culture is related to governance. The third function of culture is spiritual utilisation.

I am glad to point out to you that on the third function of culture, we Africans are probably more advanced than the rest of the world. This is why you can see that although we are the poorest continent in terms of economic growth, we are often not as sad and depressed as Europeans or Americans." Master Folie argued, taking a little sip of water from his pint glass. I admired his style of exuberant presentation. He was a tall charismatic man, of a good age, and was delivering his lecture to the first year students or "freshers" as they say in Winneba campus. "A person without a good culture is one without pride, and a person without pride is one without a clear sense of direction and the belief in his or her own ability to function or be without constant approval or authorisation from others. A nation without a unifying culture to bond its people together is a broken nation which lacks a strong sense of national identity. A generation without culture is a lost and desperate generation without hope. However, one generation of enlightened Africans with a strong sense of positive cultural identity can change and transform this continent from our ailing economic misfortunes within the blink of an eye," he argued.

"My message to you, therefore, as aspiring teachers, is that it is you, the people of this generation, who can make that critical difference between failure and success. It is you who can determine the direction of Africa. It is not the old men like me with grey hair or any man you see of your father's generation. You are what I call the new rebellious or email generation of Ghanaian teachers." Adam Folie spoke to the heart of the youth, attracting loud applause. It seemed that all the young trainee teachers liked his vivid description of a rebellious generation. The generation he described as ambitiously intelligent global citizens and cultured individuals who are not going to be satisfied any longer with less than they deserve!

"Now, I want us to move on to look directly at some aspects of our culture which are in urgent need of reforms. Let us take the African extended family as a starting point," he said, turning the page of his notes.

Our Extended Family System

"According to the first rule of nature, everything we see on earth is related to another. The moon is related to the stars and the stars are related to the sun. The sky is related to the earth because it produces the rain, which fills our seas, rivers, oceans and lakes. The sea is related to man because it provides the fish we eat and the means of transport of our goods from country to country. Here, on Planet Earth, the aeroplane, which carries people from one corner of the world to another, is related to the birds, which fly in the air by flapping their wings. Even the bird is related to the chicken, a crocodile is related to the lizard and the tree is related to man, not only because it provides us with the fruits we eat but also because without the oxygen the tree produces for us to breathe, a man cannot survive on earth for one whole day. Every single being you see today is related to a family, every family is related to a village, town, community or a tribe. Each tribe is related to another and that is why there are over 53 related tribes, which make up our country of Ghana today. And finally, there are over 53 related countries, like Ghana, which make up the African extended family which we are talking about right now," said Master Folie. After a little deliberation, he asked the students to discuss the impacts of the extended family from their own personal experiences.

"If you have any positive or negative personal experience about growing up in your village or have been affected in anyway by your extended family, please stand up and let us here your story," he said. One student stood up to say something to the class.

"Sir, my name is Lawrence Bawina and I am from Wa in the north. I am sad to say that I grew up in a wicked extended family. My uncle was evil to me, especially after my father's death," said Lawrence.

"What did your uncle do to you when your father died?" asked Master Folie.

"When my father died, he left 33 pigs to my Uncle Peter, but he sold everything and married three new wives. I was 17 and my uncle removed me from boarding school, I was in my final year by then. When I left school, he forced me to work on his farm. Anytime I refused to go to his farm, he threatened to kill me. One day I was sleeping, he came into my room and set me on fire. He wanted to kill me that night. That is why I have a big scar on my face." Lawrence spoke and stopped to shed some tears. "In fact, I wish that in the whole world, no one else should have an uncle as wicked as my Uncle Peter. I had to escape the north and run to Accra. I hustled and worked on the street for three years before I got some money to continue my education. I should have been a teacher by now, but my Uncle Peter frustrated and ruined my progress," Lawrence claimed. Everyone sympathised with him as he spoke. Whilst I was listening to his story, I reflected on my own childhood to assess the nature of my extended family and my life growing up in my village in the north, like Lawrence Bawina.

Polygamy

"Now I want us to spend some time to assess polygamy as a feature of the extended family and how it impacts our socio-economic development. First of all, what is polygamy? Is polygamy good or bad to society?" Master Adam Folie asked before immediately proceeding to answer himself.

"Polygamy is the practice of marrying more than one wife. It is a practice as old as the story of heaven and earth. The question today is, if polygamy is good or bad for you, the future generation of Africans? My answer to this question is two fold," said Master Folie.

"Yes polygamy is good and bad like everything else in this life. Sometimes, polygamy is good. If you look back into history, then you can see why. In the past, many things happened here in our continent and without a vital survival strategy and effective reproductive method like polygamy our population could have been wiped out to extinction. We have to remember that slavery and civil war have created a huge dent in our population at key moments of time in the history of this continent. It is true that during most civil conflicts, men die at a disproportionate rate compared to women. In Rwanda, for example, the current population is estimated to be around 70 per cent women. This is because of a brutal genocide in 1994. We shall hear a brief story about the Rwandan civil war later in this lecture. But the point I am trying to make is that if you are a Rwandan woman today and you are single, it may not necessarily be fair on you to be governed with a strict policy of one man one wife." Master Folie spoke and took a deep breath before stepping ahead.

"On the other hand," he said, "I say no to polygamy because I don't think it is necessarily a good force for economic development. In the past, I would say yes because, a long time ago, if you were a Ghanaian rural farmer, the best thing you could do to make money was to recruit as many wives as you could to help you on your farm. The more wives you had in those days, the more children you had to help cultivate your farm. The land was plentiful, so you could farm as much as you wanted. Today, the Ghanaian reality is different. The economic conditions are changing rapidly. Let me give you a practical example: 20 years ago Ghana's population was only 12 million people. Today, as we speak, Ghana's population is approximately 24.3 million. This means twice the number of people as 20 years ago are now competing for the same amount of land and resources. So, even if you marry many wives today and have plenty of children, you may not necessarily have enough farmland to produce enough food for everyone in your family."

"The other problem is that, every child is now supposed to attend primary education by law in Ghana. So, a man with five wives and 20 children today may not necessarily have the same labour force on his farm as compared to a man 20 years ago with five wives and 20 children," he argued. The lecture continued until the teacher invited the students to contribute their thoughts and experiences.

"Sir, I believe that polygamy is good for Africa. It is what makes us different from the Europeans and the Americans. Don't you think that some European men would also like the privilege of two or three wives?" Joseph asked.

"Joseph, how many wives does your father have?" asked Master Folie.

"Four, but I want to marry only two wives when I have enough money to maintain them and keep them both happy. I think four would be too hard to control. They would probably kill me early like my four mothers did to my father."

"Sir, I am completely against polygamy because I believe that it breeds rivalry among the children. It also leads to jealousy and hate among the wives. I will never share my husband with another woman!"

"Sir, I also oppose polygamy. I think it is a thing of the past and a very barbaric culture which must be banned in Ghana or anywhere else in Africa. As a matter of fact, I believe polygamy is greediness. The wives do not have any freedom of choice to do what they want. To me, it's just like another form of slavery. How can one man be able to look after two wives equally and be able to keep them both satisfied? I would feel very offended if my husband came to me one night and said, 'Darling, I want to marry another wife.' I don't think I would feel happy at all. I would be thinking to myself, am I not good enough for him? What is he going to get from the other woman that I cannot provide?" she spoke with passion and courage.

"Hold on a minute, the problem is that many women in Ghana prefer to have a man to look after them and take care of their needs," said Felix Atta. "They know that a man is married but they also insist on being taken care of. If a man has got enough money to marry his wives and look after their needs, why not?" he asked.

"Sir, my name is Georgina, I think it is up to the individual situation," said Georgina. "Some women may prefer a polygamous relationship because, as they say, competition is sometimes a very good thing. If you compete with another woman for the one man's attention, it gives you a different thrill and a different kind of satisfaction, especially when you get him to spend quality time with you. And it may be a good thing that when I am fed up with him, I can send him off to the other woman, so that I can have a rest. My only problem with polygamy is that it is only one-way traffic," Georgina said, causing some laughter in the lecture hall.

"What do you mean when you say polygamy is one-way traffic?" asked Master Folie.

"What I mean is that, if a man is allowed to have as many wives as he can, what happens if I also want to marry more than one husband?" Georgina asked and fuelled the debate to an entirely different level altogether.

"No, that is not according to the law of nature. This is a completely stupid suggestion," said Joseph. "Practically, a woman cannot have more than one husband. It is biologically wrong and it is impossible to practice. That is what the dogs do, not human beings."

Tribalism

"The last issue I want to discuss today is African tribalism," said Mr Folie after we returned from a break. "What is tribalism? What are the positive and negative impacts of tribalism in Africa? Why has tribalism affected more people in Africa than anywhere else in the world? First, let me try to define what I understand as a tribe. A tribe can be described as a small or large ethnic group of people who share the same cultural identity and the same language, or at least a common mode of communication." He told his class that throughout Africa, there are thousands of tribal and ethnic groupings, each of which can be said to be similar or completely different from each other in terms of their way of life.

"As you all know, there are at least 54 unique tribes which make up our country Ghana. Nigeria has over 200 unique ethnic profiles and the figures vary according to population and the size of the country in Africa you are talking about.

On the positive side, a tribe is like a family of dedicated people, united by common identity or a common goal. The Zulu tribe in South Africa is one of the most established tribes in our continent. In the past, the Zulus have united to fight off colonial impostors and won many great wars against colonial rulers. One such wars, was the Boer War against the British," he mentioned, adding that during the Boer War, the Zulu tribes of South Africa successfully fought and defeated the British in a humiliating battle because of the formidable degree of unity and fearless dedication to Zulu tribal sprit and identity.

"Here in Ghana, as well, we have the Ashanti tribe with over four million people who are all united under one King called the Ashanti-Hene. As you all know, the Ashanti tribe is one of the most peaceful and prosperous tribes not only in Ghana but also in Africa. Every Ashanti man and woman worships the Ashanti-Hene as their spiritual leader or supreme commander." Just like the Zulus in South Africa, Adam Folie said that the Ashanti tribes of southern Ghana have also fought and removed the British from Ashanti land during colonial rule. "In fact, it is true that the Ashanti tribes were extremely influential in helping to unite all the other Ghanaian tribes to fight against colonial rule. The lesson to note is, positive tribalism can bring a strong sense of spiritual identity or provide strong political leadership to a people of a common land or common identity." Master Folie continued relentlessly. The lecture hall remained quiet as he spoke.

"Negative tribalism, on the other hand, can only be described as one of the most deadly diseases in Africa. In northern Nigeria, for example, the Hausa are the Muslim majority. The rest of the tribes, such as the Ebo and the Yoruba, are the Christian minority. On most occasions, the Hausa, the Ebo, the Fulani and the Yoruba all live in peace and harmony together. They all go to trade at the same markets, eat at the same restaurants, live and work in the same neighbourhood. Yet, sometimes, they wake and take their machetes to fight and chop off each others heads. Why? Because the Hausa man that day suddenly decides that he hates the Yoruba and the Fulani man hates the Ebo.

Throughout the continent of Africa, there are many examples of this kind of barbarism, which is completely destroying our ability to function and work together as a family of interrelated people. This kind of tribalism is the most dangerous source of all evil conduct in our countries," said Adam Folie.

"I have given you an overview of the positive and negative impact of tribalism. Now I want to hear what you think as students and as future ambassadors for your country, Ghana. What role do you think tribalism can play in twenty-first century Africa? Let me hear your views," said the teacher. One student immediately raised his hand and stood up to share his views.

"Sir, my name is James, I come from Dagara. I like some aspects of my tribal way of life, but sometimes I think some Dagara behaviour and cultural practices are archaic."

"What aspects of your tribal way of life do you regard as archaic?" asked Master Folie.

"The first problem I have with my tribe is ignorance. We don't trust or respect anyone from a different tribe. As a result, a Dagara man is not allowed to marry a woman from another tribe. I think this is very unfortunate because my girlfriend right now is an Ashanti woman. But, if I venture to marry her or take her to the north, my family will disown me or even kill me for going against the tribal rules," said James. Before he finished his testimony, another student had her hand up to make a comment.

"Sir, I am sorry but I just want to say that I completely disagree with James when he said his culture is archaic. We can't blame the culture; you have to blame the people." She argued that culture is the most changeable thing in this life. But it is the people who have to change the culture and not let the culture rule their fear. "It is up to the people in your tribe to evolve or change according to the modern day reality of life. I believe that it is up to us; we can either evolve with our culture or remain in the past and continue to live in the dark ages. Personally, I am very proud and happy to be a Fanti girl!" she exclaimed.

What is Gold is also a Stone

After attending the lecture, I paused to reflect on my own personal journey and how culture has made me come this far in my life. Approximately 15 years ago, I migrated to the UK after meeting and falling in love with a Scottish woman in the north of Ghana. She was working as a volunteer science teacher in Tumu in the Upper West Region of the country. About two years after moving to the UK, I sat one day and cried, feeling like a failure. I told my wife I wanted to return home to Ghana as I felt it was almost impossible for me to fit into the Scottish society or way of life. I was sacked repeatedly from job after job, and the only reason I could think of for this was my culture. I felt that perhaps my Ghanaian culture was incompatible with the Scottish way of life. The problem was that I adored my distinctive African personality. Things were so bad for me that, when I was eventually sacked on my tenth job in two years, I decided that enough was enough!

I was about to blame society for my failings but then I paused and looked to myself. Why did my boss sack me today? I asked sitting in the staff canteen with my can of Tango. I went to the office to ask.

"Big man, you are far too bubbly for this working environment, you have to find a new environment which suits your personality" said Jimmy, the boss. I left his office rushing as fast as I could to get home and consult my *Oxford English Dictionary*. I was desperate to find out the meaning of "bubbly". I thought to myself, maybe, that is why everyone has been sacking me.

During my journey home, I thought the word "bubbly" was a very negative adjective, such as thief or liar (although I knew I was neither). I was cheered when I got home and discovered that the word "bubbly" meant over-excited, loud, lively and cheerful. I couldn't stop laughing. How can you sack someone for being happy? I am sure if you can find happiness to buy in the market, it would be more expensive than gold and diamonds put together.

Anyway, the sudden realisation that came to me was that instead, of reacting negatively to Jimmy's words, I could learn a good lesson from the advice he gave me. I realised I was in the wrong environment with my bubbly personality.

To cut a long story short, I went through weeks of soul-searching and praying to God to open my eyes and show me what a bubbly man could do for himself. I prayed to God so much, asking Him to show me what I could do with my life. I started feeling a little bit bored sitting in the house after several weeks of being unemployed. One day, I was invited to a local school to take part in a multicultural day celebration. It was a few months after September 11 and the headteacher knew I was Muslim, so invited me to talk to the children about the positive image of Islam and the similarities between Islam and Christianity. I was delighted because there was a prevailing negative impression about Muslims which I believed was unfair. I took my djembe drum with me to the school and after telling the children a little bit about my faith, I played the drum and the children clapped their hands along. It was a wonderful experience as the drum proved to be a big hit with the children. I realised that they were more interested in my culture than my religion.

"That was a new beginning for me in Scotland. My culture, which I thought was becoming a hindrance, suddenly became the saviour of my life in Scotland. I got invited by a few other schools around Glasgow, after a while I accumulated enough feedback and confidence to set up my own business.

From the onset, I received positive feedback from all the schools I visited. All the children started to treat me like a star, and I knew from that point I was onto something unique. I realised that being different or having a different cultural background is not the problem in this life. It is how we portray our culture that can make the key difference between success and failure. In other words, we all have a role to play in this life and it is not what role you play but how well you play that role that really matters. In my own case, it was how I used my djembe drum from that day in the school that helped me to come this far in my life.

Anyway, after years of visiting hundreds of schools, playing drums and telling the children stories my own Grandma had told me in my childhood, my name started to spread like a small bushfire among Scottish schools. Many of the headteachers I worked with described my services as a distinctive addition to positive global education. The children looked at me as a positive example of Africa, which is the reason why they all address me as Chief Chebe.

Chapter 16: The Purpose of Education

"Brother," he called, "you go pass Art Centre before you go to the ministry? Yesterday all, everybody day ask your matter for Art Centre. I talk them say you go come today." Shaibu spoke standing in front of the mirror. That day, I had an afternoon appointment to go and see the Ghanaian Shadow Minster for Education. After Shaibu got ready, we left the house and entered the tro-tro from the OSU Police Station bus stop.

"Yes Accra, Accra, Accra," the driver mate shouted at the top of his voice trying to attract more passengers on the way. When we reached the Art Centre, I went first to see my friend Mark. I hadn't seen him for two weeks.

"He has gone to the timber market to buy some wood. He said he wanted to make a new xylophone, I think it is for that American man," said Patrick. His shop is next to Mark's. I was surprised to see that Mark's shop was completely fixed. That day, I sat and waited for more than an hour before he arrived on his bicycle, sweating heavily as if a bucket of water had been thrown at him.

"Small boy, come and get some coins. Go and get me some ice water from Fuley-ra, the big Frafra woman in that shop next to the mosque over there," he pointed. The little boy collected the coins and took to his heels before Mark turned his attention to me. He was still slightly out of breath. "Indo, sisan, itanu fiala paa," he said, which translated as my friend, now you're looking much better. He shook my hand and gave a broad smile. "Long time no see. Every day I ask Shaibu when I will see you. I am glad the Lord Jesus brought you to me today. Let me park the bicycle before I show you the new xylophone I made for you." Mark spoke untying the wood from the back of his phoenix bicycle. I asked him how he fixed the shop.

"I found that stupid Benin man. He came and did it last week. In fact, he has been asking of you every day. He said he wanted to speak to you about something important, let me send for him. Hey, Razak, come here. Go and call me that crazy carpenter around the corner. You know him, the one with the last shop towards the sea." He carried the wood into the shop and shouted. "My brother, come and see your new xylophone. I finished it three days ago. The sound is just wonderful," he said, before using the two beating sticks to give me a demonstration. "Here is a seat, sit down and try it for yourself." Mark said and brought out a female xylophone to give me an accompanying beat. We sat facing each other in front of the shop. A few people came and stood and watched us play our traditional song.

"I have never seen a London Boga so interested in culture," Patrick whispered to his wife. Everything was going fine until Thunder arrived and interrupted the flow.

"Hey, Ghana man, where have you been? I heard you got bad malaria and I was worried for you. I want you to come to my shop. I have something to tell you," he said. I stood up and shook Thunder's hand and followed him towards the coast. "I have a good business idea for you. You are the only one I can trust. I can see that you are a very honest man and you will never cheat me, or will you?" he asked in Hausa language.

"No, I will never knowingly cheat you or anyone else in this life. What is your business idea? Tell me."

"OK, see," he showed. "Look this photo, Ibe me build this house with my own hands and my own tools."

"Wow, this is a beautiful wooden house," I marvelled with the photo in my hand.

"This three bedroom house, Ibe me build am." Thunder told me that although everyone in the Art Centre knows him as a carpenter, what they didn't know was that he was a good business man in Benin. After looking through the photos, I asked Thunder what he wanted us to do together.

"I want to do business with you," he said. Before we finished the conversation, Shaibu came around.

"Brother," he called, "Kadi brought some chop. Make we go leave this crazy Benin man, i day talk too much. Logo Am!" Shaibu said and pointed his hand angrily at Thunder-Man.

After lunch, I left the Art Centre and took another tro-tro to Independence Square where I dropped and walked by foot to the Parliament House to meet the expert.

"Education is the process of teaching a person or a people to gain knowledge and understanding about something important," said Mrs Lamptey the shadow Education Minister. "To be educated is to be knowledgeable, enlightened and cultured." The problem, she said, is: there are currently far too many educated African men and women who are not enlightened or cultured. "I believe that a person who possesses only knowledge without adequate and proper understanding of his her own culture is an educated illiterate. This is why I argue that we need to change the way we teach and educate our children so that we can teach them to be proud of our culture." I asked the Minister why she thinks the African citizen is not proud of his or her culture. Is it because we see our culture to be too primitive to associate with?

"I think this is just a feeble minded excuse to say the African culture is backwards. If you have a sore hand, do you cut off that hand because it is painful to live with?" she asked adding that it is up to those with a good education today to help change, improve, modify and add greater value to the African way of life. "In my view, the current education system in many African countries can only be described as a direct colonial inheritance and this is something we have to unite and change before Africa can develop to her fullest capacity as a great continent."

After listening for some time, I asked the Minster what she thinks we can do to develop a new educational system in Africa which can serve our needs and help us translate our dreams into a living reality in the twenty-first century. In her response, she said, "We need reverse colonisation or decolonisation as Kwame Nkrumah used to say." Mrs Lamptey told me that before we can bring the African dream into reality, we need to first of all find a way to wipe out the poisonous residue of slavery and heal the mental damage which has been inflicted on us by colonialism. So what is the way forward? I asked. "Debugging of course, if a computer has been infected by a nasty virus, what do you have to do to that computer before you can store new information into it?" The shadow minister told me what one has to do with a computer virus is exactly the same thing one has to do to a broken or corrupted brain. "We need a new educational formula. We have to reformat and defragment our collective mentality today so that we can teach our children to know and do better for themselves tomorrow."

After listening to the opposition Minister for Education, I went to see my former Headteacher, Teacher Moses. I wanted to know what he thought about the current education system in Ghana.

"It is not only in Ghana, it is true that; the education in most African countries is more or less a mental trap to process and take away all best brains and talents abroad. Just look at you, for a good example," he said and continued after taking a sip of pito from his calabash. Pito is a local cider brewed daily in Ghana. "If you look at the situation in Ghana, for example, a child is trained to become a lawyer, doctor, accountant or banker. But, no Ghanaian child is formally trained in school to become a good farmer, a traditional healer or a good miner. Our current education system does not necessarily encourage the early development of life skills, such as carpentry, bricklaying, mechanics and hands-on skills which can equip our young boys and girls with the ability and the know-how to do practical work: meaningful work which can add greater benefits to society. That is to say, we are not necessarily being trained or educated in subjects which can immediately add socio-economic value to our own lives in our own local environments."

My teacher, Moses, argued that the best way forward is to teach our children the practical life skills which can help build our societies rather than relying on a one way system which is not in our best socio economic interest. "From my experience of 40 years as a teacher and now a retired director of GES," he said referring to the Ghana Education Service, "I am convinced that if you teach a Ghanaian child whose aim is to become a doctor or a scientist, for example, then there is no doubt that, given the right opportunities and chances, the likeliest and final destination of that child will be America or somewhere in Europe, like the UK, where you live yourself," he said, pointing his finger directly at me. Teacher Moses told me that this is the reason why there are more Ghanaian doctors working abroad than those working to maintain the desperately needed Ghanaian Health Service (GHS) at home.

"Don't you think that if half of the educated Ghanaians abroad return home to build their own country, Ghana will be one of the best countries to live in the world within a generation?" He asked. I continued to nod my head whilst praying silently that one day indeed, enough Ghana doctors will return from abroad to build our own GHS. Why not? I totally agree with my former headteacher that if a third of all the skills and knowledge Africa has outside return to Africa within a decade, this will mark a new transition towards real progress and kick of a new educational revolution in Africa.

At the end of the conversation, Teacher Moses told me that it is not the method of education that is problematic in Africa but the principles and the values systems which underpin it that must be changed from a self-centred me, I and winner take it all culture to a more communal educational system which better suits our extended family and social living lifestyles.

"The point is that, in true African philosophical reasoning, we are because we belong to the Kingdom of God and not because we came from an accidental blast, atoms, bacteria or monkeys, as

European scientists may choose to argue. Hence, the urgent need to teach and train our future generations to develop themselves not only as successful individuals, but active agents and benevolent ambassadors' of the bigger African society. Education should not only teach us how to take and receive for ourselves but a good education must also teach us how to give to others who need our help in society."

Chapter 17: Dawn of a New Day

"Bang, bang, bang," someone hammered at the door. I was flat on the mattress. I stood up quickly to open the door, and discovered it was Shaibu and my two brothers from Pulima.

"Bro, why did you not phone to let me know that you are in town? You have kept the whole family worried about your whereabouts. In fact, the other day Kpunti was going around spreading negative rumours about you."

"What rumour? What have I done?" I asked in bewilderment.

"Some people say that you have been deported from the UK. That is why you are back home stranded." Babs spoke his concerns before Muzay got the chance to say hello to me.

"What is the purpose of your visit?" Muzay asked before Shaibu brought in some drinks from the bar across the street. I told my brothers that I was home to research a book on the African Dream.

"That is a fine idea, but you don't have to suffer like this to succeed with your dream. You need to take good care and look after yourself here in Ghana. Home is not easy, as you know. I mean, the word of mouth is too strong in this country!" Muzay warned before the conversation turned serious.

"Big Bro, don't you think that this room is too small for you and Brother Shaibu to live in? I think we will get you your own place so that you can feel more comfortable. We can arrange for our sister Sarata or Alima to come and stay with you to help you with your book-writing project."

"Look, my brothers, I like your offer but I prefer to stay here. I am home to learn a hard lesson for myself. Fortunately, as you can see, my Brother Shaibu is looking after me very well. If I wanted to be comfortable, I would not need to come home."

"That is true," said Muzay. "But right now, we are not happy with the way people are gossiping about you. I don't feel happy going to my bed with the knowledge that my brother who has helped to make me who I am today is back home suffering on his knees. Babs and I owe a huge part of our lives to you because you sent us both to university and paid all our fees. Luckily, we are both working now and earning money. We can look after you and make you as comfortable as possible. You need your own space and we have to get it for you." Muzay spoke and brought tears close to my eyes. On further persuasion, I agreed that they could get me a place outside of Accra, so that I could find the peaceful and tranquil setting that a writer deserves to produce his magic words.

"I have a friend in Kokrobite. His name is Toroba. Sometime ago, he said he had a room to rent. Kokrobite is a very nice place to hide and do your work," Shaibu remembered. In the end, I agreed that since Kokrobite is a small seaside artists' village, it was a good idea to get a place there as a writing retreat. I convinced myself that Kokrobite would give me the tranquil atmosphere that I required to ignite my writing brain. I agreed that if anytime I came to Accra, I would stay with Brother Shaibu, but I could still hide away to stop the escalating rumours about my stranded status. That day, Brother Shaibu cooked some jollof rice. After food, he took Babs, Muzay and me to OSU bus station where we caught a tro-tro to Accra Circle. From the Circle, we took a bus to Keneshie Market where we got the last tro-tro to Kokrobite.

"Welcome to the House of Judah," I read the sign on Toroba's gate. It was a brown metal gate with a newly built brick wall about chest high around the whole building.

"Ocean View Restaurant," said the sign of a pub on the right as we opened the gate into Toroba's compound. It was a huge compound with about four acres of land. There was a small building to the left, which was completed. I stared at the master building, which stood lavishly in the middle, on top of the hill, like a ruined castle without the roof!

"Wow, this place is so big," I commented.

Unfortunately, Toroba was not around, but his boy, Malam Yahaya, was there.

"Hey, Fulani man, where is your boss?"

"Rata, please don't call me Fulani man, my name is Malam Yahaya," he said carrying two papaws towards the uncompleted building.

"Sunday, come here and eat your lunch," Malam Yahaya spoke to his horse in Hausa. It was a big red horse with dark eyebrows.

"Toroba go to seaside, i say iday go bath," said Malam Yahaya. We left the compound and followed the path to the coast to find my new landlord; and that was it. That was yet another new beginning and a new page to my journey.

After the move, time passed and Ghana beamed with election fever every day. As D-Day drew closer, every second, minute and hour that passed added to the pain of the unknown and the relentless agony of waiting.

In the last week of the American presidential election, tensions grew to an alarming extent both home and abroad. According to all the exit polls at the time, the election race between Barack Hussein Obama and John McCain was too close to call.

At the local level, Ghana was also going through a heated presidential election campaign. The 2008 Ghanaian Presidential Election became a hot potato for many Africans inside and outside of the continent. Ghana is regarded as the "Gateway to Africa" and one of the best examples of a good working democracy in Africa. Hence, the reason millions of African patriots like me sat on thorns and watched eagerly to see how the people of the happiest African nation were going to turn at this important crossroad. Many people watched once again to see if Ghana could show or demonstrate what the rest of the world often thinks is impossible in Africa, a free and fair election. I was extremely glad to be home at the time and to be witnessing this monumental turning point in my country's history.

As there was no doubt that the world was about to change, I also felt that Africa too was about to step up somehow in the right direction once and for all!

At the heat of the election hysteria, the whole country bubbled at boiling point. Many ordinary Ghanaian citizens felt that after eight prosperous years of positive economic development, the wealth accumulated at the top did not trickle down to them as promised by their government. Some questioned why the wealth of the nation has failed to improve the living standards of the ordinary people. I have to admit that at many points in my time at home, things were hard for me as well. There were days I would wake up in Kokrobite without a penny to buy food or clean water to drink. Those days were hard for me but every inch of daily struggle taught me a new lesson in life. For example, hunger taught me how to be patient and how to trust in God. But sometimes, it also made me question whether there is really a good God in charge or responsible for the welfare of all human beings.

I often asked myself, why would a good God sit comfortably in his Heavens and let the man and woman he made in his perfect image suffer so much undignified pain on earth, especially the pain of an empty stomach? I tried to reach far and wide for an answer but, at the end of the day, I came to the humble conclusion that perhaps it is not really God's fault that we suffer on earth. Because, God has given us everything he can give. I remember once Malam Yahaya told me that if God gave the human being any more chances, man will soon try to overthrow or even try to kill God! I laugh every time I remember some of the remarks people made during my most difficult times of hardship at home.

Going back to the Ghanaian Presidential Elections, the battle ground between the two main contestants was based on division between the top half and the bottom half of the country's population. The ruling party candidate Nana Akufo Addo was the most popular candidate from the Ghanaian oligarchy. Born on 29

March 1944 in Swalaba, Accra, Nana Addo was raised and brought up in privilege. His father's residence, Betty House in Accra, was effectively the headquarters of Ghana's first political party, the United Gold Coast Convention (UGCC), which was formed on 4 August 1947. Amazingly, three of the Big Six (founding fathers of Ghana) were Nana's blood relatives: J.B. Danquah (grand uncle), William Ofori Atta (his direct uncle) and Edward Akufo-Addo (his father), who became the third Chief Justice of Ghana and later a ceremonial President of the Republic from 1969–72. As a successful businessman, Nana Addo rose from his privileged upbringing to become one of the richest men in Ghana with many business contacts both home and abroad.

From the onset, the Opposition candidate, Professor John Atta Mills, and his NDC party looked destined to cause a political upset by mobilising the masses under the catchy slogan "Time for Change". Professor Mills was a Fanti man from the central region of Ghana, but was born in the mining town of Tarkwa in the Western Region. He attended the prestigious Achimota School where he completed his A levels in 1963 before going on to study law at the University of Ghana in Legon. Mills spent his professional life as an academic both in Ghana and internationally. In 1968, he studied at the London School of Economics and later received his PhD from the University of London. As a career academic, Professor Mills spent over three decades jetting between Ghana and the United States before deciding to turn his vastly accumulated intellectual wisdom to politics with a mighty dream to transform and advance Ghana into a strong, prospering social democracy in Africa.

From my personal perspective, even before Election Day, I felt that Ghana had already won a major victory in the calibre of both presidential candidates. As an independent or self-appointed election observer, I felt that the two presidential hopefuls were remarkable, dignified and respectful in the way they conducted their election campaigns, both on the streets and on the national media channels. I felt confident that both men were capable of leading our country at this crossroad. There was a lot at stake, especially, since Ghana had just discovered crude oil on her shores. Time went by like the passing wind and each day felt like a festival, even without the luxury of money to play with. I met tens of people with anxiety, hope and belief that, one day soon, their prayers may be answered. As I have mentioned before, the election hysteria and the anxiety of the people was not only in relation to domestic issues but also concerned what was happening across the Atlantic.

"If one black man can rule America, then all African men standing together can rule the world for a change. This is time to make our own moves," Justice spoke as we all squeezed into a taxi to head to town from Kokrobite. It was the eve of the election in America and we were on our way to a prayer camp at Labadi beach in Accra. Justice and I, with a few other friends, including Abraham and Peter, all arrived at the beach that night just before the midnight prayer began. There were hundreds of die-hard Obama fans beside the roaring ocean. There was a full gleaming moon. Many people sat together and gazed at the bright stars, telling stories; others were playing drums and dancing to the music by the ocean.

"Justice, you see the angle of this moon?" asked Abraham. We all looked up. "The moon is the God of the sky and the two bright stars you see on each side of the moon, one is Prof. and the other is Nana," Abraham said referring to the titles of the two Ghanaian presidential candidates. There was a large group of people about 50 metres from the main stage at the beach front. As I walked with my friends, the sand began to get into my sandals. We edged forward and joined those sitting around an open flame. There was a pastor among them holding an old bible in his hand. Everyone prayed and chanted happy chimes in anticipation and hope that Obama would win the election the next day.

"Obama is the first true son of the world for a very long time," said Malam Yahaya. He was holding a Qur'an. That night, Malam Yahaya came to the beach on the back of Sunday.

"Let's forget about America and the rest of the world and celebrate a truly deserved African victory tomorrow. Now, the Congo man is free to decide his own destiny," said the Rasta man. Ras Kunta was one of the many musicians who were lined up to perform that night. At exactly one minute before midnight, all the music and dancing beside the main stage stopped. Ras Kunta counted the people in from ten seconds down until the clock turned to midnight.

"Hip hip," shouted Kunta.

"Hurray!" the crowd voiced back.

"Me brethren, now I want to introduce an important guest. Ladies and gentlemen, please put your hands up for our visiting pastor tonight, Prophet Samson Ibo from Enugu State, Nigeria." The clapping continued as the pastor took to the stage. "Jah Rasta Farah," Ras Kunta said loudly before handing the microphone to the guest speaker.

"My Ghanaian brothers and sisters, it is with extreme aggrandisement I am appointed by the mighty Lord Jesus, to come to Labadi Beach tonight and stand in front of you in this bright moonlight." I looked up to the sky and it was lit with billions of shiny stars. "The noise you hear from the sea is an example of the strong power of the almighty God. And whatever you think is impossible for a human being is never impossible by the power of God. So, as we gather here tonight to pray for victory tomorrow. I want you all to close your eyes and join me in prayer. I want us to pray to our kind Lord to open the door to victory for Obama tomorrow, in Jesus' name, Amen," said the pastor.

"Amen," the whole crowd roared like a pride of lions standing beside the sea, rejoicing in the anticipation of victory.

"We are gathered here tonight in front of the sea to pray to our Lord Jesus to open the way for our brother Obama. God, we pray for you to give Barack Obama the key to the White House, so that he can show the world what a man of African pedigree can do for his country America. If God can show to the world tomorrow, that an African man can rule America, then this will mark the final testimony that the African man can take charge of his own affairs. I have a dream," he said responding buoyantly to the amazing crowd. "I have a dream that one day Africa will be so prosperous that people will come from everywhere in the world, including Europe, to look for employment in Africa," Pastor Ibo prophesised before stepping ahead to stir up some serious emotions.

"My Ghanaian brothers and sisters, I want to ask you all a question, I only want you to give me your most honest and sincerest answer," the visiting prophet stood, glaring at his audience.

"Pastor, what is the question you want to ask us?" the crowd shouted.

"Ghanaians, can you do it? Can you come together as nation and work together to make your Ghanaian dream come true?"

"Yes, we can," they replied and cheered. Their voices echoed into the sea, touching souls and spirits from the distant past. "Your brothers and sisters, the Nigerians, do you think they can make it?"

"Yes they can," replied the crowd.

"What about the Congolese, the Tanzanians, the Namibians and the Northern and Southern Sudanese?"

"Yes, Pastor, they can make it." As you can imagine, the spirit of the occasion was simply indescribable. There were a few Ghanaian radio stations at the beach, broadcasting the whole event live to the rest of the nation.

"Finally, I want to ask you one last question, but I don't want you to disappoint me. I want you to raise your voices to the sea if you believe, as I do, that after Obama's victory tomorrow and with the

Lord behind us, nothing will ever be impossible again in Africa," the pastor paused looking at the crowd with a broad smile. "Africa and her people, can we unite and reason with one mind to develop our countries and build better sustainable communities for our future generations? Do we have the courage, the bravery and the combined intellect to work together to ensure that every child in Africa can get clean water to drink, good food to eat and medicine to cure our headaches and stomach pains? My Ghanaian brothers and sisters and fellow Africans around the world, we are here tonight to witness the birth of a new nation and the shaping of a new world. This is the dawn of a brand new day in Africa. The question is:" he said and held back his breath.

"If Obama can get the key to the White House tomorrow as promised by the Lord, do you think we the people of Africa can come together and make our dream come true?"

"Yes, we can," the crowd screamed and yelled in together.

"Let us pray for Obama's victory to translate into meaningful progress in our beloved Ghana, Nigeria, Ivory Coast, Zimbabwe, Botswana, Zambia, Morocco, Libya, Angola and Kenya," Pastor Ibo went on and on until there was eventually a change of wind direction. Ras Kunta returned to the centre of the stage and announced the first band to take to the stage. The music sizzled the crowd, creating a beautiful and infectious atmosphere of pleasure and hope beside the roaring ocean. The party continued all night long.

After the prayer camp, we went back to sleep at Kokrobite which is an hour's drive from Labadi. Early in the morning the following day, my Malian friend, Alhaji Banbara, went to town and bought a sheep, which he arranged to roast with some goats at the beach later for a victory party. The day flew as I struggled to catch a little afternoon nap.

Eventually, the evening arrived and the polling stations began to close in a few states. There was tense anticipation in the air as exit polls still remained too close to judge. That evening, Alhaji Banbara promised that everyone could drink from his pocket. He invited many friends and good neighbours to his private beach party to celebrate Obama's victory. At the ceremony, there was a sacrifice of one big ram, goats and four chickens. Before the rituals, Alhaji spoke a few words.

"My brothers, sisters, friends and family, I want to begin by thanking you all for coming out in your numbers to join me to celebrate the victory of our Kenyan brother tonight," Alhaji Banbara spoke with a bottle of beer in his hand. "As a Mali man, I am very happy living here in Ghana. The people of Ghana make me feel at home. You all know how happy I am here; maybe sometimes too much happiness is my weakness."

"That is true," said Diana, one of Alhaji's numerous concubines.

"You also know that, although I am a Muslim by faith, I am an original Fawfaw by religion and culture. You know how much I believe in the spirit of our ancestors. Manchia," he called the name of his friend, the eldest son of the Kokrobite village Chief.

"Manchia, I want you to take this knife and slaughter the sheep and the rest of the animals. The blood will go to our ancestors who are watching us as we pray together for unity. As for the meat, we will put it on the fire right now to go with the booze," Alhaji spoke before handing a sharp knife to Manchia.

The drinking and dancing continued, and it didn't take long before the flames of the fire rose high into the sky, overlooking the mighty ocean. Over 200 people, I counted, all happily mingling and sharing one positive loving vibration. Wine, beer and champagne flew around regardless. It was as though the beer was brewed from the bubbling sea in front of us.

The crowd grew bigger as exit polls from America began to appear on the screen. When the fire burnt down leaving the glowing charcoal, the Chin-Changa boys, took some of the red roasting charcoal to fill their grills and BBQs. Eventually, the meat was permeated with spices and spread on the fires. Soon, the aroma of the meat changed the atmosphere as people queued to get the best slices for themselves. We all enjoyed ourselves whilst waiting excitedly for the arrival of the first election results.

In the cool breezy background, there was some nice patriotic music playing. The favourite tune of the crowd was "One Love" followed by "Africa Unite for the Benefit of your People" both sung by Bob Marley. There were hundreds of others at the beach all having their separate parties. Everyone sang and danced to the tunes in harmony, whilst watching the giant screen on Alhaji's seafront balcony.

It was an all-night affair, until one man appeared on the screen. Suddenly, everyone stood quiet and listened. It was Senator McCain, the Republican presidential candidate.

"Thank you. Thank you, my friends," he greeted. "Thank you for coming here on this beautiful Arizona evening. My friends, we have come to the end of a long journey," said Senator McCain. "The American people have spoken, and they have spoken clearly. A little while ago, I had the honour of calling Senator Barack Obama to congratulate him." Immediately he paused, the crowd on the beach cheered wildly. I looked up into the sky and the moon shone brighter than usual. It did indeed feel like the dawn of a brand new day!

"In a contest as long and difficult as this campaign has been, his success alone commands my respect for his ability and perseverance. But that he managed to do so by inspiring the hopes of so many millions of Americans, who had once wrongly believed that they had little at stake or little influence in the election of an American president is something I deeply admire and commend him for achieving. This is an historic election, and I recognize the special significance it has for African-Americans and for the special pride that must be theirs tonight. But we both recognise that, though we have come a long way from the old injustices that once stained our nation's reputation and denied some Americans the full blessings of American citizenship, the memory of them still has the power to wound," Senator McCain continued, adding that, "America today is a world away from the cruel and frightful bigotry of that time. There is no better evidence of this than the election of an African-American to the presidency of the United States. Senator Obama has achieved a great thing for himself and for his country." As McCain stood in front of the glittering global media and spoke with absolute dignity and respect, I couldn't agree more, especially when he said it is only after turning their backs to bigotry that the people of the United States of America have managed to accept an African-American man as their president. In my view, bigotry does not only divide people but also destroys healthy societies. The biggest source of bigotry in Africa right now is tribalism. In Nigeria, for example, a Hausa man will never allow himself to be ruled by a Fulani man, even though they may speak the same language and worship the same Allah. Equally, an Ebo man will prefer to have a Russian or Chinese friend he can trust, rather than a Lagos man from his own country. This type of extreme behaviour does not foster national unity and patriotic love for the interest of the nation above the individual interest.

As I listened to Senator McCain, I couldn't help thinking, yes, true leaders are those among us who have the courage to lead, the ears to listen and above all, the dignity to accept defeat. I said to myself that if we really are serious about making meaningful progress in Africa, then, our new generations of African leaders must learn from patriotic American citizens like Senator John McCain: "These are difficult times for our country and I pledge to the President Elect tonight to do all in my power to help him lead us through the many challenges we face. I urge all Americans who supported me to join me in not just congratulating him, but offering our next president our good will and earnest effort to find ways to come together to find the necessary compromises to bridge our differences and help restore our prosperity, defend our security in a dangerous world, and leave our children and grandchildren a stronger, better country than we inherited."

After his gracious speech, the whole of Accra screamed loud and far into the deep ocean, sending the waves of love and thanks across the Atlantic. For many Africans who watched the 2008 American election, Senator McCain's response to defeat is something we all hope our African leaders and politicians can emulate. African politicians must stop inciting tension and tribal warfare as soon as they lose an election. Those who are defeated in elections must show enough love for their country by stepping out gracefully like McCain did in America.

"If McCain was a racist or tribal politician, he would have told his supporters that they should take their arms onto the street and fight to stop a Kenyan man from ruling America," said one commentator by the beach.

"Democracy is an unpredictable game with both good and bad seasons. A true democrat is one who is prepared to take the good with the bad; like Mr McCain," said another man. He was standing next to the burning flames.

"It is daybreak, Africa, time to wake up. This is the time for one Africa, one love, one political ideology, one religious understanding, one currency, one Olympics, one African pope, one king, our own African Saints starting with Saint Nelson, one African science, one happiness, one culture, one story, one path, one road, one motorway, one language, one common market, one family, one people with a common destiny; that is the only way we can win in Africa!" Alhaji spoke to the heart of the jubilant crowd before proceeding to make a victory toast. "Please raise your glasses and join me in a big cheer to our mighty brother Barack Hussein Obama, the new President of the United States of America and the crowned King of Africa."

Chapter 18: Appropriate Democracy in Africa

"Obama Brother, where have you been hiding? Now that your brother has got the key to the White House, I don't see you here again. I hope you are not hiding and chopping the dollars on your own," Sister Ama remarked. "Sit down. Let me bring you a Star to celebrate Obama's victory, he has done well for himself and America. Africa, as well."

"Madam Ama, make you bring me two tots of Opiemu to cool my temper. Something day disturb my mind," Thunder said entering the bar. He dragged a chair towards my table. "Hey Ghana Man, where you go? Long time I no see you. Every day iday look for you everywhere."

"Now iday Kokrobite, I be so way you no day see me for Art Centre."

"When you day go back to Kokrobite? I beg, if you day go back today, I go follow you to Kokrobite. I get something I want to talk give you." Thunder spoke and took a gulp of his drink. Opiemu is a Ghanaian brandy with a gentle touch of some carefully selected roots from the A-Fram Plains in the Western Region. I finished my beer and left to go to the Ugandan Embassy with a big question in my mind!

What is Democracy?

"There are five basic necessities of life, and democracy is one of them," said Ambassador Inga. I asked him what he believed the other four necessities of life were. "The other four are food, water, oxygen and sex." I couldn't help laughing at the top of my voice. Ambassador Inga was tall and slender with a small beard and thick dark hair. He was wearing a white shirt and red tie. You often think of politicians as uncool, boring and a manipulative group of liars.

So, it was nice and refreshing to come across one with a palatable sense of humour.

"On a serious note," he said, "the term democracy comes from two Greek words. The first word is 'demos' which means 'people' and the second word "kratos" means power. When you put the two words together it becomes DEMOCRACY: People and Power. As for the question as to why democracy fails in Africa, I believe it is due to a lack of commitment. I believe democracy fails in any society which does not fully subscribe to the true values and the basic principle of democracy." Ambassador Inga told me that democracy on its own is not an automatic magic bullet or the perfect solution to all human problems. "It is how you embrace democracy in society. Let me give you an example, God, as you know is good and kind to us all in this life. Yet, there are many who follow or worship God and still do bad things every day. You cannot claim it is because of God those people do bad things. That is the same with democracy. It is a very beautiful concept which glitters like gold, but it is all down to interpretation, commitment and better practice."

I asked Inga to explain why he said democracy has failed in Africa because of a lack of commitment to true democratic values. "You see, in this life you are either honest or dishonest about what you do. You cannot pretend to be democratic and arrest everyone who opposes your views." Ambassador Inga argued that democracy is not about expensive elections which even Mugabe can organise every four years to fool his Western enemies. True democracy is about openness, accountability, exemplary leadership, patriotism, oneness and the love of the country above the individual interest. The Ugandan Ambassador told me that in his view, wholesale democracy itself has been a bit problematic in Africa because sometimes the values enshrined in pure capitalistic liberal democracy can be contradictory to our cultural ways of life.

"This is why I say, it is not just democracy we need in Africa but a new 'Appropriate Democracy', which respects the values and norms of our traditions, cultures and our living aspirations. Appropriate Democracy is the only way forward in Africa. There is no other way, apart from organised chaos!"

I was totally intrigued as the Ambassador took his time to emphasise the dangers of an over-liberalised free market democracy in Africa.

"Culture is a big issue. Normally, democracy puts too much emphasis on choice and individualism, which may perfectly suit nuclear family environments. The problem is that, in Africa, the concept of individualism is everything against our culture of communal living. Let me cite one man, one vote as a feature of democracy which disrespects the value of our traditional institutions." I wrote and wrote with joy, respect and admiration. "One man, one vote assumes that all human beings in all societies are equal. But we know that this is sometime untrue. In every society including the jungle, we know that some are less equal than others." Ambassador Inga argued that in any typical African village, the chief and his elders have the majority say in what happens in the village: culturally, socially and economically. "If you ask the village chief and the village elders to cast the same vote as the rest of the villagers, you may be undermining their local authority and the traditional values that have kept that village going for hundreds and thousands of years. This can cause silent tension which can lead to conflict."

"So, if the principle of one man, one vote conflicts with the values of our traditions and customs, what can we do to address this problem through appropriate democracy as you described?"

"The answer is simple but complex, at the same time and maybe even controversial. If you have a village with 500 people during an election, you can give 50 votes to the chief to exercise as the head of that village. In return, you ask the chief to demonstrate a certain quality of leadership, which can be enshrined into the rules and regulations of traditional rule." The Ugandan ambassador argued that: "In Europe and America, one man, one vote works because each man is only entitled to one wife; simple. The situation as you are fully aware is slightly different in our continent. If a man has three wives, I think he should have more say in the society than a man with no wife! Equally, it is possible to argue that women who have children should have more votes than men."

Finally, I asked Ambassador Inga how he thought of the significance of an Obama's victory to the dreams and aspirations of the new generations of African people. "Obama is critical to the survival of the African race because he has shown us what one black man can do with determination. Let us see it this way," he said, as I began to shiver with goose bumps. "Are you OK my brother? Let me turn down the air-conditioning," he stood up with the remote control in his hand.

"If the one man we call Barrack Obama can unite white Americans, black Americans, and green, yellow, purple, pink, poor and rich Americans to vote for him as president: what do you think one million Africans can do together for Africa?"

"What can one million ordinary Africans in the world do to make the African dream come true?" I asked.

"One million people can make any impossible dream become possible, but first you have to come out with a way to attract, bring together and convince one million Africans to believe in themselves and what they can do together as a foundation force for positive change in Africa."

As Inga spoke, I began to think about the Tipping Point: word of mouth epidemics. I remembered Mr Gladwell's idea of the critical mass, which, in this case, represents the one million African Foundation forces that Ambassador Inga described.

"How can you convince one million Africans to follow the African Dream?" I asked.

"Simple, I believe that you can get one million Africans on the internet today. Think about a website such as www.1000000africans.com!" Inga exclaimed and continued. "If one million dedicated African people can connect together on one website, they can contribute £10 each. That will amount to ten million pounds. What do you think you can do with ten million pounds today in Africa?"

"Wow, that is a lot of money," I said.

"Ten million pounds in Ghana, Kenya, Uganda or any other country in Africa today can build ten new ecovillages, five new model towns and one new green city. If one million Africans can come together and make this happen, then everyone in Africa will see that what we doubt is possible can be made a living reality." Ambassador Inga told me that there is nothing in this world that can stop one million Nigerians, Angolans, Congolese or Ghanaians from coming together every year and contributing £10 each to build ten villages, five towns and one city in their countries. "If we do this every year from now onwards, how many new towns, villages and cities do you think we can build in Africa by 2050?"

The more I spoke to people from all walks of life, the greedier I got. Why does democracy succeed almost everywhere else in this world apart from Africa? Is it to do with the culture alone?

"No, democracy is nothing to do with culture, it is all about interpretation," said Nana Yaw, a taxi driver who was driving me to the Ghana International Conference Centre one late morning. He told me democracy fails in Africa because we don't properly understand the meaning of it. That day, I was invited by a government official to attend a gathering of ECOWAS leaders in Accra. For those of you who are not familiar with the term ECOWAS, it is the Economic Community of West African States. The summit was organised by the Ghana Government to discuss the impact of good governance in civil society. As we approached the Conference Centre, Nana Yaw explained that the situation in Africa is far from genuine democracy. "Our leaders always trick us by promising to do big things for the country during election times. They make big empty promises before they get into power. But, the moment they get into power, they turn their backs on us. Some of them even turn into wolves and monsters. Before you realise, they start to abuse the power we gave them." Nana Yaw told me it is this insincerity and the trickery of our politicians, which he describes as African demo-crazy. "If we are not crazy, why can't we rule ourselves properly for a change?" he asked as we pulled to a halt in front of the Ghana International Conference Centre.

The Importance of Good Governance in Africa

"Fellow leaders, distinguished ladies and gentlemen from the press and heads of institutions, I am enchanted and honoured to be your chair for this important seminar today. The theme of my address is: The Pillars of Good Governance in Twenty-first Century Africa. It is my belief that our blessed continent has everything good in abundance apart from good governance. But, first of all, let me start by asking you all to join me in congratulating Barack Obama for becoming the first African-American President of the United States. It is truly amazing how high a man can climb with determination and effort. I am sure you will all agree with me that Obama's victory represents a new source of hope for all Africans today," said Mr Aliu Mahama, the Vice President of Ghana. He was chairing a meeting of an influential group of foreign ministers and other political leaders from the 16 West African countries about the need for a new democratic direction in the continent.

"I want to begin my address by borrowing the use of two important phrases which are essential to the future of our continent: Democracy and Governance. Of course, as we all know, sometimes democracy and good governance are two in one. But, there are other times when we are better served by separating the two words, so that they can be better understood." Aliu Mahama paused for a few seconds.

"By democracy, I wish to refer strictly to the power dynamics or the decision making process in a country. For example, who decides how resources are distributed. Who decides how much is spent on the military, education, health, the environment and so forth. Who rules the country and why?"

"Now, governance or good governance for that matter, relates to appropriate structures and credible state institutions which can administer, deliver and monitor the policies that have been made by the democrats, who are, after all, seasoned politicians, like us in this conference centre today. Good governance is like culture, a basic necessity of life. Democracy, on the other hand, is like a religion: very important, sometimes crucial but not always necessary. The point I am making here is that, although good governance is always a necessity for the economic prosperity of a nation, democracy is not. In other words, full-scale, free market, liberal democracy is not always a necessity for economic prosperity as we can see in China today. Of course, the best scenario is good governance through proper democracy." Aliu Mahama spoke.

"Distinguished ladies and gentlemen, as you are all aware, Ghana has, over the past two decades, made remarkable progress in terms of both democracy and good governance and, from our experience here in this country, we have come to the shared understanding that, there are four pillars or broad institutions which can make democracy work for the benefit of the common good in Africa. These four institutions are: Union government as in the case of the African Union, regional governments such as ECOWAS, country governments and local governments.

Functions of Union Government

"Union government must play two important basic functions to facilitate our renewed efforts to make democracy work in Africa. The primary function of the African Union is advisory and advocacy. The second function of Union government is to legislate and develop policies of strategic matters of common interest such as democracy, the environment, agriculture, defence, foreign policy and the African economy," said Vice President Aliu. As he spoke, I began to see the light. At long last, it is good that our politicians are beginning to talk like leaders and not just economic pawns, who, in the past, used to play the role of the imperial fools.

"Ladies and gentlemen, I want to emphasise that although the African Union has a limited role to play in the day-to-day governance of the African population, its limited contributions are critical to the strategic development of our continent. The advisory or advocacy role of the Union government should be aimed at providing clear strategic framework and joint intellectual footpath for regional and country governments to follow and function properly. At the same time, Union government must also make few but essential laws that can assist, guide and, in some cases, force our country leaders to deliver their promises to the people."

"For far too long, the nature of our Union Government has remained stagnant like a talking shop. Hence, many of our youth see the African Union as a toothless hunting dog with no power or teeth to bite and take concrete action to build credible institutions to support the economic growth of our citizens. As a matter of urgency, this appalling state of lavish, expensive talks and inaction must come to an end. We in Ghana believe this is the time for a change of direction from the bottom of the pyramid to the top. On behalf of the government of the people of Ghana, I therefore want to bring forward the motion that Union government must exercise its mandate to the people by providing strong legislation on common matters of strategic interest to the whole continent."

"As a matter of fact, we in Ghana believe that the African Union must bring new laws in Africa which will prohibit any one individual politician from staying in government as a president or prime minister for any period over 12 years," the speaker said, attracting a warm round of applause from the delegates.

"I want to use this vital opportunity to stress the importance of a better functioning political union in the wider region. If we are strong in our governance and co-operate with each other as a family of nations, we can move forward with a strong collective bargaining power to trade with the rest of the world. In this exciting future ahead, we must abstain from dictatorial regimes and expensive governments, which bear no fruits for the citizens of our individual countries. If we are united and strong, we can test the power of our unity by demanding a fairer African image in the world." Aliu Mahama added, "It is no longer acceptable to run the world on the premise that Africa is a Third World continent and therefore deserves only third class treatment." He argued that if we are united as a family of nations, we can change the feeble and ill-informed characterisation of Africa and demand a better role in the global decision-making process. "For instance, if we work together as a people, we can ask for a permanent seat in the United Nations Security Council as part of our democratic right to a fairer representation in global governance."

Importance of Regional Governments

"Now, let us turn our attention to the role of regional authorities and the vital contribution they can play in delivering the values of true democracy. I want to begin this part of the discussion by stating categorically that the strategic importance of regional authorities, such as ECOWAS, can never be overstated in any way or form. As a matter of fact, ECOWAS and other regional organisations in the East, South, North and Central Africa will serve as the foundation block and vital pillars to Africa's reunification. So, before we can get a fully functioning African Union, we must first develop better regional co-operation in our subregions to pave the way," the Vice President of the Republic of Ghana continued. "Regional governance is the key to the total reunification of Africa and the role of ECOWAS is paramount." Mr Aliu Mahama insisted that ECOWAS is the only region in Africa that is almost completely united on Pan-Africanism. He pointed to the fact that, without any exceptions, the Anglophone West African nations, including Nigeria, Sierra Leone, Gambia, Liberia and Cameroon are all completely passionate, dedicated and committed to the urgent need to reengage and reunite Africa as one devolved nation.

"Even among the Francophone West African countries, with the exception of one or two notable bad apples, they are dedicated to Pan-African Unity," Mr Aliu Mahama said frankly, raising some eyebrows in the room. All the representatives of the French-speaking countries stared at each other to see where the finger of blame was being pointed. The Vice President continued with his frank dialogue arguing that apart from West Africa, which has a clean sheet, the rest of Africa is still suffering from too much external control. "Southern Africa, for example, is suffering from the remains of apartheid, East Africa is struggling away from colonial ownership and North Africa is struggling over a conflict of interest with their Arabian identity. And, most tragically, as we speak, we know that our sister nations in Central Africa are being bought and paid for by newly emerging hyper-powers such as the Chinese, the Indians and the oil-rich Arabian business network. Therefore, I want to conclude that the overwhelming danger of doing nothing right now to unite ourselves is that, sooner or later, our countries may be bought and used by the outside world as their private laboratories for social experiments and economic playing fields."

The Duties of Country Governments

Moving on from the role of regional governments, Mr Aliu stressed that African country governments have the most crucial role to play in this new direction of appropriate African democracy.

"The government of Ghana strongly believes that the duty of our country government is delivery of security. By security, I mean economic security, political security, social security and cultural security. These four broad areas are what the Ghanaian government, Nigerian government, Tunisian government, Angolan or, for that matter, all governments of Africa must concentrate on from now into the future." Mr Aliu Mahama argued that in order to achieve the above goals, country governments must build and develop strong, long-term internal institutions that are independent from government interference.

"Democracy cannot work and achieve its deserved goals anywhere in this world without the development of a strong vibrant and well functioning civil service system," said Mr Aliu Mahama. "In my 30 years or so experience as a public servant in Ghana, I have seen that democracy has largely failed in many of our countries because of the lack of strong independent civil service structures. There are many things we can all learn from our colonial masters," he said and smiled broadly. "If we take Great Britain, as an example, there are two ways people are ruled and governed: first, we have the politicians, who make up the governments of the day, which change from one political season to the other. Politicians like us are seasonal workers because we come and go every now and then. In Great Britain, the legislative arm of government makes the laws and the executive arm ensures that the laws of the United Kingdom are properly implemented.

The second and, perhaps, most importance source of governance in the United Kingdom is through the State and its permanent civil service structures, which actually deliver the goals of the country. For the civil servants to do their jobs properly, they must be immune or protected from political prosecution and needless harassment by seasonal politicians and government officials like us today at this conference." I was taken aback by the frankness of the Ghanaian Vice President. It is not very often you see our government officials speaking from the bottom of their hearts.

"The biggest mistakes we have all made in our past governments is the unnecessary amalgamation of these two important roles: that is the role of government and the role of the state or the civil service," said the speaker. He insisted that if we continued to reduce our civil service institutions to the position of a toothless dog, then all we end up with is a situation where the power of the government of the day can be abused, misused and wasted on the short-term agendas of our seasonal politicians. "For African countries to grow through better democratic governance, we need strong, independent, and dedicated civil and public service systems which are capable of serving the needs of our people."

The Role of Local Government

"Finally I want to touch briefly on the vitality of our local authorities. Local government is the best way of involving the people in a true and proper democratic government. Everywhere we are, we all belong to a local community. The people in a city are living under a local authority. London is the national city of Britain, but the people of London are governed by a local Metropolitan authority.

Local government involves traditional rule and that is why in Ghana every village has a local authority under the leadership of the village chief. The situation in Ghana is far from perfect as there are hardly any notable perfect systems anywhere else in the world. What is striking, however, is the impeccable contribution of our local authorities to the civil society. I want to finish here by highlighting the complex dynamics of the local government system in Ghana and how it is helping good governance in our country.

Let me say to you that, by local governance, I mean the active engagement and direct participation of local people in decision-making processes from household level to the African Union level.

The Government and the people of Ghana believe that at every level of society, people should be empowered to contribute and add their own value to the decision-making process. That is why we encourage all our citizens to understand that within the family unit, each member should have some reasonable amount of say in what happens in the day-to-day running of family affairs. Above the family level, each compound in the village should have a compound leader and, in every village, there should be a village committee, which helps the chief and the village elders and opinion leaders in the village to administer local justice.

From the village level, we have the district assembly system, which serves as the main link between all the villages and towns within a district or constituency. The district assemblies can make local legislation, which is legally recognised by the national or country government. The district assemblies can also raise local taxes, which can be used in addition to the revenue they receive from national government. This will allow them to deliver goods and services to the communities they represent directly at the local level.

Equally, we have regional administrations in each of the ten regions in Ghana, which serve as links between the district assemblies and national government.

Ladies and gentlemen, I want to share with you Ghana's strong commitment to open and accountable democratic governance, which we believe is the only way forward in Africa. I can assure you that the Ghana Government strongly believes that at every level of society, there must be local representation and maximum individual involvement. Hence, we hold to the value that for democracy to work and deliver its intended goals, the people in our countries must not only be allowed but also be actively encouraged to take part in the decision-making process at every given opportunity.

Finally, I want to finish my talk with you by highlighting the importance of one key ingredient, without which democracy is just as vague a word as culture and which on their own do not offer any great benefits to any nation of the world. As a matter of fact, you can have the best ideas and best plans for your country as a leader or a government, but if you don't put credible systems into place to measure the progress of your actions, then you may continue to behave like a blind man without any weapon who is hunting in the forest full of dangerous species.

In a democracy, checks and balances are like performance indicators in a corporate environment. So, if, for example, the Government of Ghana presents a vision to push Ghana above middle income status by 2020, how do we know whether the actions that the Ghana government is taking everyday of the week, month and year are taking us any closer to that dream? We need free and fair elections to make appropriate democracy work for the benefit of our people. We in Ghana have turned our backs on the days when elections were rigged to suit the incumbent parties alone. That kind of democracy led us through many decades of brutal dictatorships and unnecessary hardships. In Africa as a whole, many of our countries went through genocides and civil wars as a direct result of bad leadership. Those were the days when democracy failed us in Africa. Now we are stepping forward towards a new direction.

Distinguished ladies and gentlemen, I believe that yesterday is history, tomorrow is not yet for us, but today is what we have to think and improve our ways of lives. What we need now to succeed is good governance through sincere, honest democracy, which gives people the maximum say in how they live their lives. It is the conclusion of my country government that Africa and her people must rise up today after what we have witnessed in the United States of America. Obama shows us that impossible change can be accomplished through hard work and determination. Let us work together in Africa and free ourselves from our dark days! Let us value our people above all the gold that glitters in the world. Let us follow the proper road to our own democracy and work together today so that tomorrow, we can reap what we sow.

Finally, I wish to convince you that people only prosper when they have the freedom and the opportunities to do things for themselves and the society they live in. And democracy is the only thing that can bring freedom to us all. In conclusion, therefore, I want to say that there are no two ways. There is only one way to true democracy in Africa and that's our own African Democracy!" The Ghanaian Vice President spoke deep from the bottom of his heart and attracted a standing ovation from foreign ministers and other senior diplomats from all 16 West African States.

Africa is moving forward!" Vice President Aliu spoke enthusiastically as he left the stage.

Chapter 19:   Black Economy

"The word economy comes from the Greek word 'oikonomia', which means the management of household resources," said Martin Dawda, a senior policy adviser to the Ghana Government. I had met Mr Dawda in his office at the Ministries, near Ghana Independence Square. "According to the *Oxford English Dictionary*, the word economy also means administration, management, method, regulation and systems." I asked Martin Dawda why he thought most African countries have so far failed the dreams and economic aspirations of the people.

"To answer your question properly, I have to refer you to the words of a wise man. According to Dr Kwame Nkrumah, the difference between a good economy and a bad economy is better planning." Martin Dawda explained that, apart from better planning, there is another silent factor critical to the economic success of a nation.

"Motivation is the key to the engine of economic growth." Mr Dawda said that, the people in the United Kingdom pay their taxes because, they are motivated by what they get back in terms of good hospitals, good roads, clean water, good electricity supply, unemployment and other social benefits. "If you compare Britain to Nigeria, you can see that the people of Nigeria are not in any way less capable or somehow more economically incompetent than the British. Yet, Nigeria is poor and Britain is super rich. Why?" Mr Dawda argued that when Nigerians go abroad, they are the most intelligent, hardworking and loyal employees. The same is true about Ghanaians abroad. "We are good loyal servants to others, but in our own countries, we are economically disloyal. There is not enough motivation to do the right thing for the country. Why should people pay taxes to corrupt politicians when they don't provide the people with clean water, good roads or electricity?"

Mr Dawda argued that without motivation and belief, people always doubt what they can do for themselves.

"Just look at the African Union, for example, how long has the AU been going on? Why do we not have our own African currency yet?" Mr Dawda explained that the reason why we have failed to create a single currency in Africa is because of self-doubt. He said that, because we don't believe in ourselves, even if we go into meetings and come out with the best ideas or the best plans, we end up creating enough doubt and negative reasons why what we planned to do cannot work. "The truth is that doubt is not good for positive economic development under any circumstances," Dawda said pointing to the fact that Dr Nkrumah propagated the importance of a strong African Economic Union based on the intellectual logic of a single currency long before the Europeans started dreaming about the EU.

So, if doubt is the reason for our economic lunacy in Africa, what creates the doubt in us? What is the reason behind Africa's economic inferiority complex?

"This is a very good question which I believe we must take our time to address properly, before we can gain the confidence to move Africa forward," Mr Dawda said, adding that it is about time we redefine the meaning of Africa itself. "Africa is not just a dark continent full of poor black people, slaves or malnourished children. Africa is greater than the poor and monolithic depiction of the term black. We are Africans and we are naturally richer and more colourful than any other continent in this world."

"So, if Africa is the greatest continent in the world, why are millions of Africans living in material poverty in the 21st Century? Is it because of incompetence?"

"No, we are intelligent. We know what to do but there is no motivation as I said to do the right thing." I asked Mr Dawda what we ought to do now to build a better economic union in Africa.

"We have to develop a new African vocabulary. The Bible tells us that the word of mouth is mightier than sword. As human beings, we are governed and controlled by words. So if we use the wrong words and the wrong terminology to describe ourselves as Africans, we will always end up with a failing status." I asked Dawda why he thought we needed a new African dictionary.

"In the past, Africa has been negatively associated with everything bad, especially in relation to the colour black. Let me tell you why I believe in words: if you are walking on the street, for example, and someone calls you a bastard, you are very likely to feel upset, but if that same person were to say hello or good afternoon, your immediate reaction would be very different. This is why I believe that the wrong depiction of the words we use and the meaning we attach to them has a huge psychological effect on the way we govern ourselves and the way we run our economies." I was taken aback by Dawda's assessment on the reason for the doubt in the minds of African people, especially in relation to economic development.

"If you take the *Oxford* or *Collins English Dictionary* today and open it, you will see that the word black, for example, means hopelessness, gloom, dirty, resentful, angry, wicked and harmful. In most cases, the use of the word black usually refers to something negative. For example, the term 'black economy' means illegal economy; 'black market' refers to a place for buying illegal goods; 'black magic' refers to the use of magic for evil purposes; 'blacklist' refers to the list of people and organisation deemed as untrustworthy; 'Black mark' refers to a discredited note against someone and finally, the phrase 'black sheep' refers to a person who is regarded as a disgrace or failure in society. Unless we can find enough positive words to describe ourselves and our living conditions, Africa will remain blacklisted in the stock markets of the world!"

Mr Dawda told me that if we want to find a definitive solution to Africa's economic conundrum, we must be fully prepared to put Africa's past economic record through serious microscopic analysis. "In the past, we encountered many economic problems. Some these problems were external but many others were our own internal faults. In my view, therefore, the only way forward is to learn one big lesson from all our past economic mistakes. To achieve this, we must put Africa through an MOT." He argued that we must treat Africa like a broken car that needs major repairs. "It is only through a compulsory MOT that we can check, repair and rebuild the engine and the body of the African economic machine."

External Examination of Africa

I felt a bit lost for a few days wondering what steps to take next. Although I strongly believe that Africa's number one enemy is the African people themselves, I was still curious to find out who else might have contributed to Africa's economic woes of the past.

IMF and Structural Adjustment

"You see, the IMF is like an irresponsible doctor who always prescribes bitter quinine to some of his patients, irrespective of their complaints or illness," said Mr Baga, a veteran social economist at the Ghana Community Development Foundation. He told me the IMF (the International Monetary Fund), the World Bank and the World Trade Organization (WTO) are all excellent examples of Western institutions which operate against Africa's economic interest.

The IMF is a global development bank, established mainly by Europe and America through the recommendation of the famous "Brentwood Commission". The bank was established in the immediate aftermath of World War II to help with reconstruction of Europe and Japan.

"Like the conduct of an irresponsible doctor, the IMF does not care whether one is suffering from bilharzia, diarrhoea, malaria or cholera, it will always prescribe the same thing for all of its African patients," Mr Baga began, lambasting the IMF structural adjustment policies, which he argued have been one of the key factors in Africa's negative economic growth, especially from the late seventies until the end of the nineties.

"Like many other global institutions, the conduct of the IMF can be said to be institutionally racist. Let me explain myself by telling you a little story about the conduct of the IMF which led to mass suicide in many African countries throughout the eighties."

"Both the IMF and the World Bank were initially very successful in supporting and overseeing the reconstruction of Europe and Japan. The problem is that, after the completion of European reconstruction, the IMF and the World Bank continued to enlarge their remits as global financial institutions and later became major lenders to many developing nations – or to the so-called Third World countries."

The question is, if the IMF was so effective in helping with Europe and Japan's reconstruction after the World War II, why did the same IMF fail so miserably in helping African nations to prosper after independence from colonial rule?

"This is where a question of legitimacy comes in," said Mr Baga. "How can we, the people of Africa, today continue to trust or believe the IMF and the World Bank when we know well that their prescriptions have bitterly let us down in the past? How can we still continue to collect expensive loans with negative conditionalities and poisonous attachments when we know that the structural adjustment policies propagated by IMF have in the past done very little – or absolutely nothing – to reduce our economic pain and suffering?" Mr Baga asked before stressing that, in Africa, the IMF consistently behaved like a hypocritical financial institution which consistently robs the poor to give to the rich."

"Mr Baga, in what way do you think the behaviour of the IMF differs towards Africa as compared to Europe?"

"That is a very good question. Let me use Great Britain as an excellent example of inconsistent behaviour by the IMF," Mr Baga said and paused. He took a hard look at me and said, "When Britain went to the IMF and the World Bank, respectively, for loans after the World War II, the British did so with a strong national master plan. The leading British economist at the time was a gentleman called John Maynard Keynes. He argued that, in order for Great Britain to successfully reconstruct following the disaster of World War II, the British Government must first acquire large loans which it must spend on recreating or redeveloping public infrastructure. Keynes argued that this was a necessary catalyst to ignite the engine of the British economy. He believed in direct government action." I was pleasantly surprised at the depth of Mr Baga's understanding of the British system. I asked him how he knew so much about the British economy.

"I did my masters degree at the London School of Economics about 15 years ago," he said, before returning to the story of the reconstruction of Great Britain after World War II. "Fortunately, at the time, the then British authority was a Labour Government which also believed in the development of a strong public service system as a fairer way of public wealth redistribution. So, after listening to all the advice from the leading economists of the time, the British Labour Government set out to build a strong National Health Service, which was capable of serving every British citizen free of charge at the point of need. The Government also developed an ambitious plan to build a new first-class public education system, as well as creating and building an excellent road and rail system to connect the point of production to the point of consumption of goods and services. This, as well as the development of other public infrastructure, became the catalyst for decades of excellent economic prosperity in Great Britain," said Mr Baga. He explained that in order to achieve their set objectives, the Labour Government of the day collected huge loans from the

World Bank and the IMF to build the British National Health Service, or the NHS as we know it today.

"In my well-informed position as social economist," said Mr Baga, "I can argue that the fundamental difference in approach between the two scenarios is freedom of choice. The British were free to choose where their priorities were positioned, which, in this case, included the building of strong health and education systems by the government to serve as a positive catalyst for economic growth. My concern with the IMF is that it never permitted any African country to experience the same freedom or the same opportunity to prioritise our own agenda. Throughout the years of structural adjustments, the IMF promoted an economic agenda which led to a fallacy of composition."

"My brother, I beg, what is a fallacy of composition?" I interrupted.

"The fallacy of composition in economics is like putting all your eggs in the one basket, which is a very dangerous and risky business." Mr Baga went on to explain that, "Throughout the late seventies and early eighties, both the IMF and the World Bank propagated this missionary idea that, in order for Africa to grow, the individual countries in Africa must specialise only in what they produce most, and thus concentrate on producing more of it with the objective of selling to the world market. In practice, this meant that a country like Ghana was actively encouraged or persuaded to put all her effort into producing cocoa for export. Both institutions handed out big loans for Ghana to specialise in cocoa farming, but little did the Ghanaian Government and the poor cocoa farmers realise that the IMF and World Bank were busy running around offering the same advice to all the other cocoa-producing countries, including Ivory Coast, Cameroon, Brazil, Columbia and Indonesia.

At the beginning of this experiment, many Ghanaian farmers thought that all their prayers to the Lord Jesus Christ had been suddenly answered. Furthermore, the same IMF and the World Bank encouraged Kenya, Uganda and several other African coffee-producing nations to put maximum national effort and resources into producing more coffee for the world market." According to Mr Baga, what happened after years of expensive economic experimentation beggared belief. "Without question, the result in many cases was catastrophic to say the least. In the early to mid-eighties, what was supposed to have been a God-given miracle to African cocoa farmers soon turned into a living hell in just over one decade.

I mean, what happened was that, after several years of bumper harvests of cocoa beans by all the leading cocoa-producing countries in the world, the world market was eventually flooded with too much cocoa. This led to a sudden dramatic cut in cocoa prices worldwide. The basic problem here is that, to a poor Ghanaian cocoa farmer, the cocoa bean he produces has no other value apart from exchange for cash." Mr Baga explained how many cocoa farmers ended up destitute as world cocoa prices completely collapsed in the mid-eighties.

"Unfortunately, many farmers had received cash loans from the IMF and World Bank, which they were obliged to pay back. With no incomes to live on and the threat of going to jail, a lot of farmers ended up taking their own lives through suicide and other unexplainable sudden deaths." Mr Baga told me that this is part of the reason why Africa is in so much needless debt today. He argued that in most cases, the debt most African countries owe to IMF and World Bank is deeply questionable.

"It is Illegitimate Debt!" he exclaimed. I asked Mr Dawda to explain what he meant by Africa's illegitimate debt.

"If you know of the brutal and corrupt nature of a despot, like Mobutu Sese-Seko of Zaire, and you continue to give him fat loans to enrich himself and his inner circles of cronies, then from the perspective of moral economic negligence, I can argue that Africa does not owe a coin to anyone in the West," Mr Baga said, adding that although the whole world knew that Mobutu was one of the most despotic dictators in the African continent, throughout his term of office, he remained one of the greatest American allies, and was a very good personal friend to President Nixon and other Western leaders up until his death in 1997.

MMM Syndrome in Africa

"All charities are not always good and benevolent. This is the reason why I believe that, apart from religion and tribalism, the next biggest threat facing the future of Africa is the looming aid crisis," said Mrs Anita Doe, a senior anti-aid campaigner in Ghana. She was speaking on Joy FM about the threat of neo-colonisation in Africa. "We don't need any more handouts: what we need is a hand up to climb the economic tree so that we can pluck and eat our own fruits." According to Mrs Doe, the affluent Western world today is using international Aid to control the domestic socio-political and economic agenda of Africa for their own strategic economic interest.

"Let me tell you a fact. I believe that Western aid is the newest disease in Africa today."

"Mrs Doe, can you explain to Joy FM listeners why you believe aid is becoming a looming threat to Africa?" Mr No Nonsense, the notorious radio presenter asked.

"Please don't get me wrong, I am not preaching here against human generosity towards other humans but what I am saying here is that it is not all that glitters that is gold. In other words, there is a fundamental difference between genuine aid and bogus aid. I am also getting increasingly worried about aid conditionality. Let me give you a good example, last year, the British government threatened to freeze the aid they give to Malawi because a Malawian court decided to jail an openly gay couple in the country because homosexuality is against the Malawian law." Mrs Doe continued highlighting the dangers of aid dependency in Africa. "I am not a cynical person and I am not against being generous to others. My only concern is that, if they say there is no such thing as a free lunch in America, how come America is spending millions of dollars on aid in Africa? Why is it that a benevolent America does not send us the tractors, the working tools and the machines that we need to work and improve our own living conditions? Why can't they help our African farmers to grow our own food instead of sending food aid to Africa? We know that many of these international donor countries are now competing for power and influence in Africa because they can see that the future of this world belongs to Africa. My personal worry therefore is to do with the types and calibre of aid workers that are often sent by the rich countries to come and work in Africa."

Mrs Doe argued that although we do not have to be cynical, there is an urgent need to be suspicious about the conduct of some aid workers. "In fact, there is this popular notion that, many Western aids workers in Africa often fall within three categories known as the 3M syndrome. This means that most of the Western aid workers you see in Africa today are either: Medics, Missionaries or Mismatches."

Mrs Doe warned that it is up to we, the Nigerians, Congolese, Ghanaians, Zimbabweans, Gambians, Ethiopians or Africans as a whole to stop relying on foreign donors and their handouts. "This begging bowl behaviour or aid dependency in Africa is leading so many people to become lazy, thieving, corrupt and weak-minded citizens." She emphasised that at the present time, aid conditionality and aid delivery by rich nations to Africa raises huge and unanswered moral, ethical, political and socio-economic questions.

"Let me tell you about a recent encounter I had with an aid worker at the Irish Bar in OSU just last week."

"Please go ahead," No Nonsense instructed.

"I was sitting with some friends in the bar. It was there I met a group of young ladies, one of whom was from California. I had a great conversation with her right from the very onset! Her name was Rebecca, and she told me she was born in New York but grew up in California. Rebecca told me she loves travelling around the world to help the poor, especially in Africa. I asked her how long she has been in Ghana. She told me she has been in this country for only six weeks but she already feels madly in love with the Ghanaian way of life."

"So, what happened next?" Mr No Nonsense asked, sounding a bit impatient.

"After our initial introduction, I asked Rebecca what she was doing in Ghana. She told me she was a breastfeeding adviser to northern Ghanaian women, based in the Upper East Region.

"Mrs Doe, can I ask you to explain why you sound so disappointed with Rebecca, the breastfeeding American aid worker in Ghana?"

"Well, my reason is to highlight precisely some of the growing concerns which I expressed earlier about misfits and mismatches. I am a mother, I have six children of my own whom I breastfed until they were grown. In this country, 99 per cent of mothers, like me, breastfeed their children. So, I found it hard to believe that vital American aid money to Ghana can be used to send a 22-year-old childless American schoolgirl to come and educate Ghanaian women on the benefits of breastfeeding, don't you think it should be the other way round?"

"You mean it should be Ghanaian women who are sent to the United States to advise young American women on the importance of breast milk?" Mr No Nonsense asked laughingly.

"Precisely, so far as I am aware, only 3 per cent of American women breastfeed their children as compared to 99 per cent of Ghanaian women who breastfeed our children until they are at least six months old. The other problem I had with Rebecca was her age and obvious lack of experience.

"How old was she again?" No Nonsense asked.

"She told me she was only 22 years old and single. I told her to use her time in Ghana to find herself a boyfriend, rather than wasting her time to offer empty advice on something she knows very little about!"

Internal Review in Africa

Now that we know the problems the outside world is creating for us in Africa, what is left is to look at our own internal behaviour that is holding us back from economic progress.

"The point to note is that whenever you point your finger to others, the rest of your own fingers often point back to you. So, in my view, Africa's biggest problem is the African man himself," said Professor Wisdom from the African Union Economic Forum in Accra. Professor Wisdom told me that Africa is suffering from a leaking pot syndrome. "In pure economic terms, an average African man is a net economic liability to his country. The average Ghanaian man, for example, is like a giant leaking drum," he said, adding that it doesn't matter how much water goes into this drum, so long as it continues to leak away from all directions, the drum will remain empty." I asked the eminent professor to explain what he meant by a leaking-drum syndrome.

"By leaking-drum syndrome, I mean the wilful throwing away and reckless wastage of our vital natural and human resources. If you can imagine the combined economic resources of Africa like all the water in the Atlantic Ocean, then you can see that, no matter how much it rains, if the water in the mighty ocean continues to escape from all directions everyday, the sea will go dry in no time. This is exactly the situation that is happening to our beloved continent."

Professor Wisdom told me that every single day Africa is bleeding from self-inflicted wounds. "There are individual leakages and there are public leakages," he said before clearing his throat.

"Think about an average Ghanaian man and woman and follow what they do in a day. You will soon discover for yourself that the lifestyle he or she lives adds very little value to the Ghanaian economy," said the AU economic spokesman.

"Let us take the daily life of a 35-year-old male Ghanaian civil servant as a classic example. Let us call this man Kojo. When Kojo wakes up in the morning, the first thing he will use is a Chinese toothbrush and Chinese toothpaste to brush his teeth; after that, he will go to the bath and have a quick wash with British soap before using a European-made towel to dry himself; when Kojo leaves the bathroom, he will go into his bedroom to get ready for work. In his bedroom, Kojo will wear a fake pair of Armani pants made in China (because he is very unlikely to be able to afford the original ones from Italy with his meagre salary); the socks Kojo wears will come from Germany or Britain, despite the fact that they are still likely to have been manufactured in India or China in the first place. He will then proceed to step into a pair of Dutch trousers, pull on an Italian shirt and tie, and slip his feet into a pair of Italian shoes to complete his dress.

Depending on his ranking in the civil service, Kojo may have an Indian cup of tea before proceeding to have a Ghanaian breakfast. This is the first time he would have added a little bit of economic value to his own country. After his breakfast, Kojo will leave home quickly and head to his office using an American, Japanese or German car to travel to work, although most likely in the form of taxi or tro-tro," said the professor.

"For lunch, Kojo may choose from two alternatives, depending on his income. The sad economic truth is that the average Ghanaian well-paid civil servant is more likely to have an American fast-food takeaway for lunch than the local Ghanaian dishes. As you know yourself, the educated Ghanaian elite prefer anything foreign to locally made Ghanaian products.

Anyway, irrespective of whatever lunch he chooses to have, it is likely that, after his food, Kojo would then like to wash down his throat and cool his body with a nicely chilled American Coke or Fanta. The leaking pot syndrome continues all day and, after work, he will get back home via Japanese, German or American manufactured cars again!" said Professor Wisdom. He explained that although the vast majority of the Ghanaian population are farmers, for example, Ghana still imports 87 per cent of her rice from China, India or anywhere else apart from Africa itself! Ghana also imports 79 per cent of its chicken from Italy, Thailand and other ridiculous and unnecessarily far away destinations, thus causing further expense and huge air pollution to our innocent planet.

"The economic side-tracking continues unabated when Kojo, the average Ghanaian civil servant, returns home to enjoy his evening rice balls and groundnut soup with chicken, of which it is worth noting here that, aside from the rice and chicken, 87 per cent of tinned tomatoes are imported from Italy and other countries in Europe. So, in short, almost everything we use as individuals in Africa comes from somewhere else. That is why I said the average African man is like a giant leaking oil drum." I listened with a certain amount of disbelief, as I have never for once looked at the situation in this particular way. To a large extent, everybody in the world is affected by globalisation but the impact in most cases seems to be negative in relation to Africa.

"Africa imports almost everything including our basic necessities. This is not only a big insult but also creates doubts in our ability to function on our own. Just the other day, somebody told me that even the sewing needles we use in Ghana to patch up our old clothes are imported from India," Professor Wisdom continued.

"After food, Kojo is likely to settle down on his couch with the rest of his family to watch some TV, if he is fortunate enough to have one. Unfortunately, the television set in his living room is most likely to come from China, Britain, Germany or any other part of the world apart from Africa! The sad truth is that the vast majority of the television programmes in Ghana are also foreign-made programmes which are geared towards getting the average Ghanaian man and woman to think, reason, behave or act like Europeans or Americans," said the Professor.

"This trend of economic side tracking continues on and on, and repeats itself day after day, not only here in Accra, but in every other major African city. This is why I argue that, by diverting away from our collective intellectual path, the people of Africa will continue to suffer unnecessarily from our own self-inflicted internal economic bleeding. The sad news is that, unless we change our behaviour and consumption patterns in Africa and begin to patronise our own produce, we will continue struggling to cope with inappropriate and highly expensive lifestyles, which may continue to serve the strategic economic interest of the rest of the world at our own expense." Professor Wisdom warned, adding that, "It is insane for Africans to continue to play the role of the sewing needle, which is capable of solving or patching up other people's problems around the world apart from our own."

Professor Wisdom directed me to Mr Ibrahim Kanton, the Head of Policy Development at GIMPA, Ghana Institute of Management and Public Administration. A few days later, I went to GIMPA to ask Mr Kanton what he thought about the concept of public leakages in Africa.

"Public leakages have crippled our continent since independence. That is why I believe the problem of post independent Africa can never be blamed on the West. If you think that one corrupt dictator in Nigeria alone can take as much as six billion dollars and deposit all of it in a private security bank in Switzerland or somewhere else outside of his own country, then you can just begin to understand why Nigeria as a country has not been able to build the first-class national health service or a state of the art educational system which can educate its people to be proud, able and committed to adding greater value to the wider Nigerian society and way of life."

As I listened, I remembered that Margaret Thatcher of Great Britain once famously said – and I agree – that, "Nigeria is the only country in the world that does not require any economic assistance or international aid of any kind from anywhere else in the world because they have everything they need."

"My friend, if you think for once that this tendency of economic insanity is only a Nigerian phenomenon, you would be wrong to do so. Mobutu of Congo claimed that he was personally richer than his own country, despite the fact that 99 per cent of the money he stole from his people was all securely deposited in Western bank accounts!"

"But, surely greed is not something related to Africa alone. Why is it that the other continents have developed even though they also have greedy and corrupt politicians?" I asked.

"I don't believe that economic greed on its own is an exclusively African disease," he said. "On the contrary, it can be argued that economically, the Europeans and Americans are both sometimes greedier than Africans. Anyone who has dealt with a European, American or a Chinese politician will be aware that such individuals are just as corrupt, if not more corrupt, than the African people; and this is what brings us to your question, why is African greed so different or more poisonous than European greed, for example?" Mr Kanton asked.

"European greed resembles the state of a hungry man who seeks to look for an opportunity to make his own living conditions better. And so, if you look at the style of European politicians, for example, even if they are corrupt, their corruption is an economically productive corruption, which continues to recycle their internal resources within the same economy, thus ensuring that there is always enough to feed both the rich and the poor." Mr Kanton argued that African greed, on the other hand, can be

194

characterised as compounded stupidity and extreme foolishness at the highest level. "Can you simply imagine that someone like Tony Blair or George Bush would ever dream of taking six billion of British or American tax payer's money to come and deposit it in the Central Bank of Nigeria? The answer is an obvious 'No', and this is purely because any intelligent European leader would find it utterly insane and extremely foolish to do so when they could recycle or reinvest the stolen money in order to build factories and create more jobs for the very same people they might have stolen the money from! So, it is not the greed of taking from people that is the deadly evil but it is what is done with the stolen money which can have a positive or negative trickle-down effect on the people." I sat and listened, becoming more intrigued as Mr Kanton continued.

"Apart from bringing about sluggish economic growth, public leakages have also led to violent conflicts, tribal and ethic troubles in many parts of Africa. If you look at almost all the major internal civil wars and tension throughout Africa, you would see that, wherever there is a war, there are huge resources, such as diamonds and other precious minerals, which are cheaply used to satisfy the needs of the warlords. Consider this notion in Liberia, Sierra Leone, Sudan, Congo and Somalia. By the way, have you ever watched a movie called *Blood Diamonds*?"

"No, but I have heard of it," I replied.

"This is a brilliant movie," he said and continued. "In the past and even today, many African countries have not developed because the leaders continue to exchange our diamonds and other precious resources for AK47s and other killing machinery to use on our own people."

Mr Kanton argued that before we can stop public leakages in African countries, the enlightened African populous must stand up and push for the establishment of an inter-continental African court of economic and political justice. Mr Kanton argued that the function of such a court is to arrest and prosecute those who deliberately or knowingly become involved in leaking our important strategic country and African-wide resources. "Adopting a measure such as this will ultimately serve as a clear warning to our current African leaders that the doors are closing on dishonest leadership."

After speaking to the experts, I went to the Art Centre village to find out what the ordinary man and woman in Accra thinks about the impact of vampire agents in our struggling economy.

"Let me tell you something about economic concubines," said Alhaji Sokoto, my cripple friend. We met at Sister Ama's bar for a little drink. "An economic concubine is an expensive international prostitute or a sexual comforter whose role is to make the politician happy. She offers her clients unconditional sex on their frequent requests. Her clients, in this case, are our fat-bellied African politicians." According to the cripple, an average Nigerian MP will have at least two or three diplomatic concubines abroad at expensive destinations such as London, Paris or New York. "Our government ministers are the worst, they have an average of five of these international prostitutes who are very expensive to maintain." Alhaji Sokoto argued that in Ghana, for example, many people blame the eventual collapse of Ghana Airways on the "duplicitous and underhand activities of politicians and their expensive mistresses abroad."

"Don't mind our old politicians, they are all hypocrites, crooks, liars, thieves and sinners," she said angrily clearing some empty plates from the table. I asked Sister Ama why she used such strong words about our political leaders.

"I want to insult them because I am angry with the way they mislead us. They preach one thing publicly but in their private chambers, they do the opposite. Everyday, they come to the TV to tell us they are building good schools and hospitals for the country but they send away their children to study at Oxford and Cambridge. Why do so many African politicians send their families abroad for regular medical check-ups, when the rest of us are dying of basic diseases such as malaria? Is it not time to pass a law in Africa to ban our MPs from educating their children or taking their families for expensive medical check-ups abroad? Don't you think this will bring huge benefits to the African economy?" Sister Ama asked with rage.

Chapter 20:   African Economy

I believe that there are two sides to everything in this life. There is day and there is night. There is low and there is high. There is north and there is south as well as west and east. We have man and woman, male or female, boy or girl, father and mother. Whatever way you look at it, I am convinced that everything in this life has good and bad, including the economy of people.

In the previous chapter, we saw how the use of negative words can have detrimental impacts on our everyday lives. We saw the example of the "Black Economy" syndrome which has in the past inflicted negative doubt on the ability of our father's generation to follow the right path of action in order to succeed in the African Economic Dream.

The simple truth of life is that if you believe you are good and capable of something, you will find the way to be. On the contrary, if we believe that we are poor and there is a legitimate and acceptable reason why we are poor in Africa, we will always remain in poverty. I mean, if you think you are poor, you can start to believe you are poor and you will eventually start to behave like a poor person. It is all in the mind as Professor Mandingo said in his lecture. This is the reason I totally agree with Baba Dramani, the spokesman from the Ghana Finance Ministry that, what we need now in Africa is a new socio-economic dictionary with a new vocabulary which can help to instil a positive image of Africa in our new and competent generations of Africans. For this reason alone, I am going to refrain from using the word black or poverty to describe Africa because I believe this represents a negative past image of Africa. I believe it is not any more acceptable or legitimate to describe ourselves as poor or a people from a poor continent. Africa is not a poor place, it is just full of disorganised people and this is a poor image we can work together to change.

I want to step forward from here and portray a new positive image of a great continent by defining Africa as a land of riches and abundant resource. Africa has all what it takes to be as prosperous as any other continent in this world. I believe that Obama represents the turning of a new page in African economic development ambitions. It is up to us now to get rid of all our doubts and start building a new Africa which can fulfil the economic dreams and aspirations of our people. Belief is what makes dreams come true. With believe there is always hope and hope has brought us this far today. We have the knowledge but lack the discipline and the organisation: this is why we need an action plan.

Action Plan for Africa's Economic Revolution

Revolution comes from the word revolt, which means to stand up against injustice which affects you or your society. A little while ago, I remember watching BBC news. And then, someone amazing appeared on the screen. It was the Burmese prodemocracy campaigner, Aung San Suu Kyi talking about revolution after being released from jail by the military junta in Burma. "Revolution is radical action," she said. I remember tears came close to my eyes watching her talk with so much courage and conviction after ten solid years under house arrest. I felt yes, these are the kind of people we need in the world to show us good example. People who are in a privileged position but choose to sacrifice their comfort for the purpose of the common good.

I remembered that during that interview with the BBC journalist, Aung San Suu Kyi admitted that bringing about a revolution is a tough business, "But, life is not always supposed to be easy," she said, warning that, for a social or economic revolution to occur in any human society we "We need to offer ourselves as die-hards." The die-hards she described as the kind of people who are passionate enough about what is happening to the society. "For any revolution to succeed in any society, enough people often have to go through some amount of hardship, endurance and self-sacrifice to overturn the greatest injustice in that society." After listening to the interview, I said to myself, I wish there were enough die-hards in Africa today. I wish there were enough people who believe as I do that Africa deserve a better economic future. I wish all those who believe we can take the right economic foot steps to make our African Dream come true now, not later. I am crying this way because I believe that if enough African people and African supporters in the world believe that a new economic mentality is needed to shake up and rebuild our continent through the power of unity, this will happen within one competent die-hard generation!

My own answer to the immediate realisation of the African socio-economic dream is based on the four action points. I am convinced that unless those who say they believe in Africa are hypocrites, we can all come together and follow these key action plans to make Africa the best economic success story of the twenty-first century:

- African Union (AU)

- Country Economies

- African Entrepreneurship

- Community Interest in Africa (CIA)

African Union: Creation of a Single Currency

I believe that the AU must print a new currency by 2015. A new African currency is a prerequisite for African economic revolution. This is because we live in a world where, although money is not everything, money is one thing which is more powerful than anything else you can imagine including God. If we have one single currency, it will, in economic terms, bring about internal co-operation and encourage us to trade with each other, not against one another as we have been doing in the past.

In my opinion, the time has come for the African Union to demonstrate to its citizens that it is no longer just a talking shop for expensive political parrots, but truly a powerful civil institution with a strong ability to lead the way for positive economic change in the continent.

We already know from the Euro experience that it is not everybody who is always ready, prepared or willing to change their old habits or negative ways of thinking and doing things. So, the emphasis should be on immediate action by an effective coalition of the willing, the able and the committed. Action should start from those countries that believe in Africa and the principle of a single currency as the best sustainable way forward. It is important to engage in an ongoing dialogue with everyone in Africa about the benefits of a single currency and there should be referendums on single currency in every African nation within a decade. But, while we try to convince everyone to join the new AFRO, those countries, like many within the ECOWAS zone, which believe in Africa and the power of collective bargaining, should immediately get together and put the foundation of single AFRO into operation.

If we are serious about becoming a prosperous paradise in the twenty-first century, this is the time to take the most radical actions and radical decisions at the top of our governance. If you can imagine that the head of a man is his most important asset, then the AU is Africa's most important weapon of change. If the head or the top of an institution is rotten, nothing else attached to it will ever work or function properly. Africa needs credible leadership and the African Union is our most powerful institution to lead the way. There are many ways the AU can help to change Africa in the positive direction and as the Ghanaian Vice President said in his address to ECOWAS leaders in the previous chapters, it is time for the AU to bring the continent together through powerful legislation on areas of strategic importance such as Common Agriculture and trade.

Apart from the creation of single currency, the second most immediate thing the AU can do to kick off the African economic revolution is to build better serving institutions, which people can relate to and be proud of. A good example of this would be the building of African Union Universities in each member country as models of high standard education in Africa.

As we have learnt in the previous chapter, the brain drain syndrome has been a contributory factor in our past economic problems. At the moment, if you are an African student and you want to study at any reputable university, then you can only do so by travelling abroad and paying fees well above the board just to improve your knowledge. This is the severest and most acute type of self-inflicted mental and economic slavery, which we cannot any longer moan and blame on anyone else but ourselves. The exodus of African students to Europe and America is also one of the saddest examples of the leaking drum syndrome that is crippling our capacity to develop our economies.

If we want to make revolutionary change, we need to first revolutionise the way we learn, how we learn, what we lean and where we learn. It may sound like a big project that is impossible to achieve, but radical change requires simple action towards a high goal. I believe that unless the AU can demonstrate its credibility through radical actions by stepping in to lead us on radical educational reform, then, it is going to be really difficult to remove our people from needless economic doom in the future. I am making this proposal because of the pain and frustration expressed by our students all over the world today. The following article is a classical example, which I downloaded from the internet a while ago. This article gives us a clear picture of the problems we must do all we can to resolve immediately.

African Students Studying in the United Kingdom by Uche Nworah

The United Kingdom (UK) appears to be the favourite destination for African students; this is not surprising considering the colonial links between the UK and some African countries. Also, the United Kingdom government actively pursues a policy of making UK education the number one in the world; it markets the UK education brand all over the world in association with its many universities through the British Council and other agencies. Students are recruited using various methods such as brochures, word-of-mouth, road shows and related events, and also through technology, i.e., internet marketing. Local representatives are also appointed in some countries and are charged with the responsibility of marketing the UK education brand to local students all through the year.

According to a publication by ukuniversites.ac.uk, International student numbers in UK higher education institutions have increased by over 60 per cent in the last five years. "In 2003/04 there were 213,000 international students and 104,000 students from other EU countries in UK higher education institutions (HEIs)", the report said. These foreign students contribute about £4 billion annually to the UK economy. The average yearly tuition fee in UK universities for foreign students is £7,000 (excluding living and board) for undergraduate students. Post-graduate tuition fees are £9,000 (excluding living and board) for a year depending on the university and course of study.

There have been unpleasant stories and experiences from some of these African students studying in the UK, many of whom were conned by flashy websites only to be shocked and disappointed on arrival by the reality on the ground and the fact that some of these institutions are actually un-accredited one-flat colleges. There are also complaints against some of the older established universities as regards the quality of teaching, added value, course content as well as the general enrichment of the students' experiences. Such complaints therefore justify the Times UK Universities League Table exercise and their Good University Guide publication. It also challenges the UK's Department for Education and Skills (DFES) to improve on its supervisory and oversight functions, and gives rise to a recurring need to probe further on whether these fee-paying African students are getting value for their money. We went to town to sample the views of some African students in the UK, to get their thoughts on UK education and also to find out their plans upon graduation:

Emmanuel Osei-Tutu (business studies student at London Metropolitan University): "Studying in the UK has its positive and negative sides. On the positive side, the teachers are more helpful, probably because they also need the students to pass in order to retain their jobs. There are also the availability of computers, and technology, which are largely lacking in Ghana and in other African countries. On the negative side, the UK society suffers from moral decay; young people could easily get into trouble here by associating with bad friends. There is not enough parental control here, children and other young people are too independent, this is not so good. In this regard, I still prefer the African discipline system where the whole community watches out for each other. I am afraid in a way because there are no longer guaranteed job opportunities in the UK, as we had thought when we came, especially with the increase in the number of immigrants and also the influx of EU citizens. My advice to other African students, especially from Ghana, my home country, is to make plans of returning after graduating. After graduating, I plan to work for some time, save some money and set up a business, which will take me back and forth to Ghana."

Carlos Goncalves (accounting student at Middlesex University): "I appreciate UK education because of the ready availability of resources; you have internet access round the clock to help you in your research work. Also the libraries are well stocked. There is really no reason for not doing well and achieving top grades here. You won't believe what a difference it makes to have uninterrupted power supply in case you want to study at night, without having to resort to candles and lamps. This may sound funny, but such little things have really made a difference for me. I miss the African atmosphere though, the spirit of togetherness and so on, people back home are friendlier but then, something has to be sacrificed. I will encourage other people who plan to come to the UK to study to do so; I really see more opportunities here, as one can get a job on graduation. I plan to live here after graduating but would hope to have business relations with Angola, my home country."

Nnadubem Moghalu (law student at Holborn College): "Despite the initial culture shock and difficulties in settling down to the system, I would say that UK education is still value for money because of the quality of teaching, however this is at a risk of students becoming complacent because of the teachers' approach which is more soft-touch. Compared to the law library in my former university in Nigeria (The University of Abuja), which was housed in a small flat, I would say that Holborn College is well resourced with up-to-date law publications and periodicals. Definitely I plan to go back to Nigeria eventually, and would advise other African students to think along the same line, although opportunities abound in the UK, I believe that those of us that are privileged to have studied here should also take back our skills to improve the social and economic well-being of our people back home."

Why do we need African Union Universities?

The concept of the AU University (AUU) will be built on excellence and innovation. The AU can negotiate with the best computer manufacturers in the world to bring in the latest technology into its universities. The Chinese can carry out the construction on the first pilot AUU, whilst local construction firms within the region are enabled to deliver the final stages of this new ambitious programme. We can borrow some knowledge from America and Europe. The building of AUU will create thousands of construction-related jobs and further employment when the buildings are completed and the universities are running, as we have seen during European reconstruction after World War II.

AUU can be built on a strong social business model, which is based on concrete evidence of acute gaps in the market. From the UK example, it is clear that hundreds of thousands of African students travel outside every year to study abroad. As we have heard from the testimonies above, the reason why we travel abroad is to be able to study at good universities, which are well equipped with the right technology, information and knowledge systems. In my view, gone are the days when knowledge was possessed and distributed by the few. Today in the world of the internet, everyone can have access to any form of knowledge provided they are equipped with the right tools, such as good computers and a reliable supply of electricity and internet access. This is exactly what the AUU system should be designed to address. Apart from providing new income generating opportunities and stopping the brain drain, I believe that AUU will also serve as a symbol of pride for our future generations. This will be a good starting logic for a single currency in the continent.

Country Economies

What can individual countries in Africa do to spark an economic revolution for the benefit of the majority of the population against the tiny minority interest? I am going to take Nigeria as an example and ask: what can we do in Nigeria to bring prosperity to all Nigerians, irrespective of ethnic or tribal differences? To begin my search for a simple answer to a very complex dilemma, I phoned my friend Oga in Glasgow. Officially, Oga is an illegal immigrant in Scotland. He works as a cleaner in a Glasgow supermarket, although he has a master's degree of his own. After he finished his degree a few years ago, he was unable to get an employer to help extend his visa in the UK, so he was left with two difficult options: to return to Nigeria or go underground in the UK.

"Right now, if I had the proper option, I would go back to Nigeria tomorrow, but the situation at home is not good. In Nigeria, unless you work in government or oil business, you cannot make enough money to look after yourself and your family," he moaned. Oga cannot go home, so Oga does a rubbish job to get by in Glasgow. Everyday, he hopes and prays that one day soon, a big miracle will happen in Nigeria when everyone will change and become one. A Nigeria where people will have good jobs and good houses, where there is less crime, less stealing and cheating: less of anything negative and more of everything positive. I believe that for Nigeria to succeed as an economy everyone in Nigeria from top to the bottom must join their hearts and minds together to make it happened.

The question is, how does my friend Oga see the future of Nigeria from his underground position in the Glasgow Gorbals? When I asked Oga what he thought needed to happen to spark an immediate economic revolution in his country, this is what he had to say.

"The answer is very simple," he said and laughed over the phone. "If you want to spark an economic revolution in Nigeria, you need to take two important actions. First, we have to find a way to pay everyone in Nigerian to do something meaningful for the country. Nigeria is not like the UK or America where people are sitting and waiting for the government to come and give out benefits. What people need in Nigeria are jobs which they can do to earn a proper living." I asked him how he thinks we can pay everyone to do something beneficial for themselves and the country.

"It is a matter of will and attitudes," he said. "If the leaders are willing to create the jobs, they can do it with their eyes closed. But before we can do this, we have to address corruption in Nigeria," Oga insisted. The word corruption always sends cold shivers into my veins. In my view, I think corruption sucks. Corruption sucks because it is against the natural philosophy of life and the will of God. Those who are corrupt often persist in taking the money from the poor and wasting it in extravagances such as private jets and expensive yachts. I know for sure that we can never stop corruption completely, but I am equally convinced that we can at least reduce its poisonous impact on African societies.

What can we do to reduce corruption in a country like Nigeria, where corruption runs through every aspect of society like the blood in a human being? I have to say that I always come to the same conclusion: that, in reality, it is all about leadership. First of all, the President of Nigeria must come to the mental realisation that if your country grows rich, you, as the President enjoy better wealth, greater wellbeing and power not only in your own country but also in the world. In the twenty-first century, it is stupid for any African leader to think that when his or her people are suffering, they can continue to enjoy alone. Those days are over. The message here is that, if the President of Nigeria can reason properly in his individual capacity and believe that he wants to grow his country, he can select enough good-hearted and like-minded people into his cabinet to make this happen. No one in their right mind can assume that the task of setting Nigeria onto a good economic path will be easy. As Aung San Suu Kyi said, a revolution of any kind can be anything but easy.

My conversation with Oga continued that night over the phone. I asked him what he thought we could do about corruption in his country.

"First, we must start from the very top," he said. "We have to pay the governors and the senators good wages and then we introduce the death penalty for those who cheat the country after being paid well," he said. "Let's pay President Goodluck Jonathan and every subsequent Nigerian president five million dollars a year. Let us make the Nigerian president officially the highest paid president in the world. Then, we pay each state governor one million dollars a year. The senators, we give them a quarter of a million dollars a year to do their jobs properly. From there, we can move down to the civil servants, the doctors, the lawyers and the accountants, pay them well to do their jobs. Pay the engineers, the police, army, teachers and the labourers. Let's find a simple but effective mathematical formula to pay all these people to do their jobs properly and then Nigeria will become the best country to live on earth within 30 years from now." My friend Oga was in electric mode that evening. He convinced me even from his extreme position that, if we can convince enough people from the President down and we start to take enough consistent action now, it is not impossible for Nigeria to reach her richly deserved paradise status by 2050.

Finally, I asked Oga why he thinks that we should pay the Nigerian President five million dollars a year when there are too many people suffering in the country. "If there are too many people suffering in Nigeria, you have to understand that they are suffering for a reason. They are suffering because our politicians are corrupt. I can say that many of our potentially good politicians are corrupt because they are not paid enough to do the right thing for the nation. Let me tell you why I say we should pay Goodluck Jonathan five million dollars a year. If you don't pay him and give him a reason to think otherwise, one president alone can steal up to five billion dollars in their term of office. Just compare that to five million dollars a year," he said.

Oga also told me he believes that before the people of Nigeria can achieve their economic dreams, there has to be proper and permanent supply of electricity in the country. "Energy and power accounts for everything in this life apart from the time and conscience it takes to do things. No country in this world can grow to reach its best economic potential without the power of electrification. That is why I say the president who brings electricity to all Nigerians will be remembered forever as Nigeria's greatest hero!"

African Entrepreneurship

"What the people of Africa in the twenty-first century must know is that, when Europe and America went through the Industrial Revolution, it wasn't European and American governments that made it happen. On the contrary, it was European and American businesses and entrepreneurs who saw opportunities far away from home. It was the action of European business men which kicked off the Great Industrial Revolution," Mr Braithwaite explained before adding that: "It is sad to think that the Industrial Revolution of Europe occurred 300 years ago and yet we Africans have so far been unable to bring our acts together to bring about our own economic revolution. Now the challenge ahead is difficult but equally exciting," said Mr James Braithwaite, an African businessman in London, who I had the privilege to meet at an African Entrepreneur's forum a while back. James Braithwaite CBE, a former chairman of the South East Regional Development Agency in England and the Consular General of South Africa told the conference of African entrepreneurs that if the Africa politicians are failing to develop their countries, we must first understand that in many cases, it is because our politicians don't have the power to do so considering the wider geo-political context in which they operate.

"Fortunately, as businessmen and women in the twenty-first century, we are not as constrained by the power of remote control as our political leaders. African entrepreneurs and business leaders are free to participate in continental and global businesses in ways that has never been possible before," he said and cited the internet as a new possible platform through which new innovative African businesses can look for global clients, networks, contacts, information, technology and many more new opportunities, which he vehemently argued never existed in the past. "Let me give you a good example," he said and flicked forward his PowerPoint. "Twenty years ago, if you were a small chocolate maker in Ghana, for example, you could only sell your products to the Ghanaian or regional market. So, one can argue that the potential for that local business to grow was slim. Now, through the power of the internet, a small Ghanaian chocolate manufacturer can build a website to sell the finished products to his or her global clients. The independent Ghanaian chocolate manufacturer can use this new and powerful platform to bypass international export restrictions and find lucrative ways to sell his authentic chocolate on the internet. By building a web presence, he or she can sell directly to both final consumers and retailers. The same principles and techniques apply to Ghanaian gold jewellery or to a small-scale Kenyan coffee producer. What we have to understand is that, although these opportunities exist, they don't come to you. It is we who have to go out and seek for new innovative ways to link local African business to the international markets.

In return, African entrepreneurs abroad must create business links from our foreign destinations back to our home countries," Mr Braithwaite continued adding that: "Right now in London, Chicago, New York, Paris, Glasgow, Dublin and almost everywhere you go around the world, there are large African communities, but few of us venture into business. Why does this happen? The answer is

212

partly because we envy each other's success. This part of our mentality must change if we want to get to the next level of economic empowerment. But the second answer is the fact that we pay too much respect to paper qualifications. Every African man in the UK is busy trying to get the next masters degree. We acquire all these big certificates and we end up in low paid jobs when we can combine our skills with the limitless opportunities in the UK to set-up and run our own businesses."

What James said that day made perfect sense. I live in Glasgow and although there is now a very prominent African presence in Glasgow, the very basic goods and services we need for our daily lives are not being catered for by African businessmen and women. If I have something to send to Ghana from Glasgow, there is no African shipping agent to do it for me. If I want to send a Western Union money transfer, I have to go to an Asian shop to do so. If I want to eat some yam from Ghana, I have to go to an Asian shop to buy it. How does an Asian businessman know how to bring yams from Africa better than a Ghanaian or Nigerian shopkeeper?

Community Interest in Africa (CIA)

"There are two types of communities and it all depends on the type of community you belong to which determines your failure or success!" said Sister Grace, a senior community development practitioner at the Accra Metropolitan Assembly.

"First all, a community is a group or society of people with a common interest or common identity." Sister Rose explained that there are huge differences between "identity-based communities" and "interest-based communities."

"Let me stress here that, in practice, communities which are characterised by a common identity are usually strong on culture but weak on other areas. In this case, I want to argue that most African communities are only based on the second criteria of a

213

common identity, which is the root cause of our failure." Sister Grace told me that most African people around the world only identify themselves as Africans in relation to their skin colour. "What we don't realise is that, communities that are shaped or necessitated by a common interest like the Europeans and the Americans tend to function better in terms of economic development."

After listening to Sister Grace, I realised the reason why Africa has failed to develop in many ways. As she argued, if enough people in Africa are interested in what is happening in our continent or cared enough like I do about Africa, Africa will surely develop in no time.

After that conversation, I realised that the lack of one economic mentality or one economic community spirit is the number one evil in every aspect of African society today. We often have strong social spirits and better cultural ties but, when it comes to economic thinking, we are the most wayward, divided, undisciplined and wasteful economic community in the whole world. This negative and self-destroying collective error is something we must change without any compromise or need to think twice.

I believe that we can, and we should come together to form one economic mentality to safeguard our strategic interest as a people. I want to proceed by selecting one powerful African community to show how a better communal spirit can make the unbelievable difference between success and failure. Let's take the African community abroad as a great example.

Let us ask ourselves, Africans in Paris, London and Hamburg, what can we do as enlightened communities to contribute towards the new African Dream? Do we know that before Americans developed, they had a dream first? Are we also aware that before the Europeans developed, they had a material plan? And do we know before China grew, the Chinese had a vision. Before Africa can take off, the African community abroad must adopt a new mentality in our foreign destinations.

Let me finish this giant revolutionary proposal by telling you a little story about the Asian community in Great Britain. When Asians first came into Britain around the fifties, they faced many problems. They had language and cultural barriers. Many of the first generations of Indian, Pakistani and Bangladeshi people faced job discrimination at work and racism in the communities they lived in.

After struggling initially, the community soon learned that instead of complaining about the indigenous British population for all the negative reasons, it was better to stick together, work together to create their own economic path, which they can use as a weapon to safeguard their long-term economic interest. Without wasting their time, the Asian community in Britain quickly formed their own business links and networks. Today, in Britain, the Asian community has fully established a solid presence in every single British village, town or city. They have their own economy within the wider British economy and in Glasgow, for example, there are certain parts of the city which is 90 per cent Asian. After many decades of working together, they have even managed to change parts of the British national culture by making curry, instead of fish and chips, the favourite dish in the UK.

The question you may ask is: how did the Asians in Britain break away from economic dependency on the indigenous British population? The lesson that can be learnt from the success of the British Asian community alone, in my view, can help the African community to build a new mental direction and one strong economic path. If all the Nigerians in Britain operate as a powerful economic community, this can have huge significant economic impact on the Nigerian economy back home. Currently, we know that, the Nigerian community is huge in London but there are only a few Nigerian shops or businesses that sell Nigerian products in the UK.

Right now, if a Nigerian in London wants to cook agushi soup, he has to go to a Pakistani or Turkish shop to buy his ingredients. If a

Ghanaian man in London wants to make his light soup with goat meat, he has to go to a Pakistani or Indian shop to buy the meat.

The question now is: how can we reverse this economic leakage and unnecessary economic draining of our community resources? How can we make the right mental decisions and take the best economic choices, which can circulate or recycle our resources internally within our own African communities abroad?

The simple answer is Individual Action. The action of many individual people towards the same or similar goal is what leads to radical change! I want to assess the power of the individual and how one individual is destined to change and transform Africa from the land of the slaves, the poor and the diseased, to the land of happiness and prosperity for all. But before we proceed, let me tell you about an exemplary community event, which I attended a few years back in Glasgow. This event was organised in Paisley, a suburb of Glasgow, and was entitled: "The Taste of Africa!"

This event showcased everything positive about Africa from arts and crafts to African clothes. There were several exotic dancers and cultural performances including Rwandan warrior dancers and intricate Congolese music with plenty of amazing traditional African food to choose from. The whole feeling was homely and extremely touching. I was delighted and hopeful about the future of Africa when I set foot in Paisley Town Hall to take part in this event. I felt positive that there was a new spirit of African "can do" mentality developing in our communities abroad. The event was attended by hundreds of people from almost every single African country. There were also many local Scottish people who attended the event to experience the new "Taste of Africa", including the Lord Provost of Renfrewshire, Mrs Mary Madeline.

The highlight of the day for me came when one of the organiser climbed onto the stage to give the vote of thanks. She was dressed in beautiful and colourful Congolese clothes.

"Fellow Africans and other distinguished ladies and gentlemen, this is the second year we have gathered here to celebrate the amazing 'Taste of Africa'. As you know, this annual event has been organised to celebrate all the positive things about Africa, which make us all proud about our common future. For far too long, the image of Africa has been tarnished by the outside world and it is with so much pleasure I see that the people of Africa are beginning to see the light and coming together to tell the world the true story of Africa. I want to thank our host the good people of for accepting and welcoming us into Scotland and recognising that we can add positive value to the Scottish society and the Scottish economy.

This year, our numbers have almost doubled from last year and it is so encouraging seeing that we are coming out in our large numbers to support our own community events," said Mrs Regina Brew, the chair of the occasion. Many people clapped repeatedly before she continued.

"As you can see throughout the hall, there are many exhibiting stands with products from every corner of the continent. There is a stall with beautiful handmade clothes from Gambia and Congo beside the stage. There are craft stalls from Tanzania and Mali. There is a jewellery stall from Burkina Faso and I encourage all of you to please try and buy something from these traders. If we are serious about supporting our communities back home, we must begin to buy our own goods whilst we are abroad," she said and continued to explain her reasons.

"If a Chinese man produces his goods, there is always a market for it. If a Scottish man makes his goods, every Scottish man and woman will go out and buy it. If an Indian or Pakistani man has a shop, his own Indian or Pakistani brothers and sisters will shop from their brother's shop. If the African man opens his shop in Glasgow, Aberdeen, Edinburgh, Dundee, Manchester, London or New York, the African man fails in his business because his own brothers and sisters will refuse to buy from him. We often prefer to pass our custom to everyone else apart from the people from our own community. This is the foolish economic mentality that we have to change now," said Mrs Brew. "This is the reason why we organised 'Taste of Africa' to give Africans in Scotland as well as the local Scottish people the opportunity to buy and patronise made in Africa goods. I believe that the best way to help Africa to grow out of poverty is through trade and not charity. Mrs Brew concluded and attracted a huge cheer from the crowd.

Chapter 21: Akwaba Obama

"Yes, Ghana, we can" became the new slogan in town as people ran riot with growing anxieties about the prospect of a brighter future. From the day the White House released the statement that President Obama planned to visit Ghana; a growing hysteria resonated throughout the country and spread further into the continent. "A messiah is coming home," read the headlines of one Ghanaian newspaper.

"Akwaba Obama, our brother is coming home," read another headline.

So far as many are concerned, the choice of Ghana as the destination for Obama's maiden visit to Africa was, without a doubt, the biggest boost of confidence for the young flourishing new generations of Ghanaian citizens. The president's chosen destination also marked the best signal to the rest of the continent that Ghana is truly the "gateway to Africa" – not only in terms of history but also in terms of the hard work and great effort the Ghanaian people of today are making towards a positive Africa.

It is important to take this opportunity to reflect that, just a little while ago in December 2008, the Ghanaian people set a new world record for democracy after going through three rounds of voting before peacefully electing a new president. This scenario, as most observers will agree, could not have happened bloodlessly anywhere else in the African continent, and probably not even in some of the world's greatest democracies without the initiation of violence or mayhem on the streets. Even through difficult times and closely fought elections, the Ghanaians have proven to the rest of the African continent and the wider world, time after time, that everything in this world, including democracy, has strong roots and foundations in Africa, and that the African man of the twenty-first century is capable of doing better for himself through open and sincere democratic principle.

According to the White House, Ghana's maturing democracy and the people's commitments to good governance were the primary reasons Obama chose, amongst many other great nations, to pass his desperately awaited African message through the Ghanaian parliament.

As the people of Africa prepared to receive a Messiah, there was anxiety everywhere on the melting streets of Accra, Cape Coast, Kumasi, Tamale and every other town and village in the country. One week before Obama arrived in Ghana, I was listening to the radio in the afternoon when a big debate was sparked about the future of Africa. One man, who called himself Father Jesus, ignited the debate by telling Joy FM listeners about his vision for Africa.

"Last night I had a dream. In my dream, I saw one small mouse following and chasing five fat cats. It looked as if the five cats were terrified for their lives. I couldn't believe my eyes. It was just like a big miracle to me," he said.

"Father Jesus, what is your message to Joy FM listeners'? What is the implication of your dream and how is that relevant to Obama's visit to Ghana next week?" asked Mr No-Nonsense.

"I believe that the mouse represents the internet generation and the new enlightened African youth who are fearless in pursuit of their legitimate dreams." Father Jesus explained that the five cats represent five decades of fearless pursuit of the African dream. "I believe five decades of post-independence Africa has so far failed to make the African dream come true. It is now up to this 'mouse generation' to renew our vows and make a better pledge to make this important dream come true."

"Father Jesus, what can the mouse generation do to secure the future of Africa in economic prosperity?" asked Mr No-Nonsense. That day I was in a bus and all the passengers glued their ears to the radio station to hear what the caller had to say next.

"First of all, we must ask all African governments to give us a proper say in the day-to-day running of our country resources. We must use the power of the internet and world media to shape a new debate that can unite us as one powerful strong force. We need a referendum about the direction of our beloved continent. The question is very simple: should Africa unite under a single currency or continue to remain divided in poverty? This is a question that must be put in a referendum not only here in Ghana but also in every single African country. It is time the ordinary man and woman has a say in the way we are governed. Let us not forget that democracy is a government of the people, run by the people to the collective benefit of all the people and not just to suit the narrow interest of the privileged few. I can assure you that this is the same message Obama is bringing to deliver to the Ghanaian parliament next week," said Jesus.

Immediately Father Jesus finished his comments, another caller rang the Joy FM station to air his views.

"Mr No-Nonsense, good afternoon. My name is Osei. I am calling from the Garden City, Kumasi," the caller took his time and introduced himself properly before registering his comments. "I completely disagree with the father that the 50 years of independence has failed the people of Africa. That is a very wrong and irresponsible statement to make on national radio. I am a trader and I can assure you that, even over the past ten years, Ghana has changed dramatically for the better; especially during the time of the Kuffour Government. Don't forget that our democracy has improved dramatically. Right now, our education is good, the health service is improving and almost every village, town and city in Ghana has regular electricity. We are moving forward and not backwards. So, we have to look at the positive sides before we can condemn those who have sacrificed their lives to make things possible for us today. As a matter of fact, I think our fathers' generation has brought us far under very difficult circumstances. It is up to the new generations to make Africa a better place," Mr Osei concluded before another caller rang to add his views.

"Good afternoon. My name is Alhassan from Tamale in the Northern Region. I think Father Jesus was completely spot on. I agree with him that the past 50 years of independence has failed Africa completely. I am 69 and I am old enough to remember what happened in the past. I remember when we gained independence in 1957; Ghana was self-sufficient as we produced all the food we needed to feed ourselves. Today the opposite is the truth. Let me tell you that I used to farm over 50 acres of rice. Now, I don't have any rice on my farm because every so-called educated Ghanaian man and woman you see today prefers American long grain or Indian basmati rice. If this is what you call progress, I am afraid I disagree. Before we can make meaningful progress in Ghana, we have to ban all foreign agricultural produce. We must learn to eat our own food!" Alhassan exclaimed. Another caller echoed Alhassan's views by adding that the failure of the independence generations has been largely due to the evil conduct of our past dictators who have plundered too many of our countries into corruption states through nepotism, tribal conflicts and civil wars. He warned that unless Africa and her people refrain from dictatorial regimes in the future, the situation will not get any better.

As the bus drove from Kumasi to Accra, the hullabaloo on the radio continued into the hot afternoon until one sympathetic caller rang to ask for a tribute song in honour of a passing legend. I felt plenty of sorrow as the song was played on air. I couldn't help thinking to myself: what a shame that when one bright moon is shining on Africa, Africa and the rest of the world had just lost such a great legend and an undisputed prophet of world music in the might of Michael Jackson. "If you goanna make the world a better place, take a look at yourself in the mirror and make a change'" the song continued as the bus drove along the dusty road.

As the song continued, I prayed to my good humble lords of the heavens to forgive our brother Jackson and all the greatest men who have gone long before him. Michael Jackson, whether you liked him or loathed him, has brought more joy to this world than any other young man of his own generation. The important thing to remember is that, as he said, change is the only thing that can make our world a better place. So, as Obama prepares to come to the fatherland, my question was, are the people of Africa prepared to change and make Africa a better place in the twenty-first century?

When I returned to Accra that evening I wrote while listening to my little radio, which I had brought with me from Glasgow. I must admit that one of the best friends I had with me throughout my journey home was that little handheld radio. I carried it with me every day and to everywhere I went. I tuned to the BBC World Service regularly and other news networks across Africa to catch the flying gossip.

"Obama's visit to Ghana as the first African-American President of the United States is like the living reality of a famous dream by a great king of the past," said one commentator from Uganda. He was speaking on the BBC World Service programme "Voice of Africa". Another man phoned the programme and said, "Obama is Moses of Africa. He is coming to Ghana to lead us out of the sea of poverty," he joked referring to the biblical story of the Jews walking across the Red Sea to freedom.

"Why did Obama choose to come to Ghana as opposed to Nigeria?" asked one caller from Nigeria. By this point, there was only a few days left before his arrival and the agony of waiting was beginning to brew regional tension within the West African subcontinent. The indomitable super eagles of Nigeria were the first to make their concerns heard very loudly on Ghanaian media. "Obama is wrong in choosing Ghana over Nigeria because even though Ghana is doing better in democracy, the size of the Nigerian democracy and the many difficult challenges it faces needs greater support from America," said the Nigerian commentator on a radio interview. "After all, there can never be a truly viable and prosperous African Union without greater reforms in Nigeria. This is why I believe Obama should have come to Nigeria to tell our slowly improving, but corrupt, politicians to make fast and meaningful democratic change, not only for Nigeria as a country but for Africa as a whole."

Well, as the super eagles were busy with political point scoring, the newly elected President Jacob Zuma and his Bafana-Bafana team went on the economic goal scoring. "The Nigerians complaints are not as legitimate as the South Africans who, after all, apart from being the largest economy in Africa, also have many other great reasons to merit Obama's maiden visit to the continent," said the South African representative on Radio Africa. "Let us not forget that for the first time in history, South Africa is hosting the World Cup on behalf of the whole of the African continent!" a South African caller concluded by inviting football fans around the world to come to South Africa in 2010 and witness a new image of the twenty-first century Africa in the making. I listened with pride and joy. As I did, I also hoped and prayed that the South Africa 2010 Football World Cup should come to pass as a success not only for the Rainbow Nation but the whole continent indeed.

The North Africans were quite happy about what was happening in the region, and kept a visibly wise but low profile about the shifting of the tectonic plates in the African geo-political landscape.

"What about his fatherland?" some commentators repeatedly asked. Well, the Kenyans were, understandably, the most distinguished. Knowing very well how much Ghanaian diplomacy helped them in their own post-election shenanigans with Kofi Annan's intervention, the Kenyans showed the greatest respect to their Ghanaian brothers. Most Kenyans were happy that their son and his wife were going to visit part of the extended family in Ghana. They knew and understood that this highly spiritual home-coming was not only going to be difficult for the mighty president, but also his wife and two daughters, Malia and Sasha. It is important to mention that Michelle Obama herself can directly trace her own greatest grandfathers back to Ghana. Hence, the reason why many Ghanaians saw the first lady as a returning sister!

In fact, one northern Ghanaian chief joked on GTV that Mrs Obama is a direct family member of his. "Obama is my in-law and he is coming to Ghana because he needs to make his dowry settlement to the family." The chief said that Obama's family from Kenya were already in Ghana with their kraals of cattle. I laughed and shook my head when I heard him speak on national TV. Whatever the case, for most young Ghanaians, there was no getting away from the fact that, a truly loved and cherished brother and sister were coming home.

On the 7 July 2009, three days before Obama stepped onto Ghanaian soil, there was already a heavy American security presence on the streets of Accra. There were posters and placards everywhere. And despite all the tight security, there was a real sense of family reunion and public celebration throughout the nation. Many travellers trouped into Accra to witness the biggest miracle in the modern history of Africa.

"We Ghanaians can now boast of ourselves as America's greatest allies," a passer-by excitedly exclaimed, carrying and waving several American flags with a broad infectious Ghanaian smile of joy on his face. "Yes, we can make it together with the United States!" he declared.

Meanwhile, Obama and his family had already begun their marathon trip. From Washington, they flew to Moscow where Obama and his Russian counterparts had some frank and open discussions on the need for a renewed effort to build a safer and fairer world. A world in which East and West can reason on common grounds and make the collective progress needed to safeguard the survival of an increasingly fragile world.

From the East, Obama and his team continued to Rome, where he was given a warm dinner reception by the Pope as part of his visit to the 2009 G8 Summit of the world's richest nations.

Before he left Rome to fly to Ghana, President Obama gave an accurate emotional and honest assessment about the level of unfairness in the past, which saw his own grandfather in Kenya being referred to as a "boy" by his colonial employers throughout his working life, despite the fact he was a well-regarded and respected elder in his own community. Obama told his fellow world leaders at the G8 summit how these imbalances had led to significant negative growth in Africa for far too many decades. He cited his own personal example that, during the time he was growing up as a small boy, Kenya had a bigger and stronger growing economy than South Korea, yet Kenya has, since then, been significantly outperformed by South Korea for the past few decades, thus indirectly referring to the fact that, throughout the seventies and the early eighties, America's aid to South Korea alone was greater than the total aid America gave to the whole of Africa. And this was purely due to the fact that South Korea was highly regarded as a very important strategic cold war ally.

Obama had no time to spend on prolonged behind-the-scenes discussions after the G8 summit in Rome. He knew very well that Africa and her entire population were all awaiting his timely reunion.

On the eve of his arrival, a huge crowd of people gathered around Sister Ama's bar at the entrance of the Art Centre village overlooking the ocean. The moon was about ten days old and it shone a very bright light onto the city giving everyone a sense of godliness around Accra that night. Even the sky seemed to have dropped lower than usual and the bright moon was accompanied by two bright stars, one on each side.

Finally after many long weeks of waiting in anticipation, the President of the United States and the new King of Africa landed his plane on Ghanaian soil. During the final hour, the whole country went silent as several military jets paraded in the sky, flying low over the city. Cars stopped and many streets were closed and people stood by the roadside stretching from Independence Square all the way to the airport. The large timpani drums roared as the President and his family landed at Kotoka International Airport.

The newly elected president of Ghana, Professor Evans John Atta Mills, was amongst the distinguished crowd, which was waiting at the airport to welcome the holy brother into town. After the red carpet was laid, President Obama and his family were given a hero's welcome in Accra as the sun set. People cheered all over the city as the news of the President's arrival was shown live on Ghanaian TV.

The security was of the highest level that I have ever seen anywhere in my life. After touching the ground, President Obama was immediately taken to his secret residence, where he was permitted some peace to enjoy a rest before his extremely busy schedule the next day.

Chapter 22: Obama's Message to the African People

The doors pushed open and everyone stood to welcome the 44th President of the United States into the Ghana International Conference Centre. He was accompanied by a large entourage led by his host, Professor Evans Atta Mills. The trumpet blew catching the President's attention immediately. "I like this, thank you, thank you. I think Congress needs one of those horns," he said causing laughter in the chamber. "That sounds pretty good. Sounds like Louis Armstrong back there," he said and took to his stand in front of a fully packed Ghanaian legislature.

"Good morning. It is an honour for me to be in Accra, and to speak to the representatives of the people of Ghana. I am deeply grateful for the welcome that I've received, as are Michelle, Malia and Sasha Obama. Ghana's history is rich, the ties between our two countries are strong, and I am proud that this is my first visit to sub-Saharan Africa as President of the United States." There were loud and continued applause, forcing the President to pause for a few seconds.

"I want to thank Madam Speaker and all the members of the House of Representatives for hosting us today. I want to thank President Mills for his outstanding leadership. To the former Presidents, Jerry Rawlings, former President Kufuor, Vice President, Chief Justice, thanks to all of you for your extraordinary hospitality and the wonderful institutions that you've built here in Ghana."

"I'm speaking to you at the end of a long trip. I began in Russia for a summit between two great powers. I travelled to Italy for a meeting of the world's leading economies. And I've come here to Ghana for a simple reason: the twenty-first century will be shaped by what happens not just in Rome or Moscow or Washington, but by what happens in Accra, as well."

This is the simple truth of a time when the boundaries between people are overwhelmed by our connections. Your prosperity can expand America's prosperity. Your health and security can contribute to the world's health and security. And the strength of your democracy can help advance human rights for people everywhere.

So I do not see the countries and peoples of Africa as a world apart; I see Africa as a fundamental part of our interconnected world — as partners with America on behalf of the future we want for all of our children. That partnership must be grounded in mutual responsibility and mutual respect. And that is what I want to speak with you about today.

We must start from the simple premise that Africa's future is up to Africans.

I say this knowing full well the tragic past that has sometimes haunted this part of the world. After all, I have the blood of Africa within me, and my family's, my family's own story encompasses both the tragedies and triumphs of the larger African story.

My grandfather was a cook for the British in Kenya, and though he was a respected elder in his village, his employers called him "boy" for much of his life. He was on the periphery of Kenya's liberation struggles, but he was still imprisoned briefly during repressive times. In his life, colonialism wasn't simply the creation of unnatural borders or unfair terms of trade — it was something experienced personally, day after day, year after year.

My father grew up herding goats in a tiny village, an impossible distance away from the American universities where he would come to get an education. He came of age at a moment of extraordinary promise for Africa. The struggles of his own father's generation were giving birth to new nations, beginning right here in Ghana. Africans were educating and asserting themselves in new ways, and history was on the move.

But despite the progress that has been made – and there has been considerable progress in many parts of Africa – we also know that much of that promise has yet to be fulfilled. Countries like Kenya had a per capita economy larger than South Korea's when I was born. They have badly been outpaced. Disease and conflict have ravaged parts of the African continent. In many places, the hope of my father's generation gave way to cynicism, even despair.

It is easy to point fingers, and to pin the blame for these problems on others. Yes, a colonial map that made little sense bred conflict, and the West has often approached Africa as a patron, rather than a partner. But the West is not responsible for the destruction of the Zimbabwean economy over the last decade, or wars in which children are enlisted as combatants. In my father's life, it was partly tribalism and patronage in an independent Kenya that for a long stretch derailed his career, and we know that this kind of corruption is a daily fact of life for far too many.

Of course, we also know that is not the whole story. Here in Ghana, you show us a face of Africa that is too often overlooked by a world that sees only tragedy or the need for charity. The people of Ghana have worked hard to put democracy on a firmer footing, with peaceful transfers of power even in the wake of closely contested elections. And with improved governance and an emerging civil society, Ghana's economy has shown impressive rates of growth.

This progress may lack the drama of twentieth century liberation struggles, but make no mistake: it will ultimately be more significant. For just as it is important to emerge from the control of other nations, it is even more important to build one's own nation.

So I believe that this moment is just as promising for Ghana and for Africa as the moment when my father came of age and new nations were being born. This is a new moment of great promise. Only this time, we've learned that it will not be giants like Nkrumah and Kenyatta who will determine Africa's future. Instead, it will be you – the men and women in Ghana's parliament, and the people you represent. It will be the young people brimming with talent and energy and hope who can claim the future that so many in my father's generations never found." As I sat and wrote, the President took his time to highlight some of the reasons why the past 50 years of independence has in part been a failure. After carefully pointing out the past difficulties, President Obama turned his attention on the direction of the next 50 years in Africa.

"To realise that promise, we must first recognise the fundamental truth that you have given life to in Ghana, development depends on good governance. That is the ingredient that has been missing in far too many places, for far too long. That's the change that can unlock Africa's potential. And that is a responsibility that can only be met by Africans," he said and paused as the clapping continued.

"As for America and the West, our commitment must be measured by more than just the dollars we spend. I've pledged substantial increases in our foreign assistance, which is in Africa's interest and America's. But the true sign of success is not whether we are a source of perpetual aid that helps people scrape by – it's whether we are partners in building the capacity for transformational change.

This mutual responsibility must be the foundation of our partnership. And today, I'll focus on four areas that are critical to the future of Africa and the entire developing world: democracy, opportunity, health and the peaceful resolution of conflict."

After his excellent introduction, the noble president moved on to highlight the importance of good governance and how critical it is if we are serious about the fullest realisation of our own African Dream.

"First, we must support strong and sustainable democratic governments.

As I said in Cairo, each nation gives life to democracy in its own way, and in line with its own traditions. But history offers a clear verdict: governments that respect the will of their own people, govern by consent and not coercion, are more prosperous, they are more stable and more successful than governments that do not.

This is about more than just holding elections. It's also about what happens between elections. Repression can take many forms, and too many nations, even those that have elections, are plagued by problems that condemn their people to poverty. No country is going to create wealth if its leaders exploit the economy to enrich themselves - or if police can be bought off by drug traffickers. No business wants to invest in a place where the government skims 20 per cent off the top – or the head of the Port Authority is corrupt. No person wants to live in a society where the rule of law gives way to the rule of brutality and bribery. That is not democracy that is tyranny, and now is the time for it to end." There was a clear expression of genuine relaxation on Obama's face as he spoke deep down from the bottom of his heart.

"In the twenty-first century, capable, reliable, and transparent institutions are the key to success – strong parliaments, honest police forces, independent judges, an independent press, a vibrant private sector, a civil society. Those are the things that give life to democracy, because that is what matters in people's everyday lives.

Time and again, Ghanaians have chosen constitutional rule over autocracy, and shown a democratic spirit that allows the energy of your people to break through. We see that in leaders who accept defeat graciously – the fact that President Mills' opponents were standing beside him last night to greet me when I came off the plane spoke volumes about Ghana. We see victors who resist calls to wield power against the opposition in unfair ways. We see that spirit in courageous journalists like Anas Aremeyaw Anas, who risked his life to report the truth. We see it in police like Patience Quaye, who helped prosecute the first human trafficker in Ghana. We see it in the young people who are speaking up against patronage, and participating in the political process.

Across Africa, we have seen countless examples of people taking control of their destiny, and making change from the bottom up. We saw it in Kenya, where civil society and business came together to help stop post-election violence. We saw it in South Africa, where over three quarters of the country voted in the recent election – the fourth since the end of Apartheid. We saw it in Zimbabwe, where the Election Support Network braved brutal repression to stand up for the principle that a person's vote is their sacred right.

Now, make no mistake: history is on the side of these brave Africans, not with those who use coups or change constitutions to stay in power. Africa doesn't need strongmen, it needs strong institutions," Obama spoke pointing fingers at Mugabe and other dictators who want to be Presidents for life.

"America will not seek to impose any system of government on any other nation – the essential truth of democracy is that each nation determines its own destiny. What we will do is increase assistance for responsible individuals and institutions, with a focus on supporting good governance – on parliaments, which check abuses of power and ensure that opposition voices are heard; on the rule of law, which ensures the equal administration of justice; on civic participation, so that young people get involved; and on concrete solutions to corruption like forensic accounting, automating services, strengthening hotlines and protecting whistle-blowers to advance transparency and accountability.

As we provide this support, I have directed my Administration to give greater attention to corruption in our human rights report. People everywhere should have the right to start a business or get an education without paying a bribe. We have a responsibility to support those who act responsibly and to isolate those who don't, and that is exactly what America will do.

This leads directly to our second area of partnership – supporting development that provides opportunity for more people.

With better governance, I have no doubt that Africa holds the promise of a broader base for prosperity. The continent is rich in natural resources. And from cell phone entrepreneurs to small farmers, Africans have shown the capacity and commitment to create their own opportunities. But old habits must also be broken. Dependence on commodities – or on a single export – concentrates wealth in the hands of the few, and leaves people too vulnerable to downturns.

In Ghana, for instance, oil brings great opportunities, and you have been responsible in preparing for new revenue. But as so many Ghanaians know, oil cannot simply become the new cocoa. From South Korea to Singapore, history shows that countries thrive when they invest in their people and infrastructure; when they promote multiple export industries, develop a skilled workforce, and create space for small and medium-sized businesses that create jobs.

As Africans reach for this promise, America will be more responsible in extending our hand. By cutting costs that go to Western consultants and administration, we will put more resources in the hands of those who need it, while training people to do more for themselves. That is why our $3.5 billion food security initiative is focused on new methods and technologies for farmers – not simply sending American producers or goods to Africa. Aid is not an end in itself. The purpose of foreign assistance must be creating the conditions where it is no longer needed. I want to see Ghanaians not only self-sufficient in food, I want to see you exporting food to other countries and earning money. You can do that. America can also do more to promote trade and investment. Wealthy nations must open our doors to goods and services from Africa in a meaningful way. And where there is good governance, we can broaden prosperity through public–private partnerships that invest in better roads and electricity; capacity-building that trains people to grow a business; and financial services that reach poor and rural areas. This is also in our own interest – for if people are lifted out of poverty and wealth is created in Africa, new markets will open for our own goods.

One area that holds out both undeniable peril and extraordinary promise is energy. Africa gives off less greenhouse gas than any other part of the world, but it is the most threatened by climate change. A warming planet will spread disease, shrink water resources and deplete crops, creating conditions that produce more famine and more conflict. All of us – particularly the developed world – have a responsibility to slow these trends – through mitigation, and by changing the way that we use energy. But we can also work with Africans to turn this crisis into opportunity.

Together, we can partner on behalf of our planet and prosperity, and help countries increase access to power while skipping the dirtier phase of development. Across Africa, there is bountiful wind and solar power; geothermal energy and biofuels. From the Rift Valley to the North African deserts; from the Western coast to South Africa's crops – Africa's boundless natural gifts can generate its own power, while exporting profitable, clean energy abroad.

These steps are about more than growth numbers on a balance sheet. They're about whether a young person with an education can get a job that supports a family; a farmer can transfer their goods to market; an entrepreneur with a good idea can start a business. It's about the dignity of work; it's about the opportunity that must exist for Africans in the twenty-first century.

Just as governance is vital to opportunity, it's also critical to the third area I want to talk about: strengthening public health.

In recent years, enormous progress has been made in parts of Africa. Far more people are living productively with HIV/AIDS, and getting the drugs they need. I just saw a wonderful clinic and hospital that is focused particularly on maternal health. But too many still die from diseases that shouldn't kill them. When children are being killed because of a mosquito bite, and mothers are dying in childbirth, then we know that more progress must be made.

Yet because of incentives – often provided by donor nations – many African doctors and nurses go overseas, or work for programmes that focus on a single disease. And this creates gaps in primary care and basic prevention. Meanwhile, individual Africans also have to make responsible choices that prevent the spread of disease, while promoting public health in their communities and countries.

Across Africa, we see examples of people tackling these problems. In Nigeria, an interfaith effort of Christians and Muslims has set an example of cooperation to confront malaria. Here in Ghana and across Africa, we see innovative ideas for filling gaps in care - for instance, through e-Health initiatives that allow doctors in big cities to support those in small towns.

America will support these efforts through a comprehensive, global health strategy, because in the twenty-first century, we are called to act by our conscience but also by our common interest, because when a child dies of a preventable disease in Accra that diminishes us everywhere. And when disease goes unchecked in any corner of the world, we know that it can spread across oceans and continents.

That is why my Administration has committed $63 billion to meet these challenges. Building on the strong efforts of President Bush, we will carry forward the fight against HIV/AIDS. We will pursue the goal of ending deaths from malaria and tuberculosis, and eradicating polio. We will fight neglected tropical disease. And we won't confront illnesses in isolation – we will invest in public health systems that promote wellness, and focus on the health of mothers and children.

As we partner on behalf of a healthier future, we must also stop the destruction that comes not from illness, but from human beings – and so the final area that I will address is conflict.

Now let me be clear: Africa is not the crude caricature of a continent at perpetual war. But if we are honest, for far too many Africans, conflict is a part of life, as constant as the sun. There are wars over land and wars over resources. And it is still far too easy for those without conscience to manipulate whole communities into fighting among faiths and tribes.

These conflicts are a millstone around Africa's neck. Now, we all have many identities – of tribe and ethnicity; of religion and nationality. But defining oneself in opposition to someone who belongs to a different tribe, or who worships a different prophet, has no place in the twenty-first century. Africa's diversity should be a source of strength, not a cause for division. We are all God's children. We all share common aspirations – to live in peace and security; to access education and opportunity; to love our families and our communities and our faith. That is our common humanity.

That is why we must stand up to inhumanity in our midst. It is never justifiable to target innocents in the name of ideology. It is the death sentence of a society to force children to kill in wars. It is the ultimate mark of criminality and cowardice to condemn women to relentless and systemic rape. We must bear witness to the value of every child in Darfur and the dignity of every woman in the Congo. No faith or culture should condone the outrages against them. And all of us must strive for the peace and security necessary for progress.

Africans are standing up for this future. Here, too, in Ghana we are seeing you help point the way forward. Ghanaians should take pride in your contributions to peacekeeping from Congo to Liberia to Lebanon, and in your efforts to resist the scourge of the drug trade. We welcome the steps that are being taken by organizations like the African Union and ECOWAS to better resolve conflicts, to keep the peace, and support those in need. And we encourage the vision of a strong, regional security architecture that can bring effective, transnational forces to bear when needed.

America has a responsibility to work with you as a partner to advance this vision, not just with words, but with support that strengthens African capacity. When there's genocide in Darfur or terrorists in Somalia, these are not simply African problems – they are global security challenges, and they demand a global response. And that's why we stand ready to partner through diplomacy and technical assistance and logistical support, and we will stand behind efforts to hold war criminals accountable. And let me be clear: our Africa Command is focused not on establishing a foothold in the continent, but on confronting these common challenges to advance the security of America, Africa and the world.

In Moscow, I spoke of the need for an international system where the universal rights of human beings are respected, and violations of those rights are opposed. And that must include a commitment to support those who resolve conflicts peacefully, to sanction and stop those who don't, and to help those who have suffered. But ultimately, it will be vibrant democracies, like Botswana and Ghana, which roll back the causes of conflict and advance the frontiers of peace and prosperity.

As I said earlier, Africa's future is up to Africans.

The people of Africa are ready to claim that future. And in my country, African-Americans – including so many recent immigrants - have thrived in every sector of society. We've done so despite a difficult past, and we've drawn strength from our African heritage. With strong institutions and a strong will, I know that Africans can live their dreams in Nairobi and Lagos, Kigali, Kinshasa, Harare and right here in Accra.

You know, 52 years ago, the eyes of the world were on Ghana. And a young preacher named Martin Luther King travelled here, to Accra, to watch the Union Jack come down and the Ghanaian flag go up. This was before the march on Washington or the success of the civil rights movement in my country. Dr King was asked how he felt while watching the birth of a nation. And he said: 'It renews my conviction in the ultimate triumph of justice.'

Now, that triumph must be won once more, and it must be won by you. And I am particularly speaking to the young people. In places like Ghana, you make up over half of the population. Here is what you must know: the world will be what you make of it.

You have the power to hold your leaders accountable, and to build institutions that serve the people. You can serve in your communities, and harness your energy and education to create new wealth and build new connections to the world. You can conquer disease, and end conflicts, and make change from the bottom up. You can do that. Yes you can. Because in this moment, history is on the move.

But these things can only be done if all of you take responsibility for your future. And it won't be easy. It will take time and effort. There will be suffering and setbacks. But I can promise you this: America will be with you every step of the way – as a partner, as a friend. Opportunity won't come from any other place, though. It must come from the decisions that all of you make, the things that you do, the hope that you hold in your heart.

Ghana, freedom is your inheritance. Now, it is your responsibility to build upon freedom's foundation. And if you do, we will look back years from now to places like Accra and say this was the time when the promise was realized; this was the moment when prosperity was forged, pain was overcome, and a new era of progress began. This can be the time when we witness the triumph of justice once more. Yes we can. Thank you very much. God bless you. Thank you."

Everybody stood up clapping and cheering at the top of their voices. Tears dropped from some faces. There was a feeling of unity and greater hope, and a better sense of direction. Personally, I felt emotionally satisfied and mentally enriched and once more I could see the final stretch of the roadmap to Africa's Economic freedom. I also felt rejuvenated and energised about what can be achieved. The African Dream is alive and only we the people of Africa can stop ourselves from making progress. Through Obama's eyes, I saw a visible Africa with great landmarks, monuments and happy people sharing one love and common wealth as it should be.

"The work must start now," said one senior MP. "If we can work together to build and develop a good electricity supply, better roads with good schools and hospitals, the only difference between Africa and Europe would be the cold. We can achieve this status within the next 50 years. African Vision 2070," said the Minister of Foreign Affairs.

As Obama left the conference hall, we all continued to chant to the familiar phrase: "Yes, Africa, We Can." Accompanied by his host, Atta Mills, Obama looked remarkably relaxed and buoyant as many waved Ghanaian and American flags to show the new solidarity between Ghana and the United States. The President shook many people's hands spreading his last few words of wisdom and adding additional spice in his effort to spark a new word of mouth revolution in Africa.

The feeling for me was great and noble. I felt vindicated that my choice of Obama as the greatest connecting African salesman was correct.

Finally, the security men gently led the President away to the long black bullet-proof presidential ride; he was in a hurry to take his wife and their two daughters to visit the "door of no return" at Cape Coast Castle. The heaving crowds continued to scream and chant as they drove away, "Yes, Africa, we can!"

Chapter 23: Only God Knows!

"Obama Brother," called Sister Ama, "when are you going back to civilisation? Don't you see that it is time to go back to Glasgow? Look you," she said and stared at me from head to toe. This was one week after Obama had come to Ghana and delivered his message to the African people. "You have lost half of your weight since you came to Accra. You have to go back to Glasgow now before it is too late," Sister Ama spoke with an expression of grave concern on her face. And she was right, because after a whole year at home, I knew it was finally time to return to Glasgow to continue with normal life!

"You told me you came to write a book. Don't you have all the information you need yet? How long does it take to write a novel?" she asked teasingly. Sister Ama told me rumours have been spreading like wild bushfires about my situation at home. "The other day, your friend Razak came into this bar and said something about you which I am not happy about. You won't believe that Razak told me you have been deported from the UK. He said that is why you are back home suffering on the streets. According to Razak, you don't have the correct papers to go back to the UK. He even said he saw your passport. Others also think that you have lost your mind." That hot afternoon, I sat and sweated as Sister Ama went through the pain to tell me what "sources" were saying about my stranded conditions in Ghana.

It hurts to say that, although I believe in the sincerity of my mission at home, the actions and words and negative rumours by some people made me sometimes close to doubting the mere presence of God. Home was difficult and, by far, my worst encounter was yet to come!

"Challae, Ghana man, today I go come with u to Kokrobite. I get some serious talk," said Thunder. Mark and I were playing the xylophone at his shop front when Thunder arrived. On one or two previous occasions, he tried to follow me to Kokrobite, but I had managed to sneak away; that day was different. He sat and waited at Mark's shop until I was ready to leave the Art Centre.

When we got to Kokrobite that evening, it was around seven o'clock. Malam Yahaya opened the gate and whispered from behind. "Chief, today I no get any money to buy food. I beg, make you give me one Ghana to go and chop Banku right now. If I no eat for ten minutes, I go die," he said.

Malam Yahaya and his horse Sunday followed Thunder and me to the house. As I stood and spoke to him by the door, Thunder was anxious to enter the room. "I beg I go lie down small, I no day feel well," he said. I gave Thunder a sleeping mattress and went out to talk to Malam Yahaya, who was desperate to share some gossip with me.

"The landlord im wife came here today. He say the grass be too long for the yard. Don't worry, tomorrow, I go weed here all," he said and pointed his hand towards a group of pawpaw trees. The perfectly lit half moon took over the sky as the last shadows of the daylight receded to give way. Malam Yahaya collected some money and left the yard. I returned to my room but Thunder was already asleep. I took the bench and sat outside with a candle. I listened to BBC World Service for some time before dozing away.

It was Malam Yahaya who returned after his food to wake me up.

"Chief, I see your friend outside."

"Which friend?" I asked.

"The one you bring today. I see am, iday go Ocean Terminal."

"I thought Thunder was not well," I said and stood off my bench to check the room. It wasn't until then that I realised I must have had a deep sleep myself. It was already half nine.

Malam Yahaya and I followed each other to the beach side Ocean Terminal bar. But Thunder was not inside the local bar. "Yes, one big Frenchman came here and collected two tots of Opiemu, he was only here for two minutes," said the bar lady.

We proceeded to Big Milly's Backyard, the most popular beachside resort in Kokrobite, and probably the whole of Ghana. There was a cultural show on with a drumming group and some acrobats. There were two tall young men standing by the gates to collect entry fee.

Inside Big Milly's we shoved through the crowed for sometime before locating Thunder at the bar. He had finished his second two shots of Opiemu.

"I thought you were not well?"

"Ibe the Drink way i make better. Now iday feel hunger!" he said. We left Big Milly's and returned to the yard around a quarter to 11. By then, the moon was so bright I could see the ocean from the hill of the compound.

"I beg, I go eat something. If I no eat, I no go fit sleep tonight."

"I have got rice but the charcoal is finished."

"Make I get some wood for you," said Malam Yahaya. There was a little rain earlier in the evening, so all the wood we gathered in the yard was wet. We lit the fire but we could barely keep the flame going. After a lot of hard work, we almost gave up, but the rice was still only half cooked. With the hunger we persevered until the rest of the fire died away.

"This rice is not cook at all," I complained as we gathered to share the same bowl. After we finished eating, I ran down to the beach to get some fresh air. When I returned from the sea, Malam Yahaya had gone to his bed but Thunder was lying on the bench outside.

"I no go fit sleep. My stomach is full, I can't breathe. Iday like they put stone inside my stomach." Thunder spoke and complained about the rice we ate.

That night, I never slept a wink. Thunder kept me awake and his condition worsened as dawn approached. The next morning,

Malam Yahaya left the yard early to go to Labadi beach, where he offers weekend horse-riding lessons to beach lovers. Around 8 a.m., Thunder began to vomit and shake.

And that was it. I knew I had to act. But there was only so much I could do. I had 40 Ghana Cedis, the equivalent of 18 British pounds. I left the compound and rushed up to Kokrobite station to get a taxi. It took me about 20 minutes to get one. When I got back to the yard, Thunder was lying flat on the ground like a frozen corpse. My heart jumped as I kneeled to check his pulse. There was no sign of life.

"Let me try and blow some air into his nostrils, maybe he is just fainted." Kofi, the taxi driver, spoke and joined me to administer a few desperate attempts to bring life back to the lifeless body. After a few failed attempts at resuscitation, we gave up and decided to rush to the hospital. I held Thunder under his shoulders and Kofi took his legs to carry him into the taxi. As we drove along, I sat beside him on the backseat and checked his pulse.

When we got to the Kokrobite clinic, Thunder was rushed to a bed. "Fortunately, he is still alive, but his condition is very desperate," the duty nurse came out of the emergency theatre and gave me the news. I sighed with relief. "We may need to take him to Kole-bu," she said referring to the main teaching hospital in Accra.

Another nurse called me to whisper some words. "Sir, I need you to come to the reception and pay admission fee."

"How much is the admission fee?"

"It is eighteen Ghana Cedis but you need to pay for the drips and medical examination. That is another fifteen Ghana," she said. My heart pumped. I had already spent five Ghana Cedis on the taxi, so it meant that I had only two Ghana Cedis left out of my last 40 Ghana Cedis.

After paying the initial fees, the nurses at Kokrobite clinic gave Thunder a saline drip and battled to bring his life back in the treatment room. I was left in the waiting room, which got too warm for me. I felt restless and paced around the corridor unable to contemplate what would come next.

"Unfortunately, our worst suspicions have been confirmed. Your friend indeed has malaria A-plus. It is only Kole-bu that will save his life," Sister Grace advised. By this point, it was past midday.

I told the nurses that I had to go to town to look for money to borrow before I could take Thunder to Accra, which is an hour and half drive from Kokrobite.

I left the clinic and walked on the dusty road back to the yard. I felt frustrated: where would I get money to take Thunder to the hospital? All the people I knew and trusted well enough in Kokrobite were poorer than me. I knew that there was very little room to manoeuvre.

When I got to my room, I searched all my clothes to see if I might have kept and forgotten any money. I knew that was impossible, but faith still encouraged me to try. Lo and behold, I found a Scottish 20 pound note in my bag, which I was unable to change into Cedis when I first got home.

I took the note and rushed to Big Milly's hoping to see if the English owners may be considerate enough to change it for me.

"Mr Brian is the one who could change it for you, but he has gone to town to buy some drinks for the bar. He will be back about 4 p.m.," said one of the waiters at Big Milly's as he carried some dishes to the kitchen. I stood under the tall coconut tree and wondered for a brief moment if there really was a God.

I left Big Milly's and walked along the beach: praying for God to prove to me that he really listened to my prayers. The Kokrobite clinic shuts at 4 p.m., so I needed money to go and take Thunder or else? I couldn't bear to think of the consequences.

I walked up and down the beach and prayed hard and long before returning to see if by any miraculous means Mr Brian had returned from Accra. He had not, so I left in despair to go back to the yard. I met a friend on the way, his name is Jah Knows. Unfortunately, Jah Knows did not have any money, but he said something that immediately raised my temperature.

"I saw two guys entering your yard, I'm sure they were looking for you," he said and carried his guitar towards the beach.

"I am going to do some busking. If I get any money, I will come back and give you some," he promised and walked the opposite direction. Luckily, it was my two brothers, Babs and Muzay.

"We came here almost an hour ago. Sorry, we didn't manage to come as promised three days ago." Babs spoke first.

"Bro, you look worried, what is wrong today?" Muzay asked.

"I am not only worried but I am also relieved. I feel my prayers have been fully answered by your timely arrival." I told Babs and Muzay about Thunder and without delay, we rushed back to the clinic. From Kokrobite clinic, we took a taxi and carried Thunder to Kole-bu where a brand new chapter began.

In all, I spent four long days and nights with Thunder and, in the end, his condition deteriorated to the point where I could only grasp hard onto a slim hope. My experience at the Kole-bu hospital increased my determination to continue to seek for a better future for Africa. Every night I slept on half a bench and watched more patients trouping in and out. One night, a lady was brought in a taxi, but the hospital did not admit her because they hard no beds to offer. It didn't help that the lady had no money of her own to grease some palms. The taxi driver did his absolute best to persuade the doctors to treat her but, unfortunately, she died half an hour later from excessive bleeding. I was raging because she was never even allowed out of the taxi. How could any system fail so many of the same people it is there to serve?

Anyway, Thunder grew lean to the bone but his stomach continued to swell even bigger. I began to doubt whether he was suffering from malaria or something else entirely different. I prayed and prayed for God to come to the rescue.

"Ghana man, I beg, makes you smuggle me out of this place today. If I sleep here tonight, I go die, I swear to God," he said in a faint painful voice. "Iday suspect say Ibe my father do this to me. If I don't go to Benin, I no go survive," he said. There was one particular doctor Thunder hated from the onset. "That man, no be doctor, Ibe witch. This tube he put for my penis, i be im go kill me now," he said referring to the catheter which had drained his urine since we arrived.

Babs and Muzay arrived to visit after work and I followed them to say goodbye. When I got back into the ward, there was huge pandemonium.

"You can't just leave the hospital like this? Look at you. You will never make it home," said Josephine, the ward sister.

"This doctor, ibe witch, if I stay here tonight, igo kill me. If I go die, i no be this doctor way igo kill me," he said. He wore only his pants. I tried to persuade Thunder to return to his hospital bed but he was not having any of it!

After leaving Kole-bu, I retuned Thunder to his little stall at the Art Centre. That night, the rain fell heavily forcing us to leave Thunder's leaking hut. I begged the shop next door to put us up. His place was secure. I laid Thunder on a mat and curled myself on a bench. It was one of the worse nights in Ghana.

The next morning, everyone gathered and shook their heads.

"No, this Benin man is dead and alive!" said one observer.

"Ghana man, I beg you need to take me to Benin. If I don't reach home by tomorrow, I no go live again, I go die." As more people gathered, I went to the top side to get some money from Brother Shaibu and see how to manage the situation.

When Shaibu and I returned to Thunder's stall, there were more than 30 people gathered in front of him to witness his confession.

"Ibe five days ago, I follow that man to Kokrobite."

"When did you start being ill?" asked one fat lady. I recognised her from the last time I visited Thunder's shop.

"Whoever took you to Kokrobite must have poisoned you. What did he do to you? Look at your stomach. Tell me what happened. If you don't say the truth, we will leave you to die here," said the fat lady.

"He cooked some rice for me but I don't know what he put inside the rice. I sure say ibe the rice way iday kill me. Since that day, my stomach ibe full. I don't know why." Thunder spoke lying on a small mat and waving his hands in despair.

"These northerners are very dangerous. He is the one who poisoned you. I know a juju man in Mamobi, he is very powerful. I will take you to his place right now; he will punish the one who gave you the poison to eat. Don't worry, this Sissala man will be forced to confess by tomorrow morning!"

"Thunder, are you telling everybody in the Art Centre that I have poisoned you after all the pain I have put myself through to save your life?" I asked feeling completely betrayed. It was this point, I almost doubted God.

"Challae, there is no need to feel betrayed by this ungrateful carpenter," said Shaibu. "My brother, forget this Benin man, he has disappointed me pa-pa with his Judas behaviour!" Shaibu spoke angrily as we walked away from the drama scene.

Many other things happened during my visit home, and I have countless reasons to feel angry or sad about all the difficult problems that I faced. But, at the end of the day, I have had one of the best life experiences: the chance of relating to fellow human beings in a completely different way. My journey home taught me many, many good lessons of life including patience and perseverance.

Finally, I agreed with Sister Ama that it was time I returned to the UK. In fact, a few days later, I went to the travel agents and booked my ticket. The rest of my time vanished in a blink.

On the day I left Accra, my Brother Shaibu threw a surprise farewell party for me at the Airport Bar. Like many others, including Mark, James, Babs, Muzay, Nuhu, Osman and Ababa, Brother Shaibu helped me a great deal during my trip home. He took me almost everywhere I went, so he knew most of the people who cared to say goodbye to me at the end of a tough visit. The people Brother Shaibu invited to the airport bar included Alhaji Sokoto and a few guys from his shop, Sister Ama, Professor Yoho, Mr Kanton, Mami Dakunu from the Makola market, Professor Wisdom, Sister Adisa and Pastor Kofi. The biggest surprise for me was my teacher, Moses, who had travelled to the north but managed to return in time to join us at the bar to say goodbye.

After enjoying some refreshments together, we moved to the terminal building where we continued a lively but extremely emotional conversation until I had to leave.

"Will all passengers travelling with British Airways from Accra to London proceed immediately to the departure gate, please," a lady called from the loud speakers.

"Departure gate is this way," said one humongous man. The security man followed me towards the departure gate to collect his tip! I tried to be brave and hard, hiding my emotion, but deep inside my soul, I felt a sharp severe pain. I also felt relieved to be going back to see my dearest and most loved ones in the UK. It was truly a magical ending to the hardest journey of life. After taking a few steps forward, I paused and looked back; all my friends were still waving and waving and waving as I continued. My Brother Shaibu looked as if he was wiping some tears. I waved one final time before entering Customs and Immigration clearance. Eventually, I joined the boarding queue and followed the rest of the passengers outside. "British Airways," I read approaching the giant flying monster in front of me. It had the Union Jack colours on it. I stopped briefly to say a little prayer. Before I stepped onto the aeroplane, I asked myself one last difficult question: has this trip been worth the sacrifice, the pain and discomfort I put myself and my family through? Only God knows!

Chapter 24: Master of the Universe

After flying back to Glasgow in late July 2009, it took me several days, weeks and many months to fully reflect and recover from my trip home. I asked myself time and time again, had my trip been worth it for me, my family and the Africa I love so much and wish to rescue from the perpetual economic dustbin? Without any immediate magic bullet to unleash yet, I prayed every single day. I prayed in the morning and in the evening that one day, every African child will be able to live and grow up happily in peace and harmony with the right opportunities to fulfil their dreams and aspirations of life.

One evening, as I sat on my living room couch with my laptop on my knees, a live programme on TV caught my eye. It was the BBC Children in Need programme. My eyebrows rose as the clock clicked past midnight and the BBC announced that the viewing public in Great Britain had raised a staggering £14 million towards projects that are supporting vulnerable children in the UK.

As I sat and watched the TV, I began to reflect on the story of 2010. What a remarkable year it has been, especially for Africa. I thought to myself, if only the people of Africa can learn one BIG lesson from the year 2010, we can kick off a real African Revolution from 2011 onwards without any doubt of our ability to do so.

So, I can see your curious mind wondering, why should we celebrate the year 2010 as a year of successful beginning in Africa? And what important lesson can we learn from Africa 2010?

To get some answers, I left Glasgow one cold snowy day and travelled by train to Edinburgh to talk to my good friend Juliette, a Nigerian banker in Edinburgh. We met at a coffee shop on Lothian Road, near her office. I began the chat by asking Juliette to give me only one reason why she thinks the people of Africa should feel proud about our continent's achievements in 2010.

"Mr Achebe," she called, mixing my name as usual with the famous Nigerian writer, Chunua Achebe-Things Fall Apart. "In my personal opinion, the best news for Africa in 2010 is the story of William and Kate. William could have chosen to take Kate to the moon and propose to her, but he chose Africa," she said. My friend Juliette told me that although the wedding of Prince William to Katherine may seem unrelated to Africa; in fact, this wedding has a lot to teach the people of Africa about how to feel proud of our own continent. I sat quiet, thinking cynically to myself: why must the people of Africa feel proud about a royal affair in Buckingham Palace? What has this got to do with African development?

"Don't forget that Prince William became engaged in Kenya," Juliette said, reminding me of the fact that this important engagement was made at an exclusive resort in what has been described by the British media as one of the most beautiful places in the world. As we ordered our coffee, Juliette gave me the Daily Mail newspaper, which had a big article about the royal wedding with a glamorous photo of William and Kate on the front page.

According to the article, Prince William asked his long-term girlfriend to marry him in an isolated log cabin without electricity miles from the beaten track: "Surrounded by elephant, hyena, buffalo and leopard." The article explained that, Prince William has been so duly touched by the warmth and tranquillity of the Kenyan environment that he now regards Africa as his second home and a place where he feels safe without the pressure or the unnecessary glitz of the harassing world media.

After scanning through the article, I turned my attention again to Sister Juliette. "Prince William is my African Brother. I pray for William to have a very successful marriage with Kate. I pray that God will honour his marriage and bless him with a daughter to remind him of his mother, amen," Sister Juliette prayed wholeheartedly before standing up to put on her long black leather coat. "I need to rush back to the office. I have a meeting at half two," she spoke as we left.

I caught the train from Waverly Station. Inside the train I asked myself, why did the most famous prince in the world choose Africa as the most romantic place to propose to his beautiful bride? In the end, I completely agreed with Juliette that this news is definitely worthy of celebration in Africa. After all, there are millions of exotic and highly expensive places a future British king could have chosen to propose to his bride, but Prince William was convinced in his heart that there was no place on earth like Africa to propose to Kate!

So, from Buckingham Palace to Soccer City Stadium in Johannesburg, the people of Africa have plenty of good reasons to stand up together and feel proud of our continent. In July 2010, South Africa became the first African country to host the FIFA World Football Tournament. Personally, I regard this as Africa's greatest achievement since Ghana gained independence from British colonial rule in 1957. The World Cup, which is regarded as the best festival of sports in the world, was a tremendous success by all measures of accounts. Who can ever forget the vuvuzelas, which roared like billions of bees during each match, especially in the Soccer City Stadium in Johannesburg?

Sadly, the beginning of the tournament was marred by emotions as Mandela, the father of the Rainbow Nation, was unable to attend the opening ceremony due to the passing of his favourite great granddaughter, Zenani Mandela. She was killed in a car crashed on the way home from the World Cup opening concert. Zenani was only 14, may her humble soul rest in peace.

After reflecting through the moment of loss and sadness, the great Rainbow Nation and her people raised their shoulders high to show the whole world that Africa can deliver great success in the twenty-first century. During the rest of the tournament, our hopes of lifting the World Cup on home soil faded away after Cameroon, Nigeria,

Ivory Coast and the host nation were all blown apart at the knockout stages.

The famous Black Stars of Ghana were the last hope for the 1.5 billion African people around the world. Unfortunately, Africa's hopes were shattered during the quarter finals after Louis Suarez used both hands to block a powerful shot from getting into the Uruguay goal in the dying minutes of the game. The darling boy of Ghana and top goal scorer of the Black Stars, Asamoah Gyan was the man who edged forward to take the given penalty. He stepped forward gently in his bright red Ghanaian strip with the ball in his hand. There was a little gesture of hesitation and an expression of disbelief on his face.

I sat and closed my eyes on the couch, unable to watch. The whole world watched in their billions as the boy edged forward, holding tight onto his breaking nerves towards the penalty spot. He took a few quick steps and blasted the ball. Everybody watched on thorns as it curled towards the goalkeeper.

In total disbelief, the prayers of the whole African Nation came to vain when Asamoah's roaring shot hit the top left pole, only missing the net by a narrow margin.

It was all over for Ghana and Africa after that game. Spain, which had a flawless tournament, went on to win the 2010 World Cup for the first time in their history – Viva to the Spanish and thumbs up with maximum respect to all the people of the Rainbow Nation, you have done Africa proud!

The question now is: what lesson can we the people of Africa learn from the success of the "Rainbow Nation"? Fortunately, I travelled to Sheffield for a workshop and later I managed to catch up with my Jamaican friend, Dr Anthony Brown, a distinguished Jamaican philosopher and leading Pan-African academic. Although Anthony is Jamaican by birth, he is a true African in his spirit and ways of life. Over 20 years ago, he traced his own original roots back to homeland Ghana, hence the reason why he now officially calls

Ghana his second country. When I met Dr Anthony in Sheffield University, I began by asking if he had any idea why South Africa 2010 was such a huge unexpected success.

"First, I want to take this opportunity to congratulate the Bafana, Bafana for raising the flag of Africa so high in 2010. I believe the tremendous success of the World Cup in South Africa was due to the spirit of national unity." Dr Brown said the success of South Africa 2010 goes a long way to prove that when a nation and its people believe in themselves, what they can achieve has no impossible boundaries. "Crime alone could have crippled or tarnished the image of the 2010 tournament. Yet, everything went so smoothly. The question we have to ask is, why has South Africa done so well against all the odds?" Dr Brown said that since the end of apartheid in 1994, the people of South Africa have worked tremendously hard together to create a modern, vibrant nation with many great diverse people and cultures. He stressed that although there is still an uneasy relationship between white and black South Africans, the people of South Africa have shown their resilient ability to bury their differences and work together when it matters to every South African.

"Let me tell you something which has been generally misunderstood by millions of people around the world. Most people, for example, think that there was zero crime during the tournament because of the simple fact that there was good security. Don't get me wrong, my brother, the security arrangements at the games were impeccable, but still, if organised criminal gangs were determined to go on duty and carry out their hideous crimes, no amount of police in Johannesburg or Cape Town could have stopped their action."

Mr Brown explained that there was a unifying spirit of national patriotism about the whole tournament. As a result, there were street committees, and town committees, which worked hard at every level of community to prevent local crime during the World

Cup. "Even the criminals became vigilante volunteers because they were proud of their nations dream to host the best World Cup."

Finally, I asked my Jamaican/Ghanaian brother what he thinks are the key lessons to learn from the success of South Africa 2010 from a pan-African academic perspective.

"There are two important lessons to learn from the 2010 World Cup: the first lesson is for all the people of Africa but the second and most critical lesson is for the people of the Rainbow Nation." I sat and listened, drinking my pint of orange juice. Dr Anthony was on Stella! "The lesson for Africa is that a long time ago, we lived in Darkness, but now we can see the Light. South Africa 2010 shows that Africa is no longer a feeble continent which is suffering from impotence and incontinence." I asked Dr Brown what he thinks the people of Africa can do, now that we see the light at the end of the dark tunnel.

"After South Africa 2010, what we need now is a Nigerian Olympics." Dr Brown said insisting that a Nigerian Olympics would be the greatest African achievement and the final indication of our economic independence! "An African Olympics will dramatically boost the confidence of our youth in the twenty-first century." I asked Dr Brown to explain what he believes to be the key lesson for South Africa, the host nation.

"The 2010 tournament showed the world how prosperous and economically developed South Africa is today. Those who watched the games have seen the streets of Johannesburg to be just as great as any other city in Europe or America. The ugly truth behind the scenes is that, the vast majority of South African people have little access to clean water, good health services or proper education." My brother Anthony told me that disease, hunger and malnutrition are just a few examples of the daily hardships faced by far too many South Africans.

"South Africa is the richest country in our continent and one of the top ten industrialised nations of the world, yet 90 per cent of the indigenous population are living in poverty. This is very bad and extremely dangerous!" I asked Dr Brown why there is such a huge disparity between the rich and the poor in South Africa.

"It is because of systematic racism and economic discrimination against the indigenous population. It is sad that although political apartheid has been abolished since 1994, economic apartheid continues to divide and rule South Africa in many ways." Dr Brown told me that, in his view, the people of South Africa, both white and black must wake up to the truth that racism and negative tribalism has no proper function to play in the modern world. "It doesn't matter if you are black, white, brown or yellow, you should be able to become a president, judge, government minister, police, soldier, banker or a South African doctor based on your skills, intellect, experiences, ideas and the content of your character and not because of your pigment!"

Dr Brown warned the new generations of Africans against complacency and ignorance. "Negative tribalism and racism are not only dangerous for South Africa but the whole world. What is extremely sad and deeply disturbing is that, although racism is banned in Europe, America and every other continent of the world, racism against the black man is still alive, widely practiced and tolerated in Africa. As a man of African heritage, I see my colour and my status as a symbol of pride and a rich addition to the wider global heritage; not a sign of my weakness as my ancestor may have been led to believe."

In my opinion, every human being in this world has a good reason to feel proud of whom they are. This is why we must find enough courage to stand up together and say a BIG, BIG NO to racism in every corner of the world. We must show racism the red card because racism destroys people and societies. Hitler tried it with the blue-eyed pure master race agenda against the Jews and it led the world to a bitter war."

My Jamaican brother warned that racism and negative tribalism are both based on foolishness, narrow mindedness, ignorance and the fear of nothingness. "No man has any divine justification to feel superior over another man simply because of his race, culture or his ethnicity. Believe me my brother; God has not chosen any single race or tribe above the other. We are all children of God. So, every single human being you see in the world today is a master of his or her own diverse universe!"

Chapter 25: Global Flu of Injustice

"Chief, this place is busy," Sam said and clapped his hand. He carried a large djembe drum in a green bag strapped onto his broad shoulders. That day, Sam and I were invited to perform at a Fair Trade event in the Royal Concert Hall. This annual global farmer and ethical consumer fair is held in Glasgow to celebrate the benefits of fair trade to the world.

There were many people and stalls all exhibiting, selling and buying fair trade products from poor countries around the world.

"Chief, don't you see that there is a problem here?" Sam asked as I spotted the organiser from the other side of the hall.

"What is the problem?" I asked.

"This place is so busy with people. But, there are no Africans, apart from us and those two people over there," he said and pointed his hand towards the stage. "There are many Africans in Glasgow and fair trade is supposed to help African farmers. Why are our people not coming out in large numbers to attend and support this important event? Africans are always busy blaming the white man but I don't think it is because of the white man we are poor. Most of my Scottish friends will do anything they can to help Africa but my own African brothers in Edinburgh do not care. Anytime there is a charity event to help Africa, only Scottish people attend. How can we expect others to continue helping Africa when we the people of Africa don't care or do anything to help the situation at home?"

"Maybe the Africans in Glasgow are busy," I replied.

"Busy doing what, nothing?" Sam argued that sometimes we Africans are our own worst enemies because, where we can stand up and act to make a difference, we often choose to play the role of passive participants and dormant contributors. "We sit and wait until it is too late and then we start to moan and complain about what should have been done better."

There were two farmers from Africa at the event: a woman from Malawi and a coffee farmer from Uganda. They both spoke on stage explaining how fair trade has been helping farmers in their countries. There was a Chilean beekeeper whose speech inspired me the most about the impact of fair trade on developing countries.

"There is a global flu of injustice which is killing millions of innocent people around the world, and fair trade is the only solution we have to fight this disease," said Federico, the beekeeper. Federico argued that the current global flu of economic and social injustice is universal because it affects 80 per cent of the world population in different ways. "This injustice against the masses relates to the unequal distribution of the wealth of nations and our combined global cake! Right now, the people of Europe are facing austerity cuts in their living standards because; the 20 per cent of the people who control the world resources are growing greedier every day. This powerful 20 per cent privileged class are extremely strong, dedicated and determined to control the 80 per cent of the global cake to which we are all entitled to a fair and decent share. This imbalance is what I personally describe as the global flu of injustice!"

Federico said that a classic example of this kind of injustice is what led to the near collapse of the world economy in 2008, when the callous conduct of a canny few so called smart investment bankers in London and New York almost brought the whole world to its knees. He argued that since 2008, almost every European country has faced drastic cuts in public services with cost of food, petrol and other essential goods and services going up almost on a daily basis. Meanwhile, the same casino bankers who brought the world to the brink of financial doom are back again on track, paying themselves billions of pounds of annual bonuses for their so called hard work!

"Fair trade gives hope to many poor farmers around the world and hope is the foundation of life when people are going through despair," he said adding that when the fair trade movement began over three decades ago, fair trade coffee tasted horrible. But today, fair trade products are associated with high standards of quality.

The Chilean beekeeper finished by throwing a question to his Glaswegian audience: "What do you think our world produces the most of every year?" he asked.

"Copper," one man shouted from the audience. "Cars," said another. A few other people gave different answers but the Chilean beekeeper disputed all the answer they threw at him. "I am afraid to say that your answers are all wrong."

"What is the answer?" a voice shouted from the audience who were all sitting on long rows of blue chairs facing the stage.

"As a matter of fact, this world produces more destitute people a year than any other commodity you can think of and this is the injustice we have to fight against. In my view, fair trade is the greatest weapon and the best tool we have to overturn trade injustice in our world. I believe that fair trade is the most powerful way of addressing the imbalance of trade between the hardworking poor and the ruthless middlemen who stand between you the consumers and me the farmer."

After listening to the various speakers, Sam and I decided to take a little tour to sample the different stalls and speak to some of the people who are working so hard to bring justice to the common people of the world.

"The flavour of Africa," I read the sign above the head of one stallholder. I approached to speak to her, but she was busy trying to sell some sun-dried mangoes to a customer. I moved on to the next stall "Rainbow Turtle"; I asked the lady if she had a shop or whether she only sells at fairs and festivals.

"We have a shop at Paisley," she said.

I moved on to a group of people selling fair-trade soap from Palestine and from there, I moved to the Co-op stand which offered many free samples of chocolate from Ghana, coffee from Kenya and some fair trade wine from South Africa and Mexico. Sam went on his own way, but eventually caught up with me.

Finally, we got to one stall, which had nothing to sell, but plenty of information to offer. "Share International" I read the sign approaching two gentlemen sitting in front of a table with plenty of pamphlets and leaflets about how to save the world.

"Good afternoon gentlemen," I greeted. "Can you please tell me more about your organisation, what is it we have to share?" I asked.

"The food of the world is what we have to share to save the world! We need to share food fairly to stop millions of people from dying every single year," said one of the reps. "Food insecurity is the biggest injustice of the world."

So, how can we solve this flu of injustice and who does it affect?

"Have you ever heard of the name Maitreya?"

"No, who is Maitreya?" I asked.

"Maitreya is the global teacher, the final redeemer of the world." The two gentlemen at the stall took turns and spoke passionately about the master teacher they believe has come to save the world from the sins of self-destruction. Sam and I stood and listened.

"All the great religions on earth posit the idea of a further revelation of a teacher. Christians hope for the return of Christ, we Buddhists look for Maitreya, whilst the Muslim awaits Imam Mahdi, the Hindus await a reincarnation of Krishna, and the Jews, the Messiah," the taller of the two gentlemen read from a pamphlet in his hand. "Maitreya, the final teacher, is already appearing at several places in the world to show people the light."

"On the 11 June 1988, Maitreya appeared miraculously out of the blue at a prayer camp in Nairobi, Kenya. He was photographed addressing (in their own language) thousands of people who instantly recognised him as the Christ." According to the followers of Maitreya, the above event in Kenya was photographed and reported by major media outlets around the world including CNN.

"Chief, what those guys were saying is true," Sam spoke as we went away to prepare to go on stage. "The Bible tells us that before the end of time, kingdoms will fight against kingdoms, nations against nations, man against woman, fathers against mothers; brothers against sisters and children against parents. Don't you think that all these are already happening everywhere in the world today?"

"So, what is causing kingdoms and nations to fight against one another?"

"It is because of money," he said. "Money controls the world and people will do anything nowadays to make money. A son will kill his father because of money today and a woman will cheat on her husband because of money. Governments are lying and cheating their citizens because of money and citizens are fighting and killing fellow citizens because of money."

"So, how can we save the world from all the doom and gloom?"

"Enlightenment!" Sam exclaimed. "If you believe there is a global injustice like Federico said, then, it is only through the spirit of enlightenment that we can see the light and overcome the problems of injustice in the world!"

Chapter 26: Power to the People

In 1979, President Sadat of Egypt was killed after bravely signing an important peace agreement between Israel and the Arab League of Nations in the Middle East. Following Sadat's assassination, Mubarak who was his closest friend took over and ruled Egypt for the next 30 years until calamity broke out on the streets of Cairo.

Hosni Mubarak was born in 1948. After growing up in a noble environment, he joined the Egyptian army at the age of 18 and spent almost two decades as a hard-working loyal soldier before he was duly promoted to the rank of Air Martial – the master general in charge of Egypt's supreme Air Force.

After taking power from Sadat, Mubarak signed a peace treaty with Israel. Initially, this move isolated Mubarak from his Arab neighbours. The Arab league grumpily suspended Egypt from its tribal council. They even moved the headquarters of the Council from Cairo to Tunis.

Mubarak worked hard to bring Egypt back to the heart of the Middle East affairs.

At the domestic level, Mubarak soon established himself as the only invincible man in Egypt. From liberal autocracy to iron fist, brutal dictatorship, the people of Egypt lived under constant fear of prosecution by the secret police. As time went by, many young Egyptians began to feel disenchanted with Mubarak's regime, especially among student groups.

On one hot December afternoon, Abdul was returning from lectures when his friend told him something he struggled to believe.

"Salama-a lake," Mohammed greeted in Arabic before breaking the news. "Ben Ali has fled from Tunisia today. He has been overthrown by a revolution." Ben Ali was like the Mubarak of Tunisia: he imprisoned and sometimes killed people who spoke against him. Mohammed was shocked that ordinary young unemployed Tunisians were able to get rid of their dictator. "They said he fled to Riyadh with his family, I wish we could do the same here in Egypt. But Mubarak is too dangerous!" Mohammed warned and continued on to his IT lecture.

Abdul rushed to his flat to watch the breaking news. Unfortunately, the Egyptian Government fearful of what was going on in neighbouring Tunisia panicked and decided to block foreign news on all Egyptian television stations. Abdul got angry and left his flat. He rushed to the Cairo University library to check the news on the web but all internet access was blocked that day as well.

Feeling more angry and disappointed, Abdul left the University library and return to his flat to prepare for the next lesson. Later on, Abdul washed to go for Maghreb. On his way to the mosque, he saw a group of students gossiping about the news of Ben Ali. The people he saw were part of a secret protest group, which were already planning a student demonstration in Cairo city centre a few days from then.

The danger is real. During the last student rally, many of Abdul's friends were beaten and some of them were removed from university and sentenced to jail for treason against their own country, a country which they loved so much and wished to change with such desperation.

"We need democracy in Egypt. We are fed up with dictatorship," said one frustrated student.

"What should we do now? We have to take action against Mubarak before it is too late," Abdul spoke passionately in front of his friends.

"I hate Mubarak and his government because they don't listen to anybody in Egypt. He only listens to the Americans and the Israelis. This is the time for change." Abdul and his friends spoke along the way to the mosque, venting their unbearable frustrations.

A day after Ben Ali was stripped of power, something dramatic happened in the mid-afternoon, which changed Egypt's history. It was the burning of Hassan, a market trader who poured kerosene on his own clothes and set himself ablaze in Tahrir Square. Hassan burnt himself to death in protest against the brutal police action to demolish his shop and take away his livelihood.

"I can't believe it, see the video," Abdul said and showed the clip of Hassan's burning body to his friends.

"We cannot let Mubarak get away with murder anymore. This nation has to change, Allahu-akbar," he prayed.

"Allahu-akbar," the rest replied.

Abdul and his friends set out to unleash a new social network campaign to oust the President for his brutality against innocent people. Fortunately, they each had plenty of contacts. Mohammed alone had over 500 contacts on Facebook.

"Mubarak must pay the full price for Hassan's life." They all agreed. On the first night of their campaign, there were shockwaves at every university campus across the whole of Egypt. The students who received the call to assemble at Tahrir Square on Friday, passed the message to their own contacts. It was just like what happened with Paul Revere and his midnight horse ride that ignited the American Revolution in 1775.

Abdul and his friends ensured that their mouse-click epidemic spread so fast that they managed to gain the crucial attention of a critical mass almost overnight. Every young Egyptian who saw the image of Hassan's burnt body grew angry and supported the move for immediate and unconditional democratic change.

"Mubarak must go. Nothing more nothing less," read one campaign slogan.

Like every word of mouth revolution, the 11 faithful friends at Cairo University knew they had a damn good message to spread. It was sticky like glue, clear as daylight and simple to believe from the onset.

"Our country needs a new direction and it is we the students of Egypt today who must stand up and bring about this change. Those of us who believe in non-violent revolution must try to convince our families; fathers, mothers, uncles, aunts, and all our Egyptian brothers and sisters to come out and join the protest at Tahrir Square on Friday 28 January 2011 to make history. We must all meet immediately after Friday prayers." Many messages went out in the final hours to leave no time for the authorities in Egypt to sabotage their plans.

On the first day of protests, tens of thousands of demonstrators clashed at Tahrir Square with the brutal and government-biased Egyptian Police Force. On this critical day in modern Egyptian history, two people were reported dead in Suez, the second largest city in Egypt. According to the police's own accounts, the two men in Suez died of respiratory problems after inhaling toxic amounts of tear gas. That day, one policeman was also reported to have died in Cairo after being hit by a rock.

In a panicked reaction, Hosni Mubarak, the last Egyptian Pharaoh, ordered his loyal security forces to go on the offensive. In addition to the indiscriminate force against peaceful protesters he introduced new draconian sanctions against civil disobedience.

That afternoon, the already overbearing Mubarak regime brought in new tougher controls on the media; blocking Twitter, MySpace, Facebook, Google, Yahoo and other social media networks, which many young people relied on to spread their campaign.

There were other developments as the rest of the day drew towards a dusky evening. The sun of the earth pointed its red-yellow light and showed a bold path on the River Nile, visible for every Egyptian to see and prepare for the early evening curfew.

That day, all the protestors vowed they would not leave Tahrir Square until the government fell. "We prefer to die in Tahrir Square than to go home and die," said one protestor I saw speaking to a BBC journalist in Cairo. Most of the protesters carried Egyptian flags as well as placards. "Freedom Square," one read. "Liberty Square," read another. I sat in my house in Glasgow, glued to the television to see what would happen next. I knew that whatever happened in Egypt could have huge implications for the wider continent of Africa.

According to uncollaborated reports from Aljazeera later that evening, the son of the embattled pharaoh, Gamal Mubarak flew to the UK to seek refuge with the closest members of the Mubarak family. Many protestors were angry that Mubarak planned to hand over power to one of his sons.

Over the next few days, tension grew between the protestors and the ruthless, manipulative Egyptian police. Meanwhile, the military was beginning to show positive signs of neutrality. By culture and ancient tradition, the Egyptian Army is prohibited from shooting their own civilian population.

After the first week of protest, the Western world began to hear the alarms. America, Australia, Britain and Japan were reported to be some of the first nations to fly their citizens out of the Pharaoh's land. America began to feel unease because Egypt is one of its most trustworthy allies in the Middle East. The American Government was wary that if Mubarak went, Egypt could descend into the hands of evil and dangerous fundamentalist groups, such as Al-Qaida.

As time went by, the Western world found itself stuck between a rock and a hard place. Is it worth risking everything to support the people's revolution or is it, as they say, sometimes better to stick with the devil you know? In the past, Mubarak has been powerful in persuading the West that in the absence of an iron dictator, there might be nastier men like the Muslim Brotherhood. That day, US Secretary of State Hillary Clinton told Fox News: "We don't want to see some takeover that would lead not to democracy but to oppression and to the end of the aspirations of the Egyptian people."

On the 7 February 2011, the significantly bruised and embattled president tried to blackmail the protestors by promising to increase public workers' pay by a staggering 15 per cent overnight. The protestors refused the offer and stood their ground. They gave their ultimatum for the President to quit. "Mubarak, please leave and let us live," said one protestor. By this point, there were calls coming from America and the West for Mubarak to leave.

Tension grew to tipping point when Mubarak eventually began to show signs of departure. Early in the morning of 10 February 2011, the leader of Egypt's Supreme Military Council excited the protestors by making an unexpected announcement at Tahrir. "I am here as the commander of the Egypt Supreme Council to inform you that all your demands as protesters will be met immediately. The army is behind the people and I can confirm that President Mubarak will make his final announcement to the whole nation later today," the General announced to the extreme delight of hundreds of thousands of protestors at Tahrir Square. He was guarded by armed soldiers who led him through the crowds.

After some jubilation, they crowd stood and chanted nervously awaiting the President's final broadcast to the nation as Commander-in-Chief. The agony of silence continued as people waited for Mubarak to appear on TV. As rumours spread about the Mubarak resignation, Obama spoke from Air Force One on his way to South East Asia

"This is an historic day as we watch events unfold in Egypt. The people of Egypt are writing history as we speak. This is a new dawn of a new day," he said and thanked the people of Egypt for their courage and determination in bringing democracy to their country.

Mubarak himself took much longer than expected to address the nation.

"Good evening, my brothers, sisters and children of Egypt. It is with pleasure I stand in front of you to say that I have decided to step up as your President." As people tried to understand what he was saying, he took his time. "I promise I will be very good to Egypt and all of you, my people, from now onwards. I am angry that outsiders think they can decide what happens to us here in our own country. Don't mind these outside powers; they are hypocrites and thieves. I will not allow the outside world to dictate or control what happens here in our country Egypt.

From now onwards, I promise to listen to you and deliver any promise I make to you. In the name of God, I will remain in Egypt till September when the country will have a free and fair election..." the President continued, to the total dismay and anger of the protestors at Tahrir Square. Many people around the world simply could not believe what Mubarak said, he was calm and relaxed throughout his address. He looked remarkable for his age.

After his announcement, the seemingly invincible President told the protestors to leave Tahrir Square and return Egypt to normality. He told the protestors that if they refused to leave that night, he would not hesitate to open fire!

There were shockwaves and shivers of disbelief around the world. What went so wrong? How could the Supreme Council mislead the protestors so badly? Why did Mubarak refuse to resign as promised? Even his Vice President told Aljazeera News early that afternoon that the President was definitely going to hand over power to the Supreme Military Council.

As the questions were asked by global observers, one thing came to my mind. I believe that Mubarak preferred to jump rather than be pushed, especially by the outside world. In his own unreported words, Mubarak describes his so-called former allies as "friends today, enemies tomorrow!"

On the evening of the 10 February 2011, tensions at Tahrir Square reached breaking point. After hearing the President's refusal to quit, more and more people poured onto the streets in every major city and town in Egypt. That night, Abdul and his friends decided to call out one million people to march from Tahrir Square to the presidential palace the next day to remove the President from his office by people power. "If persuasion fails, a reasonable amount of force must be applied; Mubarak must kill us all tomorrow or leave the country immediately" Abdul and his friends wrote and sent out what they hoped would be their final blog on Facebook.

On the eleventh day of the second month of the eleventh year of the twenty-first century, history was made in Egypt. That morning, I sat on my bed with a cup of tea and toast to watch the news. Late the previous night, it was reported that Hosni Mubarak had left Cairo to go to Sharm el-Sheikh, where he had a second home that, over the previous 30 years of his dynasty had received and hosted many American presidents including Clinton, Bush and Obama.

Initially, there were conflicting reports that the President went to his favourite resort to avoid any direct encounters with the angry protestors who planned to march to his presidential palace to oust him by force. Everyone remained in limbo on the early hours of the eleventh day until the Vice President appeared on the national TV to address the Nation.

"Good morning, fellow countrymen and women, I am happy to announce to the nation that the people's President Hosni Mubarak has resigned from power as of today. He has handed over the control of the country to the Supreme Military Council, which will take charge of Egypt from now until elections in September.

On this note, I have also resigned from my position as Egypt's Vice President from today. On behalf of myself and former President Mubarak, I wish Egypt the best of times ahead." Omar Suleiman, the Vice President spoke to the delight of a restless nation.

"Yes we are free from evil dictatorship; this is power to the people," one delighted protestor reacted.

Tahrir Square roared with voices: millions of people chanting, crying, dancing, singing, waving flags, praying, wishing and hoping that their country was changing for the better.

"This is a brand new day in Egypt. I can smell a new fresh air and the feeling is so good to be Egyptian. Welcome to the new Egypt, the land of Freedom," said Abdul.

Chapter 27: African Unity

Have you ever wondered why Coca Cola is such a huge successful global brand? Why were Abdul and his friends from Cairo University so successful in toppling Hosni Mubarak, the Invincible Man? What do you know about the laws of nature and the golden rules of success? Finally, how can the three fundamental golden rules of success help the people of Africa to unite and make progress from now until the end of time?

First Rule of Success: Knowing

A long, long time ago, my Grandma Alima told me something that I will never forget. Grandma Alima told me that, although commonsense is common, you can never find it to buy in the market! It was the middle of the rainy season and we were on the farm. We had a little hut, which was made from brown clay bricks and had a thatched roof. I remember that day on the farm, we boiled some beans and just as we were getting ready to sit down for lunch, the wind started to blow, gathering and moving the dark heavy clouds from the bottom of the earth, spreading them high to the roof of the sky. Suddenly, the rain began to pour cats and dogs.

I was only 14 years old then. My sister Asietu collected some leaves from the bush and carried the boiling pot of beans to run into the sheltered hut. I followed my sister with some burning sticks of firewood, which I carried to reassemble inside the farm hut.

There was a roaring thunder and lightning as we approached shelter. Unfortunately, my sister Asietu tripped and fell. It was a disaster; everything was gone in a blink of an eye. I stood at the entrance of the hut in the pouring rain for a few sharp seconds in dismay.

All the beans were spread on the ground with the pot on one side and my poor sister on the other. She struggled to stand up from the slippery mud, I gave my sister Asietu a hand and lifted her up. She was completely covered with shivers and mud.

"What are we going to eat?" I asked loudly with a grumbling stomach. Grandma Alima shouted from inside the hut: "Children, come away from the rain and stop crying: it is useless crying over your spilled beans." The rain had quenched the flame on the wood, leaving only the smoke. Without the pleasure of any heat inside the farmhouse, we sat and curled together to keep ourselves as warm as we could. It was one of those days on the farm that I would never forget. I was very hungry and angry at the same time.

After the rains, we went out in our wet clothes to look for some shea fruits. Because of the heavy winds that day, most of the ripe fruits had already fallen from the trees and scattered in the freshly grown seasonal grass. My dog Sumaiva followed us in the drizzle and wagged its tail as we kept a hock eye on the annoying baboons. As I bent down and gathered the fruits, Grandma said something to me and my sister Asietu, which will always remain in my thoughts: "My grandchildren," she called, "please always remember this day when you grow up and become adults. Try and be generous to those you meet like the way this tree is kind to us today. This life is a struggle because some people refuse to share the fruits of their sweat," Grandma said adding that if all the people in this world shared enough love and food around, everyone would have enough to eat and live comfortably.

"Grandma Alima, why do you always like comparing people's lives to trees and animals on the farm?" My sister Asietu asked as we carried our fruits back to the farm hut. Sumaiva branched off and chased a squirrel but lost it in the bushes next to the maize field.

"Look at this tree," Grandma said pointing her brown walking stick to the large shea tree in front of the farm house. "Every tree you see on the farm was once a seed. And that is exactly the same as the people you see every day. A long time ago, your father planted his seeds in your mother's garden," she said with a little smile on her wrinkly face. She was chewing some cola nuts as she spoke. "What you must always remember is that one tree on the farm is like a drop of water in the ocean, but hundreds of trees standing together can form a big forest." On the farm that day, Grandma Alima told me and my sister Asietu that society is the root and foundation blocks of all individuals and that we are nothing on our own. She argued that without the powerful protection of society, even the strongest individuals among us remain vulnerably exposed to unpredictable dangers of life in their own neighbourhood.

I have to admit that as a little boy I never fully understood the total value of what my Grandma Alima said on the farm that day until this moment of my life. It is only now I know that my Grandma Alima was in fact referring to the first rule of nature, which is the key to the success of every single nation or individual being on earth.

According to the law of homogeneous species, every living organism, big or small, must stick together to survive the harsh realities of life on Planet Earth. For those of you who are not familiar with the laws of nature, the law of homogeneous species states that birds of the same feather flock together to succeed. In African anthropology, we say, "monkeys play by sizes".

The emphasis of this law is on the need for the individual to find identical individuals, whom they can trust, believe, play and work with to succeed without threat, fear or danger. This is the reason why all the elephants in the jungle move and graze together.

I believe the time has come for the people of Africa to pay greater attention to the law of homogeneous species and unite as a powerful race of people. It is important for our new generations of Africans to come to the immediate realisation that, although elephants are the largest and the strongest animals in the jungle, they only remain in their dominant position when they herd together as one strong family unit. As soon as one elephant is isolated from the protection of the kraal, that elephant becomes vulnerable to the unpredictable dangers of jungle life. I believe like Dr Nkrumah said that in our current state of disunity, we will continue to be the most vulnerable species on earth.

All the individual countries in Africa and all the different African tribes must think and work together to succeed, because being on our own as we know makes us weak and vulnerable. According to the law of homogeneous species, every isolated individual is a vulnerable individual no matter how big or strong you are. Even the indomitable lion can never afford to lose guard or stay away from its pride. No matter the size, when one lion is separated from its family, a powerful group of hyenas and wild hunting dogs will start to see or follow it around the jungle as a potential prey. According to the law of the jungle, all weakness attracts prey and every open wound or carcass brings vultures.

Sticking together with your relatives and maintaining good contact with one's family members is something that every jungle resident must believe, worship and practice in order to succeed.

Take an ant or a bee as a good example of the power of collective reasoning. The ant is one of the tiniest living creatures in the jungle. One ant is completely powerless and almost invisible to the naked eye. Yet, as soon as all the ants in the colony start to work together as a team of efficient ants, the work they can do together is no longer tiny in scale or size. When hundreds of thousands of little ants start to work together, they can produce more miracles than any other jungle resident you can think of, including the mighty elephants. Those who are familiar with the African jungle will tell you that, an ant castle can rise as high as the castles we build as human beings. It is also important to take note of the fact that millions of tiny little ants working together can build some of the most complex and longest stretches of underground tunnel systems you can possibly imagine.

The point I am making is that if the people of Africa start to relate better and respect our mutual brotherhood, Africa will become a paradise of good sunshine and happy people in no time – and we deserve it!

African Unity is the only way forward because, without the proper use of our combined wisdom, we will always remain as a group of vulnerable individuals and countries living in a failing continent.

I believe that today we know what we want Africa to be tomorrow, we understand why Africa is the way it is today. We know how to make Africa a better place. I believe that together, we know we can. Now what we need is the BELIEF IN AFRICA!

Second Rule of Success: Believing

Belief is the foundation of life, the source of hope and the origin of all good and bad things in every human society.

The question you may ask is: what do we have to believe to succeed? Is it necessary for an individual to believe in a God to succeed in life?

In my opinion, the answer is both yes and no. First of all, it depends on what you want in this life and how you define your own success as an individual or a society.

For example, if you think or know of a place called heaven and you wish to go there to enjoy a happy life after death, then you definitely have to believe and follow the path of a good God that can take you there. On the other hand, if your definition of success is to enjoy a good economic lifestyle in your life before you die, then you don't necessarily have to believe in any God or any supreme creator to find your success. As a matter of fact, sometimes believing in a God can slow down your chances of financial progress. In my strongest opinion, this is part of the reason why Africa is not as developed as Europe: we believe too much in God and not enough in ourselves.

Belief and faith gives birth to several children including inner strength, courage and determination. And to a certain extent, it doesn't matter how many good ideas and good contacts you have, if you don't believe in yourself or what you know, you are more prone to failure in every aspect of your life. That is why we must believe that it is possible to see a better world tomorrow. It is possible that provided we are united, we can work together as human beings to change our failing conditions. I want to warn that we don't necessarily have to start disbelieving in God in order to achieve financial progress. On the contrary, I believe that the people of Africa in the twenty-first century should endeavour to strike a fine balance between material living and spiritual wellbeing. A bit of God and reality, in my view, is the best way forward in Africa.

Belief is also directly related to the second law of nature, which is the law of gravitational force. The law of gravity states that no condition is permanent. In other words, nothing can stay up or down forever including the ground and the sky. It also means that anything that has a beginning must have an end – and this includes all pain and suffering.

In my view, President Obama has already proved to himself and the rest of the world that no condition is permanent and that it is possible to work hard and achieve change despite his own fractured and painful history as a man of African heritage. If only enough of us believe that, indeed, no condition is permanent, then we can find the necessary courage to unite as a people with the objective of making the best progress throughout the twenty-first century – and far beyond! We can make this happen if only we believe in our own worth as a people.

Look at what Abdul and his 11 friends from Cairo University have managed to achieve by believing in the combined power of the people. They managed to bring Mubarak down, despite the fact that no one previously believed it was possible to unseat him. Belief is power to the people and the best way to spread a new word of mouth epidemic in Africa.

I have to warn, however, that all our noble hopes and dreams of a prosperous Africa will continue to have little foundation without the strongest belief that our condition can change. Belief offers us hope when we have reason to feel despair. Belief also gives birth to faithfulness, which in turn breeds other important qualities, such as dedication and commitment, patience and understanding, honour, dignity, mutual respect, good friendship, better love as well as a strong will and determination to succeed.

Finally, I want to stress that, in my view, believing in Africa is not necessarily a religious doctrine but an intellectual path for the people of Africa to follow to our deserved status as the new champions of the world. If we believe in Africa, we will feel proud of Africa. If we are proud of Africa, we will eat our own African food, wear African clothes, play African music and pray every day for Africa to be a prosperous continent like Europe, America, Asia or any other continent of the world.

If you believe in Africa, you will carry a good image of Africa and portray it well with African dignity wherever you go. If you believe in Africa, you must believe in one love, one brotherhood/sisterhood. If you believe in Africa, you must believe in one African spirit, one people, diverse cultures, different tribes, several countries, one continent, one system, common languages, one currency, one intellectual path, several routes and many different roads to the Heavenly Kingdom of the one Great Mighty God of the Universe.

Third Rule of Success: Doing

In business, they say that if you want to open a new shop, the best way to guarantee success is location, location and location. I believe that in Africa, the surest way to succeed with our dream is action,

action and plenty more action. Brutally speaking, you can forget about what you want, who you know or what you believe in this life, if you don't do enough to make your dream come true, it will always remain an empty dream!

HIV/AIDS is Not the Biggest Threat in Africa, Hunger is!

No man on this earth is ever free enough to think for himself with an empty stomach. For this simple reason alone, I want to argue that the African man will continue to play the role of the economic slave in his own backyard until the day he wakes up to his fullest senses and starts growing enough of his own food to feed himself, his family, society and the wider world he belongs to.

I say this because, the history of all successful economies in the world has proven that no nation – or continent, for that matter – has been able to achieve any meaningful or sustained economic growth without first growing enough food to feed their population. From my own informed position, based on almost two decades of underground research work, I can foretell that food insecurity is the greatest threat to human progress in the twenty-first century. This problem can be seized and turned into a huge opportunity for economic growth, if we invest wisely and aim to become the major food-producing continent of the world. In my view, other forms of development will naturally follow if we make agriculture our number one development priority in Africa.

We can continue to talk, but unless we begin to do more about what we believe is now possible, nothing will change in Africa. If we are serious about real progress in Africa, we first need to grow enough food to feed all of Africa's children and not just some of the children. Growing enough food to feed all our population is not something that we should do but also something we can do and must do with speed and force. The African man will do himself justice from the simple realisation that an empty stomach is the devil's playing field and the most frequent source of evil conduct in our continent.

I believe that the level of dependency on imported food into the African continent is the biggest disgrace to our collective conscience as a people. It is ridiculously crazy and totally insane to imagine that an Africa, with a total landmass almost three times the size of Europe, still continues to import over two-thirds of our food from the 2 per cent of the European population who are directly employed in agricultural activity. I feel so shamed as an African man any time I think of the fact that Africa imports over 70 per cent of our basic food supplies, such as rice, wheat, chicken, fish and so forth, from Europe and America, although we have more productive land than any other continent in the world. Even a frog would know this is a completely wrong situation to be in!

Let me now admit why I am raving about the importance of growing our own food in Africa. The reason is this: I have experienced and felt the undignified pain that hunger brings to a human being. From my experience, I have learnt that hunger makes a clever man confused and easily misled. Hunger can force one to lose faith in his or her own society. Hunger takes away the love of God from a man of God and hunger provokes the feeling of hate and unnecessary anger against others. That is why Bob Marley sang that "a hungry man is an angry man". Hunger can make a human being feel and behave like a dog. Hunger can make a man disloyal and the woman unfaithful. Hunger breeds negative individuals and fuels problem families. Hunger destroys good communities and damages healthy societies. Hunger is the greatest source of civil conflict in Africa.

I strongly believe the most unbearable pain on earth is extreme hunger. Hunger is still by far the biggest killer disease in Africa over malaria and HIV/AIDS combined together. In fact, it is fair to say that most people, who die of AIDS-related diseases or malaria in

Africa, tend to die of empty stomachs first. This is the reason why the former President of South Africa, Thabo Mbeki once said: "It is not AIDS that kills people in Africa, but hunger."

Commonsense in Africa

The question is, what can we do with all the knowledge, commonsense and the combined belief we have to kick off a successful agricultural revolution in Africa?

First of all, I want to say that by agricultural revolution, I am referring to the radical action at every level of African society to grow, process, store and package enough food to feed our populations with surplus to store and sell to the wider world. I believe that Africa and her people have been suffering for far too long. And now is the time to turn all our big talk and best ideas into maximum food production: Africa Operation Grow Your Own Food is the only way forward. We must use all our commonsense to embark on an immediate agricultural revolution in every African village, town, city and country.

Among all the good things that I wish to see in Africa, nothing matters as much to me than my simple dream that one day in Africa, every man, woman and child will have the choice of three square meals a day. I believe this is possible within a generation of hard-working people. All it takes is commonsense to succeed. I believe that with abundant application of commonsense in Africa, we can grow enough of our own food to eat, live in our own peace and harmonious societies and enjoy the same, similar or better standards of living as the Chinese, the Europeans and the Americans. But for this to happen, there must be two important radical actions.

Firstly, all the good leaders of Africa today must unite under the AU and bring about strong legislation to minimise the growing overdependence on foreign food imports. The AU should legislate and bring about quota systems to limit the amount of foreign food into Africa to less than 50 per cent. In other words, a minimum of 50 per cent of food consumed in any African country must be produced in that country. If a country cannot produce 50 per cent of its own food, maximum support should be given to that country to improve their agricultural production capacity.

Finally, I believe with all my sincerity that for an African agricultural revolution to fully succeed we need the tools to grow our own food and we have many ways to get them. The solution is simple. We can ask the Western countries to stop giving us leaking aid from this point onwards and start sending us all the tools that we need to grow our own food. We want the West to show us the way and not to continue insisting on giving us the way. We all know that catching a fish everyday for your brother only creates long term dependency, laziness and poor excuses for your brother to sit down and do nothing to better his own living condition.

It is time for Africa to move away from the "begging bowl mentality" and start to take concrete action to change our hellish position in the world. At an AU level, our African governments must legitimately demand or force the Western world to translate half of the aid to Africa into practical tools and farm equipment, which we can use to grow and pull ourselves out of poverty. As President Barack Obama said in Ghana, the time has come for the West to respect Africa as an important global heritage and a reliable partner for collective progress in a twenty-first century interdependent Global Village. Africa needs technical assistance and we must ask for this in no uncertain terms.

We need to radically deviate from aid and tilt towards genuine international assistance, technical co-operation and self-reliance. If the Western world continues to play old games and outdated tricks with us or say no to our legitimate technical request for some unknown reason, the people of Africa must unite with our strong collective bargaining power and move to the dragon's den. We must seek assistance from the Chinese. With their level of technical advancement, the Chinese can be contracted to make appropriate farming tools for every village farmer in Africa!

If the Chinese can help Africa to grow our own food, we can send some of the food we grow to China as parity exchange. But, if the Chinese cannot reason with us on this occasion, we must pass through the house of Gandhi to seek technical co-operation. Like China, I believe that with the right incentives on the table, India has the ability to manufacture appropriate tools and equipment for our African farmers.

In the meantime, we must set a new strong agenda to advance and make our own appropriate local tools, so that we don't have to suffer later from long-term dependency, as we have suffered in the past with IMF structural adjustment policies.

Let us combine and translate half of the aid to our continent into a new Agricultural Revolution. Right now, aid has become a wasted opportunity in Africa. We spend the aid on education, healthcare, gender equality, human rights and good governance. These are all misplaced priorities because if you are hungry, you can never understand the full meaning of democracy. Equally, if a child arrives at school with an empty stomach today, how is that child able to concentrate in the classroom and learn to become a better adult tomorrow?

My best COMMONSENSE advice to all the people of Africa today therefore is: Wake up. Hurry up. Grow your own food and stop enslaving your CHILDREN!

Chapter 28: Prayer is the Key to Success

"Have you ever wondered why every American President finishes their address to the nation by saying: 'God bless America'? And why do you think people in Britain sing the praise: 'God save the Queen'?" Pastor Thomas asked the congregation. The service was held at the Woodland Methodist Church in Glasgow as part of a special thanksgiving prayer to celebrate Ghana's 54th birthday.

"My brothers and sisters and dear Scottish friends, I am extremely enchanted and humbled to be standing here in front of you all on this important occasion. The 6 March 2011, as you know, is not only a special day for Ghana, but also for Africa our Motherland. That is why today's service is entitled: African Redemption Day Prayer. Let us pray for God to unite and join us together in our hearts and in our minds. Let us pray for God to cleanse our souls, purify our thoughts and give us a common sense of being and purpose." Pastor Thomas Badiaku spoke and opened the Bible. He was wearing a dark suit and a brown tie.

"Praise the Lord."

"Hallelujah," the congregation responded joyfully.

"As we gather here to make our final redemption prayer, let us warn ourselves about betrayers and the ungodly people among us. We must remember that Judas is among us with his master Satan. Their aim is to conquer and destroy the world through divide and rule. The Bible tells us in Jude 18 and 19 that: 'In the last days of our struggle, there will be scoffers and false prophets who will purposely deviate from righteousness and the will of God. They will do so to follow their own ungodly desires.' The Bible warns that these are the men who divide you, the men who follow mere nature and do not have the spirit of God.

The Bible also says in John, chapter 11: 'Dear friends, do not imitate what is evil but what is good.' Anyone who does what is good is from God. Anyone who does what is evil has not seen God.

Let us pray to God for helping us to bring an end to our long days of darkness in Africa.

Oh Lord, we are gathered here today to thank you for all your love and compassion you show us every day. Exactly 54 years ago today, Ghana became the first African country to regain her freedom from British colonial rule. Let us give thanks and praises to the Lord for our freedom of self-determination. In this church hall today, as you can all see, there are over 500 men, woman and children from almost every nation in Africa! I want to thank our Scottish friends who have also come to join us today for this special and extraordinary service to celebrate the richness of our common humanity. Let us pray together for a brighter future in Africa. Let us pray for new enlightenment and better vision for Africa. For, it is due to lack of a clear vision that we failed to unite Africa during the past 50 years of Independence. Praise the Lord," Pastor Badiaku said and pointed his microphone towards the audience. "Hallelujah," we all cheered and buzzed along like a forest of bumble bees.

The Vision of Africa by the River Nile

"If you can imagine that the person you meet on the road has his or her eyes stitched up, do you think that person can still see and be able to separate the light from darkness?"

"No pastor, no one can see with stitched eyes," said one Gambian Lady.

"Good," said the pastor. "And just as a man cannot see without his eyes; a people without a good vision cannot see the need to reason or think together, plan together and work together to succeed." Pastor Badiaku told the congregation that we need a new vision today because Africa is at a cross road and which way we turn will determine the future. "In 2011, there are 25 nations celebrating their golden anniversary of independence in the African continent. This is the most important year in the African calendar because it is

290

the year of transition from our days of darkness into a new era of light. 2011 will be remembered as the year of African miracles. We have to celebrate this new beginning with hope and greater realisation through better enlightenment. Ladies and gentlemen," he called and stared at the audience with the old red Bible in his right hand. It was the Old Testament. "As we congregate on this special day of redemption, unity is our greatest weapon, which we can use effectively to liberate ourselves from the doom of darkness. Let us pray for African unity because the Bible tells us that: 'A family that is united is a thousand times stronger than a kingdom that is divided.'" As Pastor Thomas spoke in his eloquent way, the packed church was filled with spiritual harmony.

"My dear brothers and sisters, as I have already said, we the people of Africa today stand together at a crossroads. At this important crossroads, we have only two options. We can choose to go the right way or the wrong way! The right way is through a new galvanised spirit of oneness, better motivation, good thinking, sound reasoning, better planning, common values et cetera. This is the only way to get through the gates of the greatest Kingdom of Heaven." The pastor paused and took a sip of water.

"At this important crossroads, the wrong way the African people can turn is the doomed way, which is based on inaction, backwardness or the continuation of the wrong path of action in our current state of disunity. This is the road we don't want to take at any cost. One of the greatest quotes I have ever heard was from Sir Winston Churchill, the wartime Prime Minister of this great nation, the United Kingdom. Without quoting him word for word, Sir Winston Churchill once said that: For evil to triumph in society, all that the good people in society must do is to sit down on their lazy chairs and continue to do nothing about what is going wrong in society. Doing nothing for Africa or even too little at this crucial hour is the most dangerous path which no African man and woman can afford to take.

The good news is that, every man and woman in Africa has a choice today not to turn Africa the wrong way. If we want to turn Africa the right way, we must first change the way we do things. We can do it; we can do the right thing right now for ourselves and our family over the next three testing decades. And we know what it takes: courage. With courage, I can stand here in front of you today and prophesise that very soon, our countries and people will come together to form better economic links. We can build our cities to look modern, beautiful, clean and joyful to live in. There is no reason why Accra should not be as beautiful and comfortable as Glasgow here. If we wake up from darkness and see the light, we will enjoy the greatest benefits of our land. We will all taste the freshness of clean water from our springs and lakes. Our rivers will be full of water and fish and our farms will produce abundant food, which we can share, eat, sell and store for the future generations. Praise the Lord."

"Amen," we all replied.

"Dishonesty is a lethal weapon. Every dishonest conduct breeds enmity among friends and family. Dishonesty leads to disputes, fallouts and unnecessary conflicts which are painful and extremely costly to every one of us on this planet. Disputes and conflicts also lead to lawlessness, chaos, laziness and self-destruction. That is the negative path of the devil we wish to bury in the African cemetery as we step forward to enjoy the fresh atmosphere of a completely brand new day with a new vision in our hands." Pastor Thomas only stopped briefly to catch his breath. "Let us pray to the Lord to give us the courage to follow our own vision to success."

As I sat and listened, the humbling voice of the pastor continued to touch my heart deep inside. "Today is a brand new day in Africa. We are free because Obama has come to testify that the chains of cruelty are off our wrists. We have the intelligence and the combined wisdom to get to where we are going. Nothing is impossible because Obama has shown us that there is no mountain on earth which is too high to climb." Pastor Thomas continued saying that the moment for Africa is now or never. "Ladies and gentlemen, the future of Africa rests desperately in our capable hands. The plight of Ghana depends on the actions and deeds of every Ghanaian citizen. The future of Kenya lies in the ability of the Kenyan people to bury negative tribalism in every way or form. The progress of Nigeria relies on the ability of the Nigerians to turn their backs against political corruption. As we all know far too well, Africa has everything apart from good leadership.

We need good, sincere and courageous leadership in Africa to go through the decades of transition. So, let us pray that as we speak right now, our leaders are hearing our sorrowful voices and our tears for desperate help. Let us pray to the good Lord in heaven to cleanse the hearts of our leaders. Let us pray to the Lord to remove the sins, bad deeds and evil intentions of our leaders and replace their dirty hearts and corrupted minds with a fresh spirit of sincerity and honest conduct. Of course, a leader of a country must be entitled to the lion share. But a lion does not kill or starve all other jungle species so that it can remain the king of the jungle. On the contrary, a lion only kills what it needs every day. When it is satisfied with its own needs, the rest of the antelopes in the jungle are free and safe to live without fear. My fellow Africans, our leaders must be entitled to all the privileges at their lavish disposal, but privileges without responsibility, as we know from the past, leads to callous, irresponsible conduct based on arrogance and destructive greed." Pastor Thomas warned that the period of false prophets and fake leaders in Africa is over. "It is time to see a new generation of good leaders in Africa. Leadership is important to us because it is the key to good planning and good planning is 99 per cent responsible for both individual and collective success. This is why God planned the world very well before he made it. That is why the Universe floats in a perfect motion."

"Pastor, Praise the Lord," a voice interrupted.

"Hallelujah," voices responded.

"Pastor Thomas, I don't think the problem of Africa is poor planning. In Ghana for example, we have better plans than many countries in Europe. But, we don't follow the good plans we put together because we are very greedy. Because of greed, we envy each other's success. Africa is suffering from selfishness and greed. That is the truth," Yaw stood up and spoke before resting back on his seat. The pastor responded by arguing that in his opinion, greed is not the biggest problem of society. The real problem in Africa, he said is compound stupidity and public waste which he said is due to mismanagement.

"Greed is just an innocent victim; it is not the killer disease in Africa because greed is like blood. It is inside every human being. But greed is different from gross incompetence," Pastor Thomas spoke and continued. "Let me tell you something. I believe that the people of Africa are not greedier than the people of Europe or America. A Nigerian man is not any greedier than a German or an Italian man. As a matter of fact, if you give a quarter of the average British salary to a Ghanaian civil servant, he or she would be the happiest worker in the whole world and they will do anything you ask them to do to defend their country Ghana." We all clapped and rejoiced knowing the amount of truth in what the Pastor was saying.

"I want to tell you a little story to explain why I say greed is not the biggest problem of Africa but something else." Pastor Thomas Badiaku said and took another sip of water. He was sweating as he proceeded to tell his story. He wiped his face with a blue handkerchief.

"A long time ago, there lived a fisherman in a small Gambian village, near Banjul. His name was Baba Kunta. Every single day, Baba Kunta went to the river to catch one fish to take away home. Meanwhile, the rest of the fishermen in the village spent most of their days catching more fish to sell to the market ladies.

On one bright sunny day, Baba Kunta was returning from the river when he met a young woman carrying a wide silver basin on her head. Baba Kunta stood to one side of the narrow path to let Fatima pass by.

'Baba Kunta,' she called and approached. 'Why do you catch only one fish a day?'

'I am happy with one fish a day,' he said holding the large tilapia in his hand. He was anxious to go home and eat his fish so that he could relax for the rest of the day.

'Why can't you behave like the rest of the villagers and stay longer at the river to catch more fish. Don't you know that you can sell the fish to make plenty of money for yourself?'

'And then what? What happens if I make plenty of money for myself?'

"Money makes the world go round," said Fatima. She was shocked that Baba Kunta refused to see the point with working hard to get rich.

"Why do I have to work hard to be rich one day when I already feel rich and happy every day?" Baba Kunta asked. He laughed as he struggled to think of what to say next. He took a little gaze at the blue sky above his head. 'I have been catching one fish a day from this river for all my life. I only need one fish a day, that is why I catch one every day.'

'But Baba Kunta, what about the money, can't you see that you can make money and become rich?' Fatima asked looking perplexed. She used one hand to hold the basin on her head and waved the other one as she spoke. 'Think about the money you can make.'

'And what will I do with plenty of money? If I have money, will I grow taller?'

'No, you may not grow taller, but you can become fat," she said and smile. In Gambia, being a fat man is a sign of wealth and affluence. "With more money, you can buy a fishing boat,' she argued.

'And then what?'

'Then employ some of the village fishermen to help you. A boat full of fish a day can make you a very, very, rich and powerful man in this village. When you have money, you can do anything you want in the world. You can control everyone around you.' said Fatima.

'And then what?'

'With a boat, you can work hard for a few years and build yourself a big palace, retire and live happily thereafter."

'And what do you think I do now?" Baba Kunta asked. He looked stunned that Fatima didn't get his philosophy of one fish a day. "Why do I have to live and wait to retire before I can live a happy life?" Baba Kunta asked and carried his tilapia home." Pastor Badiaku poured with sweat. "I have told you the story of the Gambian fisherman to convince you that, it is not every human being in this world who is greed and selfish. It is not everyone in this life who wants to have millions and mansions before they can be satisfied with life. There are many people like Baba Kunta in Africa who just want enough to live on and be happy with everyday as it comes." By this point, we all stood up clapping and cheering. It was as if we were about to take off the roof with cheers.

"Ladies and gentlemen, please sit down and join me in prayers." I looked round and saw that everyone had bowed their heads, so I did the same. My friend Yaw was sitting next to me resting his head against the Bible.

"As we close our eyes, let us lean deep into the unconscious world to find the final answer to our prayer. Africa deserves better and Africa must be better. Lord you have the power to redeem us from our sins and show us your kindness and compassion.

God, you have made all men and women onto this earth. You gave us all the power to reason and make changes in every aspect of our lives; especially when things are going wrong. You ask us to pray to you as your children when we need your help. God, as you surely exist, you must be aware that something has been going wrong in Africa for over 500 years and this is the moment and time to bring an end to our suffering. Lord we are standing here in front of you and seeking for the mercy you have shown to us before. Lord we pray for you to help us bring an end to famine in Africa. Lord we have suffered enough and we cannot bear to suffer anymore in your hands. Whatever we have done wrong in the past please forgive us as we are prepared to repent for our past sins. Lord we are tired of failing and we are desperate for success. Lord we thrust that you have the power to make impossible things become possible. "

Pastor Thomas continued for sometime as we all sat in the solitary silence. My eyelids blinked with exhaustion. "Now, I want you all to imagine that you are running in a long dark tunnel. In this tunnel, you can hear many voices around you. But it is so dark you cannot see yourself or any of the people that are squeezing themselves against you. As you struggle to escape from the hell of darkness, you trip and fall down. People stumble over you. You pick yourself up and you are back on your feet running as fast as you can for your life. The thumping of the feet on the ground was like a jungle full of wildebeest. Everywhere you turn to look is so dark, as if it was the end of days. As you continue to run desperately for your life, you begin to feel that there is no end to the dark tunnel. Creeping shadows follow your every single step. You hear the voices around you crying desperately for help, but there is no one to help them or you. Now, you begin to doubt the presence of God and you are just about to give up hope. And then, you suddenly step into some water. You stop immediately frozen in fear. As you are about to take a step backward, the voice of an angel speaks out loudly: 'People, don't be afraid anymore. The era of living in the darkness is over. Open your eyes and you can see the light. You must hurry and cross the river to the other side.' Lo and behold, you open your eyes and you can see yourself surrounded by millions of people along the river bank. You join the crowd singing the songs of freedom whilst crossing the river. The smell of hope of a brighter future lingers through the air as you flock to safety.

Half way through the river, a voice from behind roared like a thundering terror. 'Wait for me to come and get you. Don't cross the river because it is full of crocodiles, sharks and other dangerous man eating river monsters.' My African brothers and sisters around the world, if you consider yourself a true African or a good human being and you find yourself among the millions passing through the Nile today, which way will you go?" The pastor paused for final effects. "Are you enlightened and courageous enough to follow the voice of the angel to the brighter side of the river, or will you be the fearful coward and the second fool in Africa who is gullible enough to go back to the days of darkness?" Pastor Thomas asked and wiped his face again with the blue handkerchief.

"We have to cross the river," one man shouted from his seat. Many others helped him to chant along: "We must cross the Nile, we must cross the Nile and we must cross the Nile!"

"As your Pastor for this special Redemption Day Service, I have done my absolute best to deliver the African gospel and bring you this far to the banks of the Blue Nile. What you all have to remember today is that Moses did not force the Israelis to cross the red sea. As we all know: You can always take a horse to the riverside but whether the horse crosses the river or not is something you have to decide!" Pastor Badiaku exclaimed and pointed his hand to the audience.

"Africans, do we have the courage and determination to succeed as one people? I want to hear the truth loud and clear from the top of your voices for one last time: Africa can we make it??????"

We roared in reply, "Yes, We Can!"

*   *   *   *   *

May God bless Africa and help us to accomplish our African Dream as he always helps those who help themselves..... Amen.

About the author

Chief Suleman Chebe is a distinguished, well-respected African philosopher, poet, storyteller and music teacher living in Scotland. A larger-than-life character, Chebe shares a positive image of Africa with the people he meets every day. His interactive drumming and hands-on "Africa Experience" workshops provide unique entertainment and training for schools, colleges, universities and corporate organisations throughout the UK, although he often travels further afield to bring a unique flavour of Africa to other European destinations, such as Prague and Dublin.

He maintains strong links with his homeland, Ghana, through his work establishing ethical trading links between rural farmers and fair-trade outlets in the UK. He is currently involved in building an Eco Centre near his hometown, Pulima. When it is completed, the Lasajang Eco Village will serve as a model international skills exchange and training centre for craftwork, carpentry, bricklaying and other essential life skills that are appropriate for sustainable community development in northern Ghana.

As a natural-born communicator and spirited social entrepreneur, Chief Chebe writes and delivers regular speeches on some of the key challenges facing Africa in the twenty-first century, with a focus on fair trade and the impact of climate change on Africa. He is a positive global activist, a dedicated pan-African artist, and most certainly one of the happiest men you could ever come across on earth today!

Highlights of Chebe's community work:

- Host/presenter of "African Affairs" with Radio Kilimanjaro – the first African Community Radio Station in the UK. (www.radiokilimanjaro.org.uk)

- Speaker and exhibitor at the annual "Fair Trade Experience" in Glasgow Royal Concert Hall

- Panel member for the Race Relation Act in the Scottish Parliament

- Founding member of the African–Caribbean Network in Glasgow

- Former Chairman of the Ghana Welfare Association in Scotland